SHIELDING DEVYN

Delta Team Two, Book 6

SUSAN STOKER

CHAPTER ONE

Devyn sat on the couch in her apartment and did her best to ignore Troy "Lucky" Schmidt. He wasn't a man who was easy to ignore. From the moment they'd met, Devyn had been drawn to him. But at the time, she was in no mood to be hit on by some hotshot special forces soldier who'd probably slept with a million women.

But as she got to know him, and all her brother's teammates, she realized Lucky wasn't a manwhore. She'd just assumed he was gettin' some every weekend because he was so damn good-looking. At six-two, he was just tall enough. Devyn loved her brother, but he was a freaking giant. She wasn't exactly short herself at five-eleven, making Lucky the perfect height for her.

Not only that, but he had the whole tall-dark-and-dangerous thing down pat. Black hair, with hazel eyes that held enough mystery to be intriguing as hell. His beard and mustache drew her all the more. She didn't know what it was about his beard that did it for her, she just knew it did. Usually, she thought beards were gross. Petri dishes that collected germs and leftover food. But Lucky kept his facial

1

hair well-groomed. It wasn't too long, it wasn't too short. And it wasn't scraggly, like those guys who resembled a fifteen-year-old trying to grow a beard.

And then there was his muscles...

She'd seen him working out with her brother a time or two, and good Lord, the man was built. She wasn't exactly surprised, since being a special forces soldier meant he had to be in great shape, but every time he moved, his muscles rippled. And that V that pointed to his groin under his shorts? It was all Devyn could do to keep from ripping his clothes off to see what he was packing in his pants.

All of which added up, in her mind, to the fact that he had to be having sex on a regular basis. He was fucking beautiful, and all the women around the Fort Hood Army post had to be on him like butter on bread. With his looks, and with a nickname like Lucky, he had to be *getting* lucky on a regular basis.

But the more Devyn hung out with her brother and his friends, the more she realized Lucky wasn't anything like she'd thought. She'd been guilty of stereotyping...and not in a flattering way. She felt bad about it, but then again, she hadn't planned on staying in Texas as long as she had. It somehow didn't make her feel as awful to judge a stranger as it would someone she knew she'd be getting to know fairly well.

Her plans had been to get the hell out of Missouri, regroup, and find a city where she could be comfortable. Get a job and get on with her life. But as it turned out, Killeen was looking like it could be that city. She loved the weather; even though it was hot, she much preferred being warm than dealing with the snow and cold that she'd grown up with in Missouri. It wasn't a huge city, but if she had the urge to go out to eat or go shopping, it had everything she could want. And she'd learned she was a big fan of traditional Mexican food, which Killeen had in spades.

And she loved her older brother. All of his friends called him Grover because their last name was Groves, but to her, he was just Fred.

They'd always been close. They were two of five kids, and life had been hectic growing up. Devyn was the youngest, Spencer was two years older than her, and Fred was two years older than him. Even though Spencer was closer in age, he had always been off doing his own thing. Their two older sisters, Mila and Angela, were seven and five years older than her, respectively, and were teenagers by the time she'd been old enough—and healthy enough—to want to hang out with them.

Devyn had spent much of her childhood in hospitals battling leukemia. It had set her apart from her siblings. And Fred had been the one to keep her company in the hospital. He didn't seem to mind sitting in her small room playing stupid board games for hours on end. He was the one who read to her. Who sang her to sleep before he left. He was her rock.

It was no wonder when she'd fled Missouri, she'd gone straight to the small city where Fred was stationed. She was determined to keep her troubles to herself, but she'd missed her big brother. Her staunchest supporter. When he'd joined the Army and moved away, Devyn had been heartbroken. She'd been proud of him, but it still hurt not to see him all the time.

So here she was.

And now, despite her best efforts, she felt as if she was perilously close to dragging him into her drama.

Devyn sighed.

"That was a big sigh," Lucky said quietly from the other side of the couch. "You want to talk about it?"

She did. Desperately. But Devyn was tired of being the helpless little sister. The one who had to be looked after and babied. The one who, every time she sneezed, got rushed into the hospital just to be sure the cancer hadn't returned. Not that she thought Lucky would treat her like that, but he was best friends with Fred. And she suspected whatever she told him would get back to her brother.

"No," she said after a painful amount of time had passed.

Lucky nodded. "Okay."

She looked over at him. "Why are you still here? You got me home; thank you. I'm sure if you called one of the others, they'd come pick you up so you could go back to the party."

They'd been at Oz's new house celebrating Lefty, Brain, and Oz's marriages to Kinley, Aspen, and Riley. She was happy for her new friends. Each of the women had been through hell, and they all deserved the best. And they'd found it in her brother's teammates. They would protect their women with everything they had. It was in their DNA to help others, and her friends were lucky to have found happiness and everlasting love.

But after she'd unconsciously answered her phone, then realized it was Spencer on the other end, she'd lost all desire to be around her joyful friends. She didn't want to bring anyone down, so she'd left.

Except Lucky had seen her leaving and volunteered to drive her home. Selfishly, she'd taken him up on his offer.

"I'm exactly where I want to be," Lucky told her, settling back on the couch as if he were planning on staying indefinitely.

Devyn frowned. She needed him to go. She couldn't get even more tied to this town. Tied to Fred's friends and teammates.

"I'll order you an Uber," Devyn told him, reaching for her phone.

Lucky put his hand over hers, stopping her in her tracks.

"Talk to me, Dev," he said in a low, husky tone. "I'd like to think I'm your friend. You can tell me anything."

"If I tell you, you'll talk to Fred," she blurted.

Lucky blinked. "You don't want your brother to know what's wrong? Why not?"

Devyn closed her eyes in defeat. She was caught between a rock and a hard place. "I've been a pain in my family's ass since I was diagnosed with leukemia," she said begrudgingly. "My parents had to drop everything to take me to doctors' appointments. I had too many hospital stays to count. No one in my family had a normal life after I was diagnosed. Even after I went into remission, we couldn't do things most families could. Visits to Disneyland were out; too many people. Too big a chance of my compromised immune system getting overwhelmed. I refuse to put my family through more than I have already."

Lucky hadn't moved his hand from hers, and Devyn had the momentary wish that she could scoot over and put her head against his chest, but she held firm. He'd probably think she was insane and wonder what he'd gotten into.

She was pretty sure Lucky had wanted to be more than friends for a while, but she'd kept him at arm's length. She wasn't certain she was staying. But it was getting harder and harder to push him away. Especially when she felt as alone as she did right now.

"I'm sure no one in your family resents you for having cancer," Lucky said.

"I know," Devyn told him. "But sometimes I wonder what our lives would be like now if I'd been normal."

"You *are* normal," Lucky said forcefully. "And who's to say what's normal and what isn't? I'm a firm believer that things happen exactly the way they're supposed to."

Devyn snorted.

"Seriously. Just because we don't like some aspects of our lives doesn't mean another way is any better."

"I'm just tired," Devyn told him, closing her eyes.

"You're still part time at your job, right?" Lucky asked.

"Yeah. But that's not what I meant. I love working at the vet clinic. Animals are so...simple. If they're in pain, they try to scratch or bite you. If they're happy, their tails wag or they purr. There's no artifice with them. As long as they have food, water, and shelter, they're good to go. Humans aren't like that. They always want more."

"More what?" Lucky asked quietly.

Devyn knew she'd said too much as it was. "Everything," she answered vaguely. Then she opened her eyes and looked over at Lucky. "If I asked, would you keep what we talk about between the two of us? Like, not tell Fred?"

She knew from the look on his face, he couldn't promise her that.

"Grover's like my brother," Lucky said. "He's taken a bullet for me, as I've done for him."

Devyn didn't like that fact. At all. But Lucky didn't give her a chance to comment.

"He loves you. A lot. He was excited when you told him you were coming here, but worried too. He didn't know why you'd give up your life back in Missouri on what seemed like a whim. It's no secret that I like you, Dev. A lot. And that if you gave me the slightest hint you might be open to starting something, I'd be all for it. But I can't—and I won't—keep secrets from Grover. Especially if it involves your health or safety."

Devyn nodded. She'd known he'd say something like that. She wasn't mad at him though. She admired the bond Fred had with his teammates. But that was why she'd kept her problems to herself. She'd never had a friendship like that, and she had no desire to do anything to harm the relationship between her brother and his teammates.

"Are you sick? Or in danger?" Lucky asked.

"No," Devyn said without hesitation. The cancer hadn't returned, thank God, and she didn't *think* she was in danger. Her issues with Spencer were irritating and stressful, but not worth shaking up the foundation of her family, and not life or death.

She'd hoped that moving so far away would make Spencer change. Would be enough for him to do what he needed to do to get back on the right track.

But as she remembered the short phone call that afternoon, she knew he hadn't changed at all since she'd left.

"Hey, sis. It's your favorite brother."

"Spencer. How did you get my number?" Devyn asked.

"Fred gave it to me. I'm hurt that you've been avoiding me," Spencer said.

"What do you want?"

"Ah, straight to the point. How very like you. I need a loan."

Devyn's stomach clenched. "No."

"Come on, sis, you know you're the only one I can count on."

"I said no. You haven't paid me back the money you've already borrowed from me."

"But this time is different," Spencer whined.

"It's never different!" Devyn told him heatedly. "You always think this is the time you're going to hit it big, but you never do! You need to stop gambling and get serious about your life."

"Like you?" Spencer sneered. "You're always leaning on everyone else. You're pathetic."

"Don't call me again," Devyn said as forcefully as she could manage.

"I'm sorry," Spencer quickly responded, trying to appease her. *"I asked Mom for money, but she doesn't have any more."*

"You took money from Mom and Dad?" Devyn asked.

"I had to! I was going to be kicked out of my apartment."

"I bet you haven't asked Fred, have you?"

"No. He wouldn't give it to me even if I did. And Mila and Angela don't have any to spare, with all those kids of theirs. You're my only hope."

"Again, no!" Devyn said forcefully. *"I'm not giving you any more money."*

"You're ungrateful for everything we sacrificed for you when you were sick," Spencer seethed. *"You ruined my childhood! You owe me."*

Devyn clicked off the phone without another word.

She wanted to talk to someone about Spencer's gambling, but she didn't think anyone would fully understand how bad it had become.

She'd given her brother money when he'd first started asking. It was just twenty bucks here or fifty bucks there. It wasn't a big deal. Then the amounts had started increasing. The last time, she'd given him five hundred dollars because he'd said his car was going to be repossessed. She'd felt bad for him.

Devyn discovered he was gambling it away every time, in the hopes of winning the "big pot."

The last time she'd seen Spencer, he'd scared her. He'd gotten really pissed that she wouldn't give him more money...

When she moved, she'd lied to everyone. Her boss hadn't hit on her. Hadn't pushed her and given her the bruise Kinley had seen when they'd helped her move into this apartment.

Her *brother* had.

She was too ashamed to admit that it had been her own

flesh and blood who had hurt her. And Fred would lose his ever-loving mind if he ever found out.

It was better if she kept her mouth shut. She didn't want to be the reason her family fractured for good. Their parents had almost gotten a divorce when she was young because they couldn't deal with the stress of her being sick. She couldn't stand it if she was the reason everyone took sides and stopped talking to each other.

And that was why she couldn't talk to Lucky. He'd tell Fred what was going on, and that would be the end of their family. She couldn't do that to them. Not after everything they'd suffered during her illness. She'd just have to continue to keep her distance from all the questions and inquiries about what was going on. Spencer would eventually get the clue that she was done funding his habit.

But now a part of her really worried about whether that would happen…because it had been months and months, and he'd still called to ask for more money. She'd made it clear before leaving Missouri that she wasn't his personal bank, but he hadn't given up.

This was why she knew it would be a bad idea to stay in Texas. Near Fred. Because she'd get too attached and not want to leave. And it was happening already. She didn't want to give up her new friends. She wanted to meet Aspen's and Riley's babies. Aspen was due in a couple months, and Riley wouldn't be too long after that. And Logan and Bria, Oz's nephew and niece, were so cute, and she loved hanging out with them.

She'd made a new life here, even though she'd known better, and she really didn't want to leave.

Then there was Lucky.

As if on cue, he asked, "Dev? What are you thinking about so hard over there?"

He really was a good guy, and not for the first time, Dev wished her life was different. "Nothing," she replied quietly.

"You know, sharing your burdens usually makes them less scary and overwhelming," he said.

Devyn chuckled. "I didn't know you were so emo."

Lucky smiled. And the sight of it made Devyn's belly do summersaults.

"I'm not. And it's true. Maybe sharing what's wrong isn't actually a bad thing. You know your brother and I, and the rest of the team, will do whatever it takes to slay your dragons."

"I know." And she did. But the proverbial dragon that might need to be slayed was her own brother. And Fred's. She just couldn't do it.

"Think about it," Lucky told her. "I won't push...tonight. But you have a whole slew of people who love and worry about you. No one messes with one of our own. That includes you."

His words were sweet and terrifying at the same time. "Thanks."

"You're welcome."

"I'm kinda tired," Devyn lied. She needed to get Lucky out of her apartment before she caved and told him everything.

"Okay. I'll head on out."

"You need me to get an Uber?" she asked.

"No. I'll call Grover. I know he'll be worried about you."

"But he's still at the party," Devyn protested.

"He won't care. He'll probably be glad to get away from all the happiness and lovey-dovey crap for a while," Lucky said with a smile, standing from the couch.

"Is that why you left?" Devyn smirked.

"No. I left because you needed me." Then he shocked Devyn by leaning down and kissing the top of her head. "See you soon," he said as he gave her a long, intimate glance, then headed for her front door.

"What was that?" Devyn whispered when she was alone in her apartment once more.

But she knew. If she wasn't mistaken, Lucky was done letting her shut him out.

She'd seen firsthand that when a Delta made a decision about a woman, he was nothing if not determined to do whatever it took to win her over.

She couldn't decide if she was thrilled with the prospect of Lucky pursuing her, or if she was scared to death.

CHAPTER TWO

"Is she all right?" Grover asked in lieu of a greeting when Lucky climbed into his Jeep Grand Cherokee outside of Devyn's apartment complex.

"She's okay," Lucky told him.

"She tell you what the fuck's going on?" Grover asked.

"No."

"Shit. Why not?"

Lucky turned to his friend. "I have a question for you."

As Grover pulled out of the parking lot, he said, "Shoot."

"How would you react if your sister told me something and asked me to keep it between the two of us?"

Lucky watched as Grover's jaw hardened. "I wouldn't fucking like it."

"Yeah. And that's what I told her when she asked," Lucky said. "I would never keep something as important as your sister's well-being from you. You're one of the best friends I've ever had, and I have no desire to keep secrets from you. I have no idea what's going on, and she wouldn't tell me, but it's pretty obvious it has something to do with your brother. I might be way off base here, but I'm thinking she doesn't want to muddy the family waters."

Grover sighed. "Yeah, she's been avoiding my parents' calls for a while now. When Spencer asked for her number, I gave it to him in the hopes they could mend whatever was wrong. Guess that backfired, huh?"

"For the record, she said she wasn't sick or in danger," Lucky said.

"That makes me feel a little better. But because she was sick for so long, she doesn't like anyone to make a fuss over her. She could have a broken arm and she'd claim that it was just a scratch."

Lucky nodded. "I'm done fucking around," he informed Grover.

"Good," his friend said without hesitation. "I told you before, and I'll say it again. If Devyn got together with you or Doc, I'd be beside myself with joy."

"She's *not* hooking up with Doc," Lucky growled.

Grover laughed. "Right." Then he got serious. "I already feel as if you're my brother, but if you were my brother legally, I'd be fucking thrilled. And if you can figure out what's going on with Devyn and make the light come back to her eyes, I'll be forever in your debt."

"I do feel as if I need to say this..." Lucky said.

"Yeah?"

"As of right now, I'm Devyn's friend. And as such, I have no problem sharing stuff she tells me with you. But if things between us get serious, that's gonna stop. Dev and I will decide together if there's something she wants you to know or not, but I'm not going to be blabbing every single thing that goes on in our lives to you."

Grover was quiet for a moment. Then he said, "I can respect that. It's hard for me to think of Devyn being anything other than my little sister who I need to protect, but she *is* an adult."

Lucky nodded in relief. He didn't mind passing on pertinent information about Devyn's health and well-being to Grover right now, but it would seem too much like breaking a confidence if he shared too much, if they ever got to the point where they were a couple. And he wanted that. To be taken into her confidence...and to be able to call Devyn his.

He'd wanted that almost since the moment he'd laid eyes on her.

The two men were quiet as Grover drove back toward Oz's house. When they arrived, Grover pulled up next to Lucky's GMC Sierra pickup truck. "Figured you wouldn't be in the mood to go back in," he said as he turned off his engine.

"I feel bad, but yeah, I need to think about what my next steps will be," Lucky said. "If you talk to Spencer, or your parents, you might tell them to back off Devyn for a while. She needs space. I have the feeling she's on the verge of bolting."

"What do you mean?" Grover asked, looking concerned.

"She hasn't unpacked. Not really," Lucky said.

"*Really?*"

"Yeah. There are boxes all over her place."

"But we helped her move in over a year ago."

"We moved the *boxes* in, but didn't stay to watch her unpack them."

"Fuck."

"If she gets any more pressure from Spencer about whatever it is he's pressuring her to do, I have a feeling she'll leave."

Grover looked over at Lucky. "I've missed her. I love all my siblings, but Devyn and I were really close growing up. I hated when she got sick and spent every minute I could with her. I didn't even want to play with my friends; all I could think about was how sad I'd be if she died. So I stuck by her side like glue. Even after she went into remission, we were still close. We're four years apart, but we might as well have been twins. I'm thrilled she's here. She's grown into an amazing woman, and I love her so much. I don't want her to leave."

"I don't either," Lucky said. "And I'm going to do everything in my power to get her to stay. But if Spencer keeps calling her, she might decide to leave to spare you whatever's happening."

"Right. I'll talk to him," Grover said.

"Good."

"Can I give you some advice?" Grover asked Lucky.

"Please do."

"Get a pet. A dog, or cat, or goat. It doesn't matter. Go to the shelter and pick out the sickest animal they've got. Then ask for Devyn's advice as to how to keep the poor thing alive. She'll be putty in your hands."

"Not sure I want to manipulate her like that," Lucky said, frowning.

"My sister loves animals. More than she loves people. She won't be able to resist helping you nurse some creature back to life. It'll give you an in."

"It's still manipulation," Lucky protested.

"Tell me you haven't wanted to get a dog," Grover retorted.

Lucky sighed. That was the thing about best friends. They knew you better than you knew yourself. "You know I have. We always had animals around the house when I was growing up. But it's not fair with how much we go on missions."

"If Oz can leave his nephew and niece in Gillian's capable hands when we head out, I think you can leave an animal or two with Gillian, Kinley, Aspen, or Riley. You know they'd love to help."

Lucky *did* know that. And he had to admit that Grover's idea had merit...though it still seemed a little underhanded.

As if reading his mind, Grover said, "Look, I love my sister. But she's stubborn as hell. Do what you have to do. Also, I appreciate more than I can say that you don't want to keep shit from me, but if you need to promise to keep your mouth shut in order to get her to admit what's wrong...I'm okay with it. All I ask is that if her life is at stake, you don't keep it from me."

"Deal," Lucky said immediately. He didn't want to keep anything from his friend, but if the subject came up with Dev again, he'd tell her about this conversation. Something was bothering her, and he desperately wanted to know what it was. Not to fix it for her, but to help her come up with a solution. Together.

"I wonder what the Humane Society's hours are?" he mused quietly.

Grover laughed and slapped him on the shoulder. "That's the spirit. And for the record, there's no way you'll get away with a courthouse wedding. My parents would have a heart attack. Mila and Angela were married in our family church back in Missouri, and that's where they'll want Devyn to marry the love of her life too."

"Jumpin' the gun a bit, aren't you?" Lucky asked as they both climbed out of the Jeep.

"I don't think I am. The guy who ends up with my sister will be damn lucky...and you're the luckiest asshole on the team. If anyone can make her fall in love, it's you."

"Thanks." Grover's confidence and approval meant the world to Lucky.

"She's a handful, but she cares more than anyone I've ever met," Grover said. "See you at PT tomorrow morning. Good thing we've got the rest of the day off afterward, so you can head to the Humane Society."

Lucky shook his head as his friend laughed and wandered back toward Oz's house and the party going on inside.

Grover had given him some good advice, and Lucky was more relieved than he could say that his friend was supportive of him starting something with Devyn. It wouldn't have stopped him regardless, but it made things a hell of a lot easier. He wasn't comfortable with keeping secrets from Grover, but he'd play that by ear. If Grover did his part and had a talk with his brother, maybe Devyn would relax. Time would tell.

In the meantime, he'd do whatever it took to get Devyn to trust him, to see that he was a man who could be relied on. Who *she* could rely on.

CHAPTER THREE

"How can I help you today?" a woman asked when he walked into the Humane Society the following morning.

Lucky couldn't believe he was doing this, but Grover was right. He'd missed having pets underfoot. He grew up on a farm in upstate New York and there were always dogs, cats, pigs, ferrets, goats, or some other furry creatures around. He could even remember one summer when his parents had decided to try to save an orphaned calf, and it had lived inside their house for three months before it got so big they had no choice but to transition it to sleeping in the barn.

"I'd like to adopt a pet," Lucky told her.

"Great!" the perky woman said. "Do you know what kind?"

"I think a cat. I travel for work, and I think a cat would be easier to have someone take care of when I'm gone."

"True. Although cats get just as lonely as dogs. Some people think they can leave their cat home alone with a jug of water and a large bowl of food and they'll be fine. But they need social interaction too."

"Oh, I wouldn't leave it alone," Lucky said. "I'd have a friend come over every day."

"Okay, good. Do you want a kitten? Older? What color? We have a lot of black cats. Unfortunately, people still buy into the myth that black cats are bad luck."

"I'm not really sure what I'm looking for," Lucky admitted. "I kind of thought I could see what you have and go from there."

"No problem. We usually have adopters fill out paperwork once they find a *fur*ever friend. If you'll follow me, I'll show you where the cats are kept and you can take your time and see if anyone *cat*ches your eye!"

Lucky barely kept himself from smirking at the woman's attempts at humor. He followed her to a door off to the left of the reception area. They passed several empty rooms, obviously spaces where potential adopters could hang out with an animal to make sure they were compatible.

The longer he'd thought about it last night, the more sure he'd become of the decision to adopt a pet. He knew Grover had suggested it somewhat as a joke, but Lucky was actually becoming excited to pick out a cat.

The woman opened a door, and the sound of barking dogs immediately assaulted his ears. Another reason to adopt a cat; they didn't bark their heads off and annoy the neighbors.

The employee smiled at the animals as she guided him past a long row of kennels holding dogs. Each space was about six feet long by four feet wide. There were blankets in most of the kennels, along with toys and bowls of food and water. A chain link fence ran along the length of the kennels, with gates leading into each small space. Most of the dogs jumped up against the wire, barking as Lucky and the employee walked past.

They were about to enter another room—which Lucky

could see held stacks of cages housing cats—when something caught his eye.

Turning, Lucky glanced at a kennel that looked empty at first glance. It was movement in the very back that had caught his eye. A shaggy brown dog was huddled in a back corner. He could see dark brown eyes peering out at him untrustingly. It wasn't barking; in fact, the poor thing was shaking and looked as if it hoped he kept walking away as fast as possible.

"Sir?" the woman asked.

Lucky pointed to the dog. "What's his story?"

"Her. A worker on a demolition crew called her in. She was living in an abandoned house that was set to be torn down. Thankfully, they didn't tear down the house before finding her inside. She had to be darted for us to capture her. She's extremely skittish, almost feral. We think she's part terrier, part retriever, maybe."

Then Lucky saw something he hadn't noticed the first time. A smaller pair of eyes peering out from between the dog's legs.

"Is that a...cat?" he asked.

"Yeah. They were found in the house together. The dog is very protective of his friend. From what we can tell, the dog had a litter, but the puppies didn't make it. She probably found the kitten and, since she was still lactating and missing her pups, adopted the kitten as her own."

Lucky's heart melted.

"We haven't had any luck in socializing them though. The dog hasn't loosened up around any of us. She had to be sedated just so we could examine her, and the cat meowed pitifully the entire time her companion was gone. Unfortunately, they're on the euthanasia list for later this week. As much as we'd like to save everyone, they need to be adopted out together, and with their skittishness, that's not likely."

"I'll take them," Lucky said impulsively.

The woman blinked. "What?"

"I'll adopt them both."

"Oh, um...I thought you said you wanted a cat?"

"I do. But I'm not opposed to a dog. And these two probably need to be adopted more than any other animal in here."

"But we haven't even gotten into the cat room," the woman said, still sounding confused.

Lucky turned to face her, cocking his head. "Are you trying to talk me *out* of adopting them?" he asked.

"Well, no, not really. But we don't even know the full extent of their medical needs. And that dog isn't going to be the best pet. She's been on her own too long. Doesn't trust anyone."

"Does she have a name? The dog, I mean," he asked.

"Not officially. But the staff has been calling her Lucky."

Lucky grinned. Why wasn't he surprised?

"I'll need to get some paperwork for you to fill out," she told him, still sounding doubtful. "If you'll come with me—"

"Can I go in there with them?" Lucky asked. "I'd like to see if I can get them used to me. At least a little bit. To try to make me transporting them to my place a little less traumatic."

At that, the woman looked extremely skeptical. "Well, it's against policy..." she said, her voice trailing off.

"Are you going to be able to get them into one of the visitation rooms without completely freaking them out?" Lucky asked.

She looked uncomfortable at the question.

"I won't let them out. I just want them to get used to the sound of my voice." Lucky wasn't sure that was even possible, with the riot of barking dogs all around them, but he didn't want to traumatize the pair by having them dragged out of the kennel and thrown into a strange room. This was what they were familiar with at the moment.

"All right. And you can change your mind at any time," she told him.

That wasn't happening.

Relieved, however, that he would be allowed to greet the new members of his household on their turf, he nodded at the employee.

She opened the door to the kennel and Lucky slipped inside.

"Rebecca?" a woman called from the door to the reception area. "I'm getting slammed up here. Can you come help me?"

The woman who'd been helping him, Rebecca, looked at him uncertainly.

"I'm fine," Lucky told her. "Take your time. I'll just be here hanging out with my new friends."

"Okay. I'll be back as soon as I can."

Lucky nodded and then she scurried back down the walkway, toward the reception area.

Lucky breathed out a sigh of relief. He wasn't sure he could gain the pair's confidence, but he was glad he wouldn't have an audience while he tried. He eased himself onto his ass at the gate, then rolled onto his belly with his legs bent at the knees so he fit in the space. Propping his chin on his hands, he gazed at the pathetic-looking dog and her kitty friend.

"Hi," he said softly. "I'm Lucky. I know that's what people around here have been calling you, but it would get confusing if we both had the same name. And while you really *have* been lucky, I think something more feminine would suit you better. How about Gretta?"

The dog didn't even blink.

"No? Yeah, maybe not. Abby? Belle? Charlie? Nikki? Pepper?" Lucky knew some people would think he was being ridiculous, asking a dog what she wanted her name to be. But when he was younger, he'd always been in charge of naming their pets, and he'd taken his job seriously. He believed that the animal would let him know when they liked one of the names he chose.

"Layla? Trixie? Ginger? Angel?"

The second he said the name Angel, the dog's ears perked forward and she lifted her head a bit.

"Angel, huh? You like that?" Lucky asked.

Of course the dog didn't answer him with words, but he saw the tip of her tail move slightly.

"Okay, Angel. Here's the deal. You're going to come home with me today. You *and* your friend. I live in a townhouse, and there's lots of room for you both. I know things have been scary recently, but from here on out, you're safe. I won't hurt you, and you'll have lots of food and water. I don't know what happened to you before, but you've got a whole new life ahead of you now. One where you don't have to worry about your house being torn down with you still in it."

Angel continued to stare at him, as if she understood every word he was saying.

Lucky moved slowly, staying prone on the ground. He wasn't looking at Angel or the cat anymore, but he stretched his hands out toward the pair, palms up. He continued talking about nothing in particular. Telling his new friends about his team and their women. He told them about Devyn, and how she was skittish too, and how he hoped to gain her trust.

Basically, Lucky wanted the pair to get used to the sound of his voice. To see that he wasn't going to hurt them.

He didn't know how long he lay on the floor, but when he felt a cold nose against his fingers, he didn't move an inch.

He kept talking, telling Angel what a good dog she was, what an amazing mother she'd been to the kitten. He felt the dog's nose sniffing his palms a bit more...then the weight of her head resting on the fingers of one of his hands.

Lucky smiled. He moved his head without picking it up and saw Angel had shifted so she could get a bit closer to him. Her dark brown eyes were focused on him, and she'd actually put her head on his hand.

"You like that, girl?" he asked. Using his thumb, he gently caressed the side of her muzzle. It was the only thing he could reach. Amazingly, Angel didn't move.

The cat, which had been nestled between Angel's legs, seemed to want in on whatever her adopted protector was getting, and she inched her way forward as well. Her head butted against his other hand, and Lucky smiled again.

The cat looked like she was in as rough shape as Angel. Her tawny-colored fur was matted in places, but she had the most beautiful and expressive green eyes he'd ever seen. "Hey. I have no idea if you're a boy or a girl, but you're awfully brave, aren't you? And look at those long whiskers," he crooned. "How about if I call you Whiskers? What do you think of that?"

The cat butted its head against his fingers again, demanding pets. Lucky didn't dare laugh out loud, in case that would startle his new friends. He acquiesced to the cat's demands and used his fingers to pet its head as well as he could in his prone position. He could see the cat was older than he'd first thought, making it obvious the pair had been together for longer than just a few weeks.

"So, Angel and Whiskers, you think you might want to come home with me? I promise, if nothing else, it'll be a hell of a lot quieter than it is in here."

Whiskers began to purr softly, Lucky could feel the vibrations against his fingers, and Angel actually closed her eyes as she lay on his hand.

Thirty minutes later, Rebecca appeared at the front of the kennel. She stared at Lucky in disbelief.

He'd changed position and was now sitting with his legs crossed, both Angel and Whiskers in his lap. The dog was probably about twenty pounds and the cat wasn't much more than five, if he had to guess.

When he'd sat up, both animals had scurried back into the corner. Lucky had pulled the blanket in the other corner onto his lap and kept talking to the pair, low and easy.

Whiskers had been the first to move, stepping closer to him and eventually climbing onto the blanket on his lap. Angel had become distressed, and had quickly joined her friend, probably wanting to protect her. But after a few minutes, and more pets, both had relaxed.

"Holy shit," Rebecca said softly. "If I wasn't seeing this with my own eyes, I'd never believe it."

Lucky smiled. "I've got a way with animals," he told her.

"Yeah, I can see that," she retorted. "You think you can pick them up? Or will they freak?"

"I'm not sure I can even stand," Lucky admitted. "I think my legs are asleep." They smiled at each other. "But yeah, I'm thinking I can probably carry them."

"We've got a crate you can put them in to transport them home," Rebecca said. "I just ask that you bring it back; we need all the supplies we can get."

"No problem," Lucky told her.

Thirty minutes later, he was in his Sierra with two very scared animals in a crate in the backseat. Lucky sighed. He hadn't planned well. He needed food and beds and leashes and collars. He'd kind of thought he'd pick out a cat, stop at the store real fast on his way home, and be good to go. But there was no way he could bring Angel and Whiskers into a store, and he wasn't going to leave them alone in his truck either.

Both animals needed a bath, badly, and they needed to be examined to make sure they were healthy. The shelter had given them shots, and even had both animals spayed, but he still worried about their overall health.

"Don't worry, guys. I'm going to call somebody, but she's good. She's gonna love you, and she won't hurt you." Lucky wanted to laugh at himself. He was talking to the dog and cat as if they could understand him. But a part of him believed they *could*. At least in theory. Animals were very good at picking up nuances of the human voice. If someone was upset or mad, they knew it. If they were relaxed and happy, they reacted accordingly.

He clicked on the Bluetooth in his car and selected Devyn's number. Grover had told him that Devyn had the day off today.

"Hello?"

Everything about Devyn appealed to Lucky. Even her husky voice. "Hey. It's Lucky."

"What's up?"

"I need your help. But I want to make things really clear from the start—your brother told me to do this as a way to manipulate you. To give me a way to spend more time with you and to make sure you're all right. But that's *not* what this is," Lucky said.

Devyn chuckled nervously. "Oooookay. That sounds ominous."

"I just didn't want Grover to say something later and have you misconstrue it. I mean, I don't think it's a secret that I want to spend time with you. That I like you a hell of a lot. But I didn't do this as a way to force you to hang with me. I want you to want that because you like me back."

"You're making me very nervous," Devyn said. "But I appreciate your honesty. And while we're being honest, I like hanging out with you already, you don't have to come up with fancy excuses."

"I appreciate that," Lucky said, although he was afraid to ask if she liked hanging out with him as a friend of her brother's, or if the possibility for more existed. He was too much of a chicken at the moment to even go there.

"So...what do you need me to help you with?" she asked.

"I kind of adopted a dog and a cat, and I have nothing for them. No food, no litter box, no beds. And I need it all. But I don't want to leave them alone in my townhouse while I go out, and I can't bring them into a store with me. I was hoping maybe you wouldn't mind picking up some stuff and bringing it to my place? And when you get there—if they're okay with it—maybe taking a peek at them to check them over? Healthwise."

There was silence on the other end of the phone for a long moment.

"Devyn? Are you still there?"

"I'm here. You *kind of* adopted a dog and a cat?" she asked.

"Yeah," Lucky sighed. "Grover suggested that it would help me get in your good graces, but honestly, I've been thinking about getting a pet for a while. I grew up with animals, and with everyone getting married and having babies, we've all been hanging out a lot less outside of work. And I'm not afraid to say it—my place is lonely. So I thought I'd get a cat. Except, then we walked by a kennel with a dog *and* a cat. A bonded pair. They were scheduled to be euthanized later this week. I couldn't leave them."

"Holy shit, Lucky's a total softie," Devyn murmured.

"Shhhhh, don't tell anyone," he joked. Then he sobered. "They're scared to death, Dev. Skittish as hell. It's breaking my heart to think about why they're so scared of people. I got them to trust me at the shelter, but I have a feeling they'll be completely freaked out when I get them home. I just...I need help."

"I can be there in forty minutes or so," Devyn said without hesitation. "Do you have their records? Did the shelter give them any medical care?"

"Yeah. They've both been spayed, so they're both female. They've got mats in their fur, and I think they're both underweight, but the shelter gave them all the required shots... rabies, parvo, kennel cough, that sort of thing."

"Okay, that's good. You know I'm not a vet, right?" she asked.

"I know, but you're a damn good vet tech. I realize I need to bring them in for a complete workover, but I can't do that when they're so scared. They need time to relax. To see that they're safe with me. That I won't hurt them. And shoving them back into this crate and hauling them off to be poked and prodded isn't going to do a damn thing to make them trust me."

"You're...This is a side of you I haven't seen before," Devyn admitted.

"What, a Delta Force Operative can't be concerned about two helpless animals?" Lucky asked, a little snappier than he probably should've.

"It's not that. It's just...most people wouldn't care this much about a stray dog and cat."

"I've seen a lot of shit on missions—animals being abused in the worst ways—and I haven't been able to do a damn thing about it. But I could do something for Angel and Whiskers."

"Do you have a preference for food or anything else?" Devyn asked in a tone Lucky couldn't interpret.

He mentally kicked himself for talking about abused animals. "No. Although neither are really young, so don't get kitten or puppy food. Oh, and I'm thinking a pink collar for

Angel; she seems as if she'd like that. Don't get retractable leashes, those are dangerous as hell. And get Whiskers a harness so she can go on walks with us. I have a feeling she won't be happy if I take Angel for a walk and she doesn't get to come too. And the dog bed should be really fuzzy. Big enough for a thirty-pound dog and ten-pound cat, because they're inseparable. They don't weigh that much right now, but I'm sure I'll overfeed them when they give me the pathetic dog and cat eyes. Oh, and toys! Get some harder ones Angel can chew on, and some of the stuffed ones. We'll have to see if she destroys them to get to the squeaker inside or not. And catnip stuff for Whiskers—"

Devyn burst out laughing.

"What?" Lucky asked.

"Nothing. So you want me to get half the store then?"

Lucky chuckled. "I'm being ridiculous, I know. But you didn't see them, Dev. They need pampering more than anyone I've seen in a very long time. You're gonna fall in love the second you meet them."

"I'm sure I will," Devyn said quietly. "Okay, I'm out of here. I'll be at your place as soon as I can. I'm not sure how much stuff will fit in my Mini Cooper though. Do you need a crate?"

"Yeah, I think I do. They'll feel safer in there. I need to bring the one the shelter gave me back to them. It'll be a place they can hide in if they need to. I'm thinking a plastic one. Medium. I can call Grover or one of the other guys to pick it up if it won't fit in your car. You really *do* need something bigger, Dev."

"Nope. I love my Mini. It's old, but it runs great and it's not boring, like a sedan would be. I'll see what I can do about the crate. I agree with you that if Angel and Whiskers are already skittish, having a crate for them is a good idea."

"Thanks for helping me out," Lucky said.

"Of course. See you soon."

Lucky clicked off the phone at the same time he pulled into the parking space in front of his townhouse. He lived in an end unit in a row with five others. His neighbors were mostly military families, and he'd never had any issues with anyone. He had no idea if Angel was a barker, but he hoped not for his neighbors' sakes. So far he hadn't heard the dog make a sound, so he hoped that boded well for his future relationships with his neighbors.

"We're home," he told his passengers. "I know this is all very scary, but I promise your lives will be smooth sailing from here on out."

CHAPTER FOUR

Devyn couldn't see out her rearview mirror, but despite that, she couldn't stop smiling. She'd never met anyone quite like Lucky. She knew her brother's teammates were good men, but she'd somehow still expected them to be like a lot of other alpha guys she'd known over the years. Way into sports, a little condescending to anyone they thought was "weaker" than them, and never allowing anyone to see anything that could seem even slightly like a flaw.

Instead, Grover's teammates were nothing like what she'd imagined for badass special forces soldiers. They were protective for sure. And didn't hesitate to stand up to anyone who was being a jerk. But they were also funny. And not scared to show their feelings. They'd invited her into their inner circle without reservations and with open arms. As had their girlfriends—now wives. All of them were, collectively, the biggest reason why she hadn't moved on. Texas was just supposed to be a short stay while she figured out what she wanted to do with her life next. Where she wanted to live.

Then there was Lucky.

She supposed she should call him by his given name, Troy,

but she'd heard Grover talk about his team for so long now, it felt weird to call him anything but Lucky. At first she'd assumed he had the nickname because he got lucky in bed a lot, but Grover had explained it was because the man had the most amazing luck with just about *everything*.

From the first time she'd seen Lucky, Devyn had felt an attraction, but she'd fought it hard. The more she got to know him, however, the harder he was to resist. She'd been able to keep him at arm's length so far, because she knew she'd be leaving eventually, and starting a relationship with anyone would be foolish.

But the attraction always remained, simmering beneath the surface. All of her new girlfriends had noticed. And after he'd made sure she'd gotten home safely when she was upset yesterday, and considering how he didn't push her to talk...it was more and more difficult to tell herself they could only be friends.

She had a feeling that when she saw him with the dog and cat he'd just adopted, she'd be a goner. That was a level of compassion she hadn't expected, not from a special forces soldier. Which was ridiculous; even though he was a Delta, he still had feelings. And she could tell even over the phone that Lucky would do whatever it took for his new pets to feel comfortable. He was already completely spoiling them, if all the crap she'd bought was any indication.

How could she *not* fall for a man who went all gooey-eyed over a pair of strays?

The bottom line was that she couldn't. She wasn't ready to tell him all her secrets, but she had a feeling he could easily convince her to open up to him before much longer.

Telling anyone about Spencer, and what she'd gone through back in Missouri, could be the death knell for her family. Her sickness had already almost broken up her parents. She wasn't all that close to her older sisters, who'd admitted once that they'd been irritated with her for getting all the attention when they were younger. Oh, they all got on pretty well now...but there was still that niggling thought in the back of Devyn's head that she was a pain in everyone's asses. The source of too much trouble.

And if she confided in Grover, everyone would take sides, and it would be a disaster. It was up to *her* to keep her mouth shut.

If Spencer wouldn't get help, that was on him; she was done being his go-to girl.

When she pulled into Lucky's parking lot, she parked in a visitor's space not too far from his truck. Deciding to leave all the stuff she'd bought in her car for now, Devyn headed for the door.

Oddly, her skin seemed to be tingling. She'd never been inside his place. He'd texted the address and invited her to come over one night when his team and their women were hanging out watching a football game, but she'd declined. She'd still been trying to keep her distance from everyone at that point. To keep from getting too attached. But that had been a huge failure. They'd all snuck under her radar.

Especially Lucky.

"Hey," he said, opening the door before she could knock or ring the bell.

Devyn jumped in surprise.

"Sorry, didn't mean to scare you. I didn't want Angel or Whiskers to freak out if they heard the doorbell or a knock. Come on in."

With every expression of concern for his new pets, Lucky wormed his way further into her heart.

Devyn walked inside, looking around curiously. The small foyer led into an open room. A dining area was on the right side of the foyer, where Lucky had a fairly large table filling the space, which was a surprise. There were eight chairs around the oval oak table. A laptop was sitting open on one end, with napkins and an open bag of chips next to it.

"Sorry, I didn't have time to clean up before you got here," Lucky told her, obviously following her gaze.

"It's fine. You didn't have to clean up for me. I'm just Grover's sister."

"You aren't *just* anything," Lucky said immediately.

Devyn stared at him for a long moment. She wanted to say something witty, something flirty, but her mind was a complete blank. So she turned her attention back to the house instead.

"This is the kitchen. It kind of sold me on the place," Lucky said, gesturing toward the huge area. A granite-covered bar bisected the big space, and she couldn't help but be impressed. Whoever had designed the kitchen hadn't spared any expense. The oven was restaurant quality; she saw an ice maker under the counter as well. The refrigerator was massive—much bigger than a normal fridge. All the appliances were stainless steel, and the sink was one of those barn sinks, deep, and it looked as if it was made out of concrete.

Devyn wasn't the best cook, though she enjoyed making complicated dishes every now and then. But this kitchen was a bit intimidating.

"The size of the kitchen took away from some of the living area, but I love it. The pantry is huge too, which means I can buy a lot of stuff in bulk so I don't have to go to the store as much," Lucky said.

"It's amazing," Devyn told him.

They walked into the comfortable-looking living area. There was a leather couch against one wall, a bookshelf stuffed with CDs and books, and a large coffee table. A recliner rounded out the room. "No TV?" she asked.

Lucky shrugged. "I've got one upstairs in my bedroom. I

don't watch a lot of television. I prefer to listen to music or read."

She liked that. She felt the same way.

"Come on, you've got to see the back deck," Lucky said.

Devyn followed behind Lucky as he led the way through the living room. They entered a small laundry room before he opened a back door. He gestured for her to precede him, and Devyn gasped as she walked out onto the deck.

They were on the ground level, but the land dipped slightly and the view was as beautiful as anything she'd ever seen. There was a fence around the yard, but because of the way the land sloped down before it leveled out, she could see over the fence to the wilderness beyond the property.

"Wow!" Devyn exclaimed.

"Yeah. The kitchen sold me, and this view solidified my decision. I probably paid way too much for this place, but I couldn't resist. And because I've got the end unit, my yard is much bigger than the others. It's as wide as it is long."

"This is awesome. Is that part of Fort Hood?" Devyn asked, gesturing toward the large expanse of land in front of them.

"Yeah. Which means no one can build a huge housing complex back there and ruin this view," Lucky said with a smile.

This part of Texas wasn't exactly known for its lovely vistas, but he had truly lucked out with his townhouse. She looked over at him. "Another one of your *lucky* finds?" she asked.

He smiled sheepishly. "I can't help it if I'm lucky. The seller was devastated to have to get rid of the place, but his mom was sick out in California, and he needed to move out there to take care of her."

Devyn simply shook her head.

"Come on, I'll show you the rest of the place. I've got Angel and Whiskers upstairs in my bathroom for now."

Devyn nodded. She couldn't believe she'd almost forgotten why she was there. "Let me run out to my car to get my medical bag. I brought it just in case."

Lucky followed her out to her Mini Cooper and grabbed as many bags of dog and cat supplies as he could. He stuffed a tan, fluffy dog bed under an arm. "Good choice," he told her.

Devyn smiled, relieved. She'd spent way too much time agonizing over which dog bed to get. She finally settled on the tan one because the clerk helping her had recommended it. He said he had one, and his dog literally slept in it all day.

They went back into the house and Lucky put everything down but the bed, heading up the stairs. Devyn couldn't help but stare at his perfect ass as she followed. She hoped she wasn't drooling.

He quickly gave her a tour of the two bedrooms upstairs, and the functional yet boring guest bathroom. Then he led her into the master bedroom.

Devyn would've known it was his without being told whose townhouse she was in.

She was immediately surrounded by his scent. It was subtle, but she'd always associate the smell of his body wash with Lucky.

Standing in his personal space felt so...intimate. He slept here. Watched TV. Probably masturbated.

God, she was being weird. She never thought about that kind of thing with anyone else. She'd gotten tours of other houses and sex hadn't ever crossed her mind. But with one glance at his king-size bed, she couldn't think of anything *but* sex.

His covers were mussed, as if he'd just climbed out from under them—

"Dev?" Lucky asked. "You okay?"

She knew she was blushing, but she nodded. "Yeah, of course."

"They're in here. I know you're a professional, but please don't make any sudden movements. Angel's really scared, and I want her to like you. I'm thinking we'll go in, close the door, then you can sit against the door and I'll sit with my back to the wall. Last I saw them, they were huddled behind the toilet. We'll just talk and give them time to get used to us. Okay?"

Devyn's heart melted even more. He sounded extremely worried and stressed. He wanted his new pets to feel safe, and it was obvious he'd do whatever it took to make sure that happened.

"Sounds good," Devyn told him.

Then Lucky surprised her by grasping her free hand with his own, before he opened the door.

He quickly shut it after they entered. Devyn got a quick glimpse of the bathroom—one sink, a bathtub/shower combo and toilet—before her attention was focused on the two fluff balls cowering behind said toilet, just where Lucky had said they'd be.

"Hey, Angel. Hi, Whiskers. It's just me. You're okay. I know the drive home was stressful, but you're safe here. I brought a friend. This is Devyn. She was the one I was talking about on our way home." He paused and looked over at her.

Devyn quietly added, "Hey, you two. I hope you know how lucky you are to have snagged this guy here. You're gonna be so spoiled. And I'm sure we're gonna have to watch your weight. I have a feeling Lucky's gonna give you way too many treats."

The animals didn't move from their hiding spot, but they didn't seem to cower away from her either. She took that as a win.

"Change of plans," Lucky told her. "Let's both sit here," he said, pulling her down onto the floor next to him. "Angel didn't flinch from the sound of your voice," he said. "I think maybe she recognizes it from when I talked to you in the car."

Devyn wasn't so sure of that, but she let Lucky take the lead.

They sat on the floor for twenty minutes while Lucky talked nonstop to his new pets. He told them about how Devyn worked with animals on a daily basis, and how she could be trusted.

He placed the dog bed on the floor in front of them and explained that it was much softer than the hard tiles they were sitting on. Devyn couldn't believe it when the cat actually crept her way out of the protective embrace of her doggy friend to try it out. Of course, Angel couldn't let Whiskers get more than a heartbeat away, so she followed.

It wasn't long before both were curled up in the bed and Lucky was scratching their heads.

"That's so mind-blowing," Devyn said.

"What?"

"You're a dog whisperer. Or cat whisperer. It's amazing."

"Naw, they just need some time to analyze new situations. Rushing them wouldn't do anything to make them feel safer. Come here," he said, keeping his voice low and calm.

Devyn slowly scooted closer to both him and the animals.

"Give me your hand."

She did, shivering slightly when he intertwined his fingers with hers.

"If you smell like me, they'll trust you more easily." Then he reached out with both their hands and gently stroked Whiskers' head.

"She's more outgoing," he told Devyn. "It wouldn't seem like it since she hides in Angel's fur a lot, but I have a feeling she hasn't been as traumatized by humans. So she trusts more easily. I'm guessing Angel's had a hard life and hasn't been treated well. But she follows Whiskers' lead."

"How do you know so much about animals?" Devyn asked quietly.

"Grew up with them. Was in 4H, took in strays, that sort of thing," he told her. "I've always been drawn to them. There were times I thought they understood me better than my family did."

"Are you close with your parents?"

"Yeah. I don't see them a lot, but I try to get up to New York to visit when I can. It's getting harder and harder for them to keep the farm going, but they love it."

"A farm, huh? I wouldn't have pegged you for a farm boy," Devyn teased.

"I know. I had a great childhood though. I'm the man I am because of my parents. They're great. Sometimes I feel guilty that I had such an easy time growing up. So many people I know struggled."

"Don't feel bad," Devyn said.

Lucky turned to her, and she felt pinned in place by his hazel eyes. In the light of the bathroom, she saw more brown than the blue she'd spotted there earlier in the sunlight. "I hate that you were sick," he said.

For the first time in a long time, Devyn didn't see pity in someone's gaze when they talked about her leukemia.

"Thanks. Honestly, I didn't know any different. By the time I got old enough to understand that other kids didn't spend most of their lives in a hospital being poked and prodded, I was used to the routine. I feel worse for my siblings. In many ways, I think my being sick was harder on them than it was on me. They didn't get a lot of attention."

"Tell me about your brother and sisters?"

She figured he didn't mean Grover, since he already knew

him very well. "Mila is the oldest. She's seven years older than me. She's married to a great man and lives in Colorado. They have three kids. I try to FaceTime with them as much as I can, but it's never often enough. Angela is next. She's five years older than me. I remember wanting to hang out with her when I wasn't in the hospital, but I was too little, and fragile, to spend much time with her. Then when she was a teenager, she was into boys, and a sickly sister was the last person she wanted to hang out with. We've gotten closer over the years, but I don't think we'll ever be best friends. She's also married, and lives in Virginia with her husband and their two kids."

"So they both moved away from home," Lucky said.

He'd removed his hand from hers, and she absently petted Whiskers on her own. "Yeah. Angela went to school at Virginia Tech in Blacksburg, and Mila went to the University of Colorado in Boulder. They met their husbands in college and never left."

"Where'd you go to school?" Lucky asked.

"University of Missouri. My parents really wanted me to stay close to home."

"And what did *you* want?" Lucky asked.

Devyn shrugged. "I had no idea. I was just happy to have more freedom than I'd had living with my folks. They were always super protective of me, not that I can blame them. Anytime I got the sniffles, they'd panic, thinking the cancer was back."

"And you moved back to your hometown after you graduated," Lucky said.

"Yeah. I got a job with a local vet and was content."

She was afraid Lucky would press for more details. Would want to know why, if she enjoyed her job so much, she'd left it and headed down to Texas.

"What about Spencer? He's two years older than you and two years younger than Grover, right?"

Devyn nodded, grateful she didn't have to talk about why she'd left Missouri...but she wasn't all that fired up to talk about her brother either. She appreciated Lucky wasn't demanding answers. He already had to have guessed things between her and Spencer were strained. He knew Spencer was the one who'd called her yesterday, and that was why she'd left the party. For that alone, she kinda felt as if she owed him some sort of explanation.

"Spence went to college in Rolla, Missouri. A technical school. He didn't graduate; came home instead and got a job at the local bottling factory. He lived with Mom and Dad for a while, but eventually moved out and got his own place."

She paused, not knowing what else to say.

"Did he resent you?" Lucky asked.

Devyn winced. "Yeah, a little. I think he felt lost in the shuffle. My older sisters were always great students, and Grover headed off to join the military. Everyone was so proud of him. Then there was me, the sickly little sister getting all the attention. He partied a lot in high school and had some pretty nasty friends. My parents weren't happy when he flunked out of college, but they were glad when he got the job at the factory and seemed to get his act together."

She wanted to say more. But couldn't. She'd kept her secrets about Spencer for so long, it felt wrong to talk about them now.

"You can trust me," Lucky said softly.

Devyn smiled as Angel headbutted her fingers, demanding more pets. She felt as if she were like this little stray. Kinda lost in what she wanted to do with her life, skittish and slow to trust...and she so very much wanted to feel safe.

"I know," she said after a minute.

"I don't think you do. But you will," Lucky stated. Then he changed the subject by saying, "I think they like you."

Whiskers was purring nonstop, and Angel had moved a little closer so Devyn could pet her with the hand that wasn't caressing Whiskers.

Moving slowly, Lucky reached out and lifted Angel onto his lap. The dog trembled but didn't fight Lucky. Devyn looked into the dog's eyes as she palpated her abdomen, checking her uncovered spay incision. "She looks good," Devyn told Lucky.

He sighed in relief. "Good."

"I mean, I'm not a vet, but her incision is healing fine. It could probably use some more fresh air, but overall it's fine. She doesn't have goopy eyes, and she doesn't flinch when I press on her anywhere. I think she just needs a good bath, food, and some time."

"I think we'll skip the bath for now. But the time, I can give her."

They went through the same motions with Whiskers, and Devyn declared her in good shape as well. The pair settled back into their fuzzy bed and sighed in exhaustion, as if they'd just walked ten miles.

"Well, at least they're not hyper," Devyn said dryly.

Lucky chuckled. "True. You hungry?"

"I could eat," Devyn said.

"Great. Come downstairs and I'll make you the best grilled cheese sandwich you've ever eaten."

"You're awfully sure of yourself," Devyn quipped.

"Yup," Lucky agreed.

They slowly stood, and he took her hand in his again, as if he did it every day.

"I'm going to leave the door open. Let them explore if they want," he told her as they made their way through his bedroom.

"They might pee on your floor," Devyn warned. She knew she should pull her hand from his, but she couldn't bring herself to break their connection.

Lucky shrugged. "Then I'll clean it up."

Lord, the man was too good to be true.

"I'll take them outside before we eat," he told her. "I think Whiskers will be easy to potty train. She does everything Angel does. I'll be the only guy with a cat who goes outside to use the bathroom. I might not need that litter box you bought me."

Devyn laughed. "That would be amazing," she told him.

"I taught one of the cats we had growing up to pee in the toilet," he said as they headed down the stairs.

"Seriously?"

"Yup. It drove my mom crazy though because we had to leave the lids up so she could go. She would've preferred for the cat to use the litter box." He squeezed her hand and pulled out a chair. "Have a seat. I'll get us fixed up."

"Can I do anything?" she asked.

"Nope. I've got this. Although..."

"Yeah?"

"Maybe you could put together the crate? And cut the tags off the toys and stuff?" Lucky asked.

Grateful to help, Devyn nodded and stood, heading for the bags they'd brought in earlier. They laughed and joked as she got to work and Lucky made them sandwiches.

Eventually, Devyn said, "Lucky?"

"Yeah?"

"I appreciate you being honest with me about talking to Grover about anything I might tell you, and about him telling you to get a pet so I'd feel obligated to come help you out. When I was sick, a lot of people talked *over* me, or just outright lied to me. They didn't think I could handle knowing the truth about my treatments and stuff. I think they got used to babying me, so they continued not telling me anything even after I got better. So...thank you."

Lucky put down his spatula and came over to the table, where she'd sat after finishing the crate. He crouched in front of her and put a hand on her knee. "There *will* be things I can't share with you. Things about my job and what we do. But otherwise, I promise that I'll do my best not to keep secrets from you.

"I want you to trust me, Devyn. To know that I have your back no matter what the situation. That might mean hearing some uncomfortable things from time to time—like me admitting that Grover's idea about a pet had merit—but I'd rather be honest from the get-go than have you find out later that I'd lied to you or hidden the truth. And besides, I know that Grover wouldn't be able to keep his mouth shut. Sooner or later, you'd hear about what he'd suggested. And the last thing I wanted was for you to think I was being sneaky. We're adults, Dev. We need to talk about things that are bothering us, or things that might be scary."

Devyn's heart was beating a million miles an hour. This was a hell of a serious conversation, and she hadn't really meant for it to be as intense as it was. "You make it sound as if we'll have lots of deep things to discuss in the future."

"I hope we will," Lucky said. "I want to get to know you better, Devyn. I want to go out with you. Date. And part of that is being honest. I've got flaws, more than I'm comfortable talking about right now when I'm trying to convince you to give me a shot." He grinned. "But you'll learn them sooner or later. I just want you to know that I'll always be on your side. If our getting to know each other turns into a relationship, you'll come first. My relationship with your brother will change, which isn't a bad thing. We'll always be like brothers, and I'll always trust him with my life, but he won't have the right to know every little thing the two of us talk about."

Devyn swallowed hard. She understood what he meant. At least she thought she did. As of now, anything she might tell him about what was going on with her and Spencer was fair game for him to pass on to Grover. But if they got serious, that would change.

She had no doubt if something really serious happened, like her cancer returned or her life was in danger, Lucky would tell Grover. But otherwise, if they were a couple, their personal lives were just that. Personal.

"I..." Devyn cleared her throat and tried again. "I want to get to know you better too. And for the record, I don't mind Grover knowing things about me or my life. We've always been close. I just...I don't want to be responsible for making the relationships between my siblings any harder than they already are."

Lucky picked up her hand and kissed the palm before squeezing her fingers. "They're all adults. Anything that goes on between your brothers and sisters is between *them*. You aren't eight years old anymore, Dev."

"I know."

And she did. Mostly. But she still felt an obligation to not rock the boat.

"So, you'll go out with me?" Lucky asked with a smile.

"Yeah."

One word. But it would change her life forever. She knew it.

For good or bad, she was going to go after what she'd wanted for months. The consequences might tear her apart emotionally, but she was so tired of doing what she thought was best for everyone else.

And the smile that crossed Lucky's face was enough to make her push her other problems to the back of her mind.

"Good," he said. "I'm gonna go get Angel and Whiskers and take them out. Then we can eat. Will you pour a bowl of food for each of them, and water too? I don't know if they'll eat, but I want to try to leave them down here while we have lunch."

"Of course. I'll also put the crate in the corner, where they can see us but feel safe in there at the same time."

"Great idea. We're a good team," Lucky said.

He hesitated for a moment, as if he wanted to say something else, then he stood and headed for the stairs.

Devyn let out the breath she'd been holding. She wanted to confide in Lucky. Badly. But she couldn't. Not yet.

Hopefully Spencer would get the message that she didn't want to talk to him. That she couldn't help him out anymore. He needed to help *himself*, and until he did that, he'd never get better. She just hoped he'd see that before it was too late.

CHAPTER FIVE

A week later, at PT, Oz asked, "So, what's up with you and Devyn?"

Lucky stopped mid sit-up. "What?"

"You and Devyn. Riley was talking to her the other night, and Devyn said that she'd been spending the last few evenings at your place. You want to tell us something?"

Glancing over at Grover, Lucky was relieved that the other man didn't seem upset. He'd said that he was all right with him dating his sister, but when faced with the reality of the situation, he might've felt differently.

"You know I got Angel and Whiskers," Lucky told his teammates. "Well, I asked Devyn if she would help me socialize them. Angel was just about feral and needs a lot more human interaction. So she's been coming over to hang out with us, to show them that not all humans are bad. She's not staying the night, if that's what you were insinuating."

"I wasn't insinuating anything," Oz said with a smile. "Just wondering."

"To answer what you *didn't* ask, but I know you're all dying to know, we're dating," Lucky told his friends.

"It's about time!" Trigger exclaimed.

"Awesome!" Doc declared.

"Sweet!" Lefty said.

Grover merely smiled.

"Happy for you, man," Brain told him. "You have to know we've all been rooting for you two."

"She's...awesome," Lucky said with a small smile.

"She tell you any more about what's bothering her?" Grover asked.

Lucky shook his head, turning to look at his friend. "No."

"Damn."

"We both know it's something to do with your brother, Grover. Have you talked to Spencer to see what the hell is going on?" Lucky asked. "I get the impression that Devyn doesn't want to upset your family. She's very concerned about not doing or saying anything that might hurt anyone. Did you know she blames herself for your parents almost getting a divorce when she was sick?"

Everyone had stopped working out, and they were listening intently to the back and forth between Grover and Lucky.

Grover ran a hand through his hair and sighed. "I've tried to call him, but he never answers. It's frustrating, but short of driving my ass up to Missouri and forcing him to talk to me, there's not much I can do. And no, I didn't know she blames herself, but it doesn't surprise me. Devyn acts tough on the outside, but I think she's actually really sensitive. She takes things very personally, and is hyperaware of what everyone else is saying or thinking."

"Exactly," Lucky said with a nod. "And whatever is bothering her has to do with Spencer. Keep trying to call him. Tell him to lay off your sister."

"I will," Grover said. "She talk to you about her ex-boss?"

Lucky blinked at the abrupt change in topic. "Who?"

"The guy at the vet clinic where she was working in Missouri. You know, the one who pushed her around and put that bruise on her side? I know something's up with Spencer, but I'm thinking this asshole might also be part of the issue. She said he had the hots for her, and that's why she quit. He could still be harassing her."

Lucky frowned. "She hasn't said anything about him to me. And if he's been harassing her long distance, I haven't seen any evidence of it. She hasn't gotten any phone calls when she's been over at my place, and her phone hasn't been exploding with texts."

"That doesn't mean he's not sending her emails or harassing her when you aren't around," Trigger said.

"True. But I don't...I just don't get the feeling that she's afraid," Lucky said. "I know that doesn't make a lot of sense, but she's not overly concerned about walking from my door to her car when it's dark, and she seems pretty laid-back when we're hanging out at my place."

"I'd still like ten minutes alone with that asshole," Grover muttered.

Lucky remembered Devyn mentioning her boss when they were helping her move into her apartment, and he'd asked about the bruise on her side. He'd been plenty pissed off about it then, but she literally hadn't mentioned the man since. That didn't mean he wasn't still harassing her or anything, as Trigger suggested, but Lucky doubted it. Maybe he'd find a way to bring it up

While he'd loved hanging out with Devyn during the last week, he wanted more. A *lot* more. He loved how comfortable they were with each other, but somehow it felt as if their relationship so far was...superficial? He'd learned a lot about her —her favorite color, how she hated bungee jumping but loved skydiving, that she loved reading thrillers, and she couldn't stand green vegetables. But he didn't know the deeper stuff.

How she felt about having, and beating, leukemia as a kid. Why she'd decided to work with animals. Why it seemed as if she was still holding a part of herself back from Gillian and the other women.

He wanted to know what made Devyn tick, and he wanted her to share things with him that she hadn't shared with anyone else.

He knew she enjoyed their time together, but he wanted her to trust him enough to completely open up. To let him see all the parts of her, including the ones she thought were tarnished. Grover said she was sensitive, but Lucky hadn't seen that part of her at all. And it bothered him.

"You guys ready to run this obstacle course?" Trigger asked.

Everyone agreed.

"I think we'll do it with full packs this morning," Trigger informed them with a smirk.

Everyone groaned. Their packs weighed upward of sixty pounds and were unwieldy at best. But no one complained otherwise. There had been plenty of times in the past on their missions when they'd had to navigate tricky terrain and obstacles while wearing their packs, and there would be future missions where they'd need to do the same thing.

Lucky actually looked forward to the grueling training. It would take his mind off Devyn for a while. Maybe.

* * *

Devyn did her best not to squirm as she sat with Aspen, feeling the woman's intense gaze on her. They'd gotten together for lunch, and Aspen was way too observant for Devyn's liking. Out of all the women she'd gotten to know over the last year, Aspen was the hardest to get anything by.

"Want to tell me how you're *really* doing?" Aspen asked.

Devyn inwardly sighed, but put on a bright smile and said, "I'm good."

She hated the look of disappointment that flashed on Aspen's face before she hid it.

"Right. You're good. You're always *good*, Dev, but it's bull-shit. Are you at least talking to *someone* about what's going on with you? You can't keep everything locked inside. It's not healthy."

Devyn was tempted to tell Aspen everything, but the woman had enough on her plate as it was. She had about two months to go before her baby was born, and she'd just had to go on sick leave at her EMT job, which Devyn knew she didn't want to do. But she'd gotten to the point where her baby belly was getting in the way of her job. Brain had been relieved when she'd conceded that she needed to stop working for now.

"It's complicated," she said softly. There was no chance anyone would overhear them in the crowded café they'd agreed on for lunch, but Devyn didn't want to broadcast her troubles to anyone who might want to try.

"It always is," Aspen said, leaning her elbows on the table. "When Brain kicked me out of his hospital room after real-izing he couldn't remember any of the languages he'd learned, I thought I was going to die. I *wanted* to die. I couldn't believe the man I loved more than anything, the man I'd liter-ally held in my arms in the nastiest water you can ever imag-ine, had figuratively spit in my face and told me to get out. It hurt. And my first inclination was to hole up and not talk to anyone."

Devyn knew all about how Brain had gotten hurt, but she'd never really heard all the details about what had happened between him and Aspen afterward. She knew they'd had a fight, but not what had brought it on. She leaned toward her, not wanting to miss a word of the story. "Is that what you did?" she asked.

"No," Aspen said, shaking her head. "I called Gillian and went off on Brain. I told her I hated him, and that he was an asshole and I never wanted to see him again. She listened to my rant and when she thought I was done, said, 'Good riddance. Now you can find a man who appreciates you.'"

Devyn gasped. "She said that?"

"Yup. And my first reaction was basically horror." She laughed. "I laid into her, insisting that Brain *did* appreciate me. That he was hurt and not thinking straight. That she didn't know the entire story about what had happened. Then I heard her laughing. She knew I just needed to get my frustration and hurt out before I could plan what to do next."

Devyn wasn't sure what Aspen was trying to say. Her furrowed brow must've communicated her confusion, because Aspen went on.

"My point is that Gillian helped me look at the situation in a different way. She let me rant and rave, then provided me the push I needed to get my shit together. We're all here for you, Devyn. We don't know what's going on with you, but we're happy to listen when you're ready to talk things through. We might be able to provide a perspective you haven't thought of before. You can trust us."

Devyn swallowed hard. *This* was why she hadn't left Killeen. She'd come because Grover was here, but she'd stayed because she knew deep down that she'd found a group of friends who liked her just the way she was. They hadn't known her as the sickly kid she'd been long ago, so they didn't treat her with kid gloves. They'd come to enjoy being around her for who she was now.

"I know," she said softly.

"I hope you do," Aspen replied easily. "We've all been through a lot of shit, but we're stronger because of the people we have around us," she said. "You've got one hell of an impenetrable outer shell. I'm not saying you haven't earned it the hard way, all I'm saying is that you're safe with us. Me, Gillian, Kinley, and Riley. We'll have your back. No matter what."

"Thanks," Devyn choked out.

"And then there's Lucky," Aspen said with a grin. "You know that man wants in there bad, right?"

Devyn was relieved Aspen had lightened the mood. "Who even says that?" she asked.

"Me. And you should know we've all been talking about you two. The girls, that is. We've kind of got a betting pool going on about when you guys are finally going to do the deed."

Devyn almost spit out the sip of water she'd just taken. "Oh my God, no you don't!"

"We do. Gillian's gonna lose; she said three months from now. Kinley's a little more optimistic and said you'd probably already made love. Riley took a month and a half from now."

"And you?" Devyn asked with a grin.

Aspen cocked her head and examined Devyn with a little more intensity than she was comfortable with. "You don't trust easily. And even though you've been here with us for a while, you're still trying to decide if this is where you want to stay. You're still working part time, even though I know the vet you work for has begged you to go full time. You want Lucky, but you're also trying to protect your heart from him. But he's gotten through, at least a little. So I said within the month."

Devyn knew she was blushing. "He's amazing," she admitted. "The way he is with Angel and Whiskers is adorable. He has the patience of a saint. He doesn't get upset when Angel cowers in the back of her crate. He just sits on the hard floor in front of it, letting her get used to the sound of his voice and his presence. And damn if every time she's not sitting in his lap by the end of the night. Sometimes I feel as if I'm exactly like his pets. Hoping to be loved and cherished, but scared to death to take what I want."

Aspen reached out and took hold of Devyn's hand and placed it on her swollen belly. Devyn didn't flinch away from the intimate gesture. "Feel that?" Aspen asked.

Devyn nodded as the tiny baby in Aspen's belly kicked.

"I spent so much time trying to fit into a man's world, being tough and pretending not to care when men belittled me and told me I wasn't good enough to be a combat medic, that I forgot it was all right to be a woman. It was okay to want to be loved, to like flowers, and to want to be a mother. Being with Brain taught me that it's okay to be *exactly* who I am. Someone who can be tough as hell in the middle of a fire-fight overseas, or crying on the couch eating chocolate while watching a sappy chick flick.

"We all want to be loved, Devyn. There's nothing wrong with that. We want people to like us, we don't want to upset the apple cart, so to speak, but life isn't always going to be perfect. People are going to think we're bitches, or that we're selfish, or a million other derogatory things. But when you find the person who loves you exactly how you are, warts and all, what others think about you kinda falls to the wayside. The assholes don't matter as much anymore. I always wanted to be a mother, but I focused all my energy on fitting in with men who didn't accept me as I am. And now I *am* pregnant—and happier than I've ever been. Take a chance on Lucky. He's a good man. One of the best."

Devyn sniffed. Hard. "You're making me cry, bitch," she told Aspen.

"Good. Because I've cried more in the last couple months than I have in years. These pregnancy hormones are no joke."

Devyn took her hand back. "Are you scared?" she asked.

"About giving birth?"

Devyn nodded.

Aspen shook her head but said, "Terrified."

They shared a smile.

"I know how it all works. Hell, I've even birthed babies before. But it's different because now it's *my* baby. I already love him so damn much it's not funny. But I know with Brain by my side, I can get through anything."

Devyn appreciated that Aspen was trying to reassure her about Lucky. The encouragement was welcome. She wasn't as sure about everyone betting on when she and Lucky were going to make love, but deep down, she had to admit it made her laugh.

Did she trust Lucky? Yeah. She did. But if that was true, why couldn't she tell him about Spencer?

The entire situation was ridiculous. Everyone involved was an adult, but somehow she felt like she was five years old again, and if she let Spencer's secret out of the bag, she'd be the one responsible for ruining her family.

"You're gonna be fine," Devyn told her. "As long as you aren't late to your own baby's birth, like you are to everything else. You'll probably cook a six-course dinner, run three miles, and save someone's life by giving them CPR, all within hours of becoming a mom."

Aspen burst out laughing. "I'm not sure about any of that...except the being late thing. Dev?"

"Yeah?"

"I really am scared."

Devyn immediately reached for Aspen's hand. "About what?"

"All of it. Scared I won't be a good mom. That I'll screw something up. You know how smart Brain is; if our son inherits his smarts, I'm gonna be *so* out of my league. Or what if he turns out to be a bully? I don't know what I'll do if he's the mean kid everyone hates."

"Take a breath," Devyn ordered. "Good. Another. You are going to be an amazing mom. Know how I know?"

"How?"

"Because you're so damn worried about it. If you didn't care, I'd be more worried. Your kid is gonna be amazing because you and Brain are so great. If he's smart, that'd be wonderful. But even if he's not, are you gonna love him any less?"

"Of course not."

"Then stop worrying about stuff you can't control," Devyn ordered.

"Yes, ma'am," Aspen said with a smile. "I'll try."

"Out of curiosity...what did you guys bet on me and Lucky?" Devyn asked.

Aspen smirked. "Four hundred bucks."

"Holy shit, seriously?"

"Yup. We each ponied up a hundred. Winner takes all."

"I can't believe you're betting on me and Lucky having sex." Devyn knew she should be more upset than she was—especially considering the gambling aspect—but it was obvious it was all in good humor.

"Yeah, well, us girls just wanna have fun," Aspen told her.

Devyn rolled her eyes. "Great, now you're quoting Cyndi Lauper."

"I'd appreciate it if you got on that, literally and figuratively," Aspen said with a giggle. "I mean, I could use the cash. We're still setting up the baby's room."

"Isn't it cheating, telling me about the bet?" Devyn asked.

Aspen shrugged. "Probably. But the way I see it, if it helps you move things along with Lucky, it's all good. Seriously, Dev, you can't do better than him. Well, maybe except for Brain, but he's taken."

Devyn wanted to tell Aspen that she'd seriously been thinking about asking Lucky if she could stay the night, but so far, she hadn't gotten up the guts. She couldn't deny that she wanted the man. He made her feel...normal. And it had been so damn long since she'd felt that way. If ever.

With him, much like with her friends, she wasn't the kid who'd had leukemia. She wasn't the "fragile sister." She wasn't the daughter her parents had to worry about. She was simply Devyn.

And she'd seen what she'd thought was lust in his eyes. It made her feel really good inside.

"Right, well, I'll be sure to tell you when we go to bed together," she teased.

"Do that," Aspen said, completely seriously. "And now I need to go home. Brain told me I'm only allowed to be out for an hour before I should go home and put my feet up."

Devyn stared at her. "Really?"

"Yup. Although, I should say that while he told me to only go out for an hour, that doesn't mean I'm listening to him."

Both women chuckled.

"He's being overly protective, but it's cute, so I'm letting it slide," Aspen said. "I'm perfectly fine and haven't had any issues with the pregnancy. But since he's worried about me *and* our baby, I'm tolerating it."

Devyn stood and helped Aspen out of her seat. "Thanks for the talk," she told the other woman.

"You're welcome. And seriously, we all love you and are worried about you. If you can't talk to Lucky, we're all here for you."

"Thanks. That means the world to me."

"Call me soon," Aspen said.

Devyn agreed and they headed out of the café. On her way back to her apartment, she thought about what Aspen had said. And she was right. She needed to stop living part-way. She loved it here and wanted to stay.

First, she finally needed to unpack her stuff. Second, she should talk to her boss about switching to full time. And third...she wanted to move things along with Lucky. She'd kept him at arm's length for over a year, despite their attraction. If they were dating, she needed to at least try to go all-in. She liked him, he liked her, and she wanted to be with him.

She'd decide on the rest later. She still wasn't sure what opening up about Spencer might do to her family. She'd table that for now, but the rest of it? It was time to get on with her life.

Skydiving and bungee jumping were all well and good, but she was kidding herself. Doing those kinds of things didn't make her brave; they were a cover for her insecurities. Dangerous stunts didn't make her past go away. She'd always be a cancer survivor. It was who she was, and it was about time she dealt with it and got on with her life.

And hopefully Lucky would be a big part of that moving on.

CHAPTER SIX

Devyn had grand plans for making sure Lucky knew she was truly ready for a relationship. More than just one of friendship. But after she got home from lunch with Aspen, Spencer called.

"Spencer, you need to stop calling me," she said in lieu of a greeting.

"Hey, sis. Long time no talk."

"Seriously, I'm done."

"Are you ever going to forgive me for shoving you?" Spencer asked.

Devyn winced. "It's not about that."

But he ignored her and kept talking. "Because I've already apologized. I was upset that day, and I didn't mean to push you so hard. It wasn't my fault you're clumsy and hit that table and fell."

"That's bullshit and you know it," she said, angry that he would spin the situation to make himself feel better about what he'd done.

"Whatever. Siblings fight, Dev. We've always been that way. Remember when you were eleven and you didn't like something I'd said to one of my friends about you, and you almost pushed me out of our treehouse?"

Devyn winced. She *had* done that. "We were kids, Spencer. It was different."

"But we're the same people. Family. And family helps each other."

And there it was. The guilt he was so good at inflicting. Especially on her. "I *did* help you, Spence. And you promised it would be the last time. And yet you came back wanting more. You need help, and until you admit that and actually go through with it, I'm done bailing you out."

"Devyn, you're the only one I can go to. Fred won't help, he'll tell me to man up or some other bullshit, and Mila and Angela don't have any money. I already owe Mom and Dad."

"You owe *me*, Spence. But you don't care about that, do you?"

"Come on, sis. You're single. You can afford to help me out."

"Actually, I can't. I'm only working part time and I've got my own bills to pay."

"But I'm in trouble this time, Dev. *Big* trouble."

Devyn closed her eyes and did her best to harden her heart. She and Fred had always been close, but that didn't mean she didn't want to have the same kind of relationship with her other brother. They were all so close in age, they should've been like three peas in a pod. But Spencer hadn't dealt well with her getting so much attention when she'd been sick, and he had pulled away from both her and Fred.

"Please, sis."

"How much?" Devyn asked, hating herself. This was why she'd moved again. Why she refused to take his calls. Because she gave in to his begging. Every time. She knew she shouldn't...but he was her brother. She loved him, even when he walked all over her.

"Fifty."

"Only fifty bucks? Come on, how much?"

"No. Fifty thousand," Spencer said.

"Fifty *thousand*?" she practically screamed.

"I know, I know! But this time it's different."

"You know I don't have that kind of money," she said, shocked.

"He's going to hurt me, *bad*, if I don't pay him back," Spencer said.

Devyn sat on the edge of her couch and rested her forehead in one of her hands. "I don't have anywhere close to that much," she repeated.

"If I can get five, I can make that work. Turn it into the fifty I need. I know it!"

Devyn felt a tear roll down her cheek. "You've said that before, and it never happens. You have a serious problem, Spence. You need *help*! There are programs that you can go through. Gambling addiction services. They can help you beat this. Please, for me, for the rest of your family, see what you're doing to yourself. To *all* of us."

"That's rich," Spencer said nastily. "You single-handedly ruined our family, and you're telling *me* to lock myself away so some doctor can tell me I'm fucked up in the head? Not happening."

"I was a kid," Devyn said quietly. "I had *cancer*. It's not the same thing."

"Whatever. Are you going to help me or not?"

"I can't," she whispered, feeling sick. "I don't have that much."

"They're going to hurt me, Dev! Maybe even kill me," Spencer told her. "And you're going to sit there and let it happen?"

"*I'm* not letting anything happen! Your actions have consequences, Spence. They always have, but you've just been too selfish to see it! You rely on other people to bail you out, then you go and do the exact same thing you've always done."

"When you read about my dead body showing up in a cornfield somewhere, don't be surprised. Maybe you won't be all high and mighty then."

"Spencer—"

But it was too late. He'd hung up on her.

Bowing her head and letting her tears fall, Devyn felt sick. She wanted to help her brother; she *did*. But she'd already given him thousands of dollars to bail him out in the past. That was why she'd left Missouri. Because she couldn't say no to him. Because he knew she was a pushover and would eventually give in and hand over the money he needed to pay off someone else he owed.

Spencer was an addict. He couldn't stop gambling. She couldn't count the number of things he'd pawned for money. He was always sure he could make back thousands more if he just kept playing. One more pull of the slot machine. One more card game. But he never did. He just got deeper and deeper into debt.

The last time she'd seen Spencer had been when he'd gone to her apartment while she wasn't home. He had a key, because he was her brother. She'd walked in on him stuffing a cardboard box with anything valuable he could find. They'd gotten into a huge fight, and he'd shoved her. She could've hit her head, but her table broke her fall.

She couldn't tell her parents. They'd have tried to convince her that she was overreacting, that her brother loved her and hadn't meant to hurt her. She couldn't tell Grover because she didn't want to hurt his relationship with Spencer. And she couldn't tell Lucky the truth about how she got the nasty bruise on her torso, because he'd probably want to kill her brother. She was in the middle of a no-win situation.

After Spencer tried to rob her and had hurt her, Devyn knew she had to leave. Get out of her hometown, away from her brother. She loved him, but he was slowly sucking the life out of himself, and he'd bring her down with him if she let him. So she'd quit her job and fled to Texas.

Intellectually, she knew this was all on Spencer's shoulders, but emotionally, she couldn't help but believe she should've been able to talk him into therapy. She felt like a failure. And now she was scared to death for Spencer. She was irritated with him, but that didn't mean she wanted someone to hurt him.

"Fuck," she whispered.

Drained, Devyn turned off her phone and went into her bedroom. She undressed and climbed under her covers. It was too early to go to bed, and Lucky would probably expect her to call or come over, but she couldn't deal with anyone or anything else today.

This was why she hadn't wanted to take Spencer's calls. Because she knew he would ask for more money. Because she knew he'd make her feel guilty. Because if anything happened to him, it would feel as if it was her fault.

Feeling the pressure of the last year weighing down on her, Devyn cried. For her brother. For being too scared to tell anyone what was going on. For the decision she knew she was going to have to make—soon.

She'd either have to be an adult and tell someone what was going on, or she'd have to move. To run like a coward. Neither option was appealing, but she couldn't go on this way.

* * *

Two days later, Lucky was done being patient. Devyn was giving him the cold shoulder and he wasn't going to take it anymore. Something was really wrong. He felt it in his gut. And it was time she talked to him. If he had to swear not to tell Grover what they discussed, he would...even if it was something dire. He didn't like the thought of keeping anything from one of his best friends, but he would if it made Devyn open up to him.

He'd called Aspen to see how their lunch went, because he couldn't get ahold of Devyn that evening, and she'd said that it had gone really well. So he had no idea why she hadn't called him since. Why she'd been avoiding not only him, but Grover too.

Well, he was done with that.

He'd sent several texts and left a few messages that she'd ignored. If Devyn thought she could blow him off now, after they'd started something...she was wrong.

Lucky knocked on her door and waited for her to respond. He knew she was home because her Mini Cooper was in the parking lot. Before going over, he'd called the vet clinic and was informed that she'd called in sick that day.

He actually hoped she *was* sick, and that was why she'd gone radio silent, but he had a bad feeling that wasn't it.

"Go away, Lucky," she said from the other side of the door.

Frowning, Lucky crossed his arms over his chest. "No. Open the door, Dev."

"I'm sorry, but I can't do this."

"Do what?" he asked.

"Be in a relationship with you."

"You are *not* breaking up with me from behind a door. You want to break up, open the door and tell me to my face," Lucky growled. He didn't believe for a second that she didn't want to be with him. Nothing had happened between the last time they saw each other until now. She was scared of something, and he couldn't help her if he didn't know what it was.

He'd been able to gain Angel and Whiskers' trust; he could do the same with Devyn. She was skittish, and he'd do everything he could to make sure she knew she was safe with him.

He heard the chain come off and then the dead bolt clicked. Devyn opened the door and said a little belligerently, "Fine. We're done. Now you can go."

The sight of Devyn scared the shit out of Lucky. She looked awful. Her hair hadn't been brushed or washed and she had deep circles under her eyes. She wore an oversized T-shirt and a pair of sweatpants.

Gently pushing on the door, Lucky stepped inside.

"Lucky!" she protested, but he ignored her. He closed the door behind him and took hold of her elbow, pulling her deeper into her apartment.

"Stop it, Lucky," Devyn said, but she didn't rip her elbow out of his grasp.

"What have you eaten today?" he asked.

"Pop-Tarts, Reese's Peanut Butter Eggs, and fourteen cheese sticks," she said a little defensively.

"Sit," he ordered, pulling out a barstool.

Devyn sighed but did as he asked.

Lucky pushed up his sleeves and went to her refrigerator to see what he had to work with.

"Why are you here?" she asked quietly as he pulled out some eggs, cheese, peppers, and chorizo sausage.

"Because you've been avoiding me. And all your other friends. Because I called the vet clinic and they told me that you called in sick. I'm here to feed you. Find out what the fuck is going on so we can move forward."

"I can't talk to you about it," she said sadly.

Lucky put the ingredients for the omelet he was planning on making on the counter and walked back around to where Devyn was sitting. He turned her on the stool and took her face in his hands. He tilted it up so she had no choice but to meet his gaze.

"You can talk to me about *anything*," he told her.

"Not this," she whispered.

"Whatever you have to say, it stays between the two of us," he said.

She frowned. "What?"

"You heard me. If you need the reassurance that I won't tell Grover anything that we talk about, I'm giving it to you."

"But...you guys are best friends. Won't that hurt your friendship?" she asked.

"It's possible. But you're more important."

Devyn gawked at him. "I don't...*Why?*"

"It's no secret that you've gotten under my skin, Devyn. I think you're beautiful, funny, a hard worker, and so damn loyal it's almost painful. I go to sleep thinking about you, then I wake up doing the same. I wonder how your day went at work and I worry about whatever's bothering you. This past week, before you decided you couldn't talk to me, was one of the best I've had in years. I loved hanging out with you, and seeing you interact with Angel and Whiskers is making me fall for you even more. If you need the reassurance that what we talk about stays between the two of us, if that's what it'll take for you to trust me, then I'm giving it to you...but there are two exceptions to me not saying anything to Grover."

"What?" Devyn asked.

"We've kind of already discussed this, but the exceptions are if your life is in danger. Or if your cancer has returned. I can't, and won't, keep those things from Grover, or the rest of the team. We'll do whatever we can to fight your demons, whether they be physical threats or your own damn body. You've kicked cancer's ass once, you can do it again. But I can't keep either of those things from your brother."

"I told you before, my life isn't in danger and I'm not sick," Devyn replied. "I wasn't lying about that."

Lucky momentarily closed his eyes in relief. Then he opened them again. "Good. Then whatever this big secret is that you're carrying, you can tell me and we can figure out what to do about it. But before that happens, you need food. Real food. You can't survive on Pop-Tarts and cheese sticks."

"And peanut butter eggs," she reminded him with a small smile.

Lucky loved seeing the quirk of her lips. This woman had a spine made of steel, she just couldn't see it. "Right, how could I forget those?" Lucky said with a roll of his eyes.

He started to step away, but Devyn grabbed his wrists, holding him in place. "Lucky?"

"Yeah?"

"I'm so scared of making the wrong decision."

Lucky's heart swelled in his chest. He wanted to slay all Devyn's dragons for her, but he knew she'd be stronger in the end if she slayed her own. "We're all scared of that, Dev. I know I am. But with friends and family by your side, you can get through anything."

"I hope so," she said softly.

Lucky couldn't help himself. He leaned down and kissed her forehead gently. "I know so," he told her. Then he dropped his hands and headed back around the bar into the small kitchen. "When was the last time you showered?" he asked nonchalantly.

"Is that your way of telling me I stink?" Devyn asked.

Lucky was thrilled to hear the light tone of her voice. "Not at all. I know better than to *ever* say that. But I'm thinking you'll feel better if you're fresh and clean."

"Nice and diplomatic," she said with a smile. "Fine. While you slave over food, I'll go shower."

Lucky smiled at her.

"How're Angel and Whiskers doing?" she asked.

"They miss you. And they're okay. Getting a little braver every day. Whiskers has gotten used to her harness and even got three feet away from Angel when I took them outside last time."

"Awesome," she said with a smile. "They don't know how good they have it with you."

"I'm hoping I can convince you to come home with me after we eat," Lucky told her.

"But it'll be kind of late by then. I'll just have to turn around and come home within an hour or so."

"Or you could stay," Lucky said.

Devyn stilled, staring at him intently.

He hated that he couldn't read her expression.

"Are you asking me to spend the night?" she asked.

Lucky admired how straightforward she was. "Yes. But it's up to you on where you want to sleep. I've got an extra bed, or there's the couch downstairs."

"What about *your* room?" Devyn asked.

It was Lucky's turn to freeze. "You can have my bed," he said quietly. "You can have any damn thing of mine you want."

"Including you?" she asked.

"Damn," Lucky said under his breath. "Yes, Dev. I'm fucking yours. I've been yours from the moment I met you. I've just been waiting for you to catch up."

He saw her swallow hard, belying the bravado she'd used to ask him where she was sleeping. "I have a tendency to get lost in my own head. To think too hard about things. But I've done enough thinking when it comes to you and me. I want you, Lucky."

"Then you have me," he managed to say. "Pack a bag with enough stuff to last a few days. I have a feeling once I've got you in my lair, I'm not going to want to let you go."

She grinned. "I have to work tomorrow afternoon."

"Damn," he said again.

Devyn climbed off the barstool but didn't enter the kitchen. She slowly backed toward the hallway where the bedrooms were. "I'm gonna go shower," she said.

"And now I've got *that* vision in my head," Lucky said, rolling his eyes.

"We've waited months, what's a few more hours?" she asked playfully.

"It just might kill me," Lucky said semi-seriously.

She stopped in the entrance to the hall. "Lucky?"

"Yeah, Dev?"

"I'm not sure I want to tell you what's going on, but I can't keep it to myself anymore. It's selfish of me, but I appreciate you not telling Grover. At least not yet."

"We'll figure it out," Lucky told her, worried as hell about what her big secret was. "And if and when the time is right, we'll tell your brother together. Okay?"

"You'd do that for me?"

"I'd do anything for you," Lucky admitted. "Including make you a big-ass omelet so you don't pass out from lack of nutrition."

She chuckled, as he'd intended. "I'm going. Thanks for forcing your way into my apartment and making me food I didn't ask for."

"You're welcome. I might not always be the most socially acceptable man, but I'll always do what's best for you. And tonight you needed to be forced out of the funk you put yourself in. To see that you've got friends who will gladly be there for you...if you'll let us."

Devyn nodded, then turned and disappeared into her bedroom.

Lucky took a deep breath and rested his palms on her counter. He had to admit things had gone better than he'd hoped. Dev had agreed to come back to his place, and to actually talk to him. Not only that, but she admitted that she wanted to stay the night. With him. In his bed.

Ignoring his hard-on, Lucky turned his attention to the food. He needed to get a decent meal into his woman, then take her back to his place and make her feel comfortable enough to open up.

The fact of the matter was that she'd scared him. Not answering his texts or calls, then when Grover had said he hadn't been able to get in touch with her either. None of the other women had talked to her, and he'd had visions of her lying helpless and hurt in her apartment. He never wanted to experience that feeling again.

CHAPTER SEVEN

As it turned out, there was no big reveal that night. When Lucky finally walked into his townhouse with Devyn, it was clear Angel had experienced a very upset tummy while he was gone. He'd put the crate in the bathroom, and they'd found diarrhea all over the floor of the bathroom and inside the crate. Both dog and cat were covered in feces.

So a major cleanup had to be done and both animals had to be bathed and comforted. It was obvious Angel knew she'd done something wrong, and she'd shivered and cowered for an hour after her bath. Lucky finally got her to relax by lying on the floor of his bedroom with her, Whiskers curled up in the crook of his body.

Devyn had changed into a pair of sweatpants and a tank top and had fallen asleep on his bed, and Lucky didn't have the heart to wake her up. It was obvious she was exhausted, and he loved simply having her there with him. So he'd put the animals back into the now clean and sterilized bathroom and climbed under the covers behind Devyn. He gathered her close, and had never felt more content than when Devyn sighed in her sleep and snuggled farther back into him.

He'd fallen asleep within minutes.

His alarm went off early the next morning, and even though Lucky turned it off quickly, Devyn stirred.

"You going to PT?" she asked.

"Yeah," Lucky told her quietly. "I'll be back in two hours. Sleep."

"'Kay. I'll get up in a bit and let the animals out."

"I'll let them out now so they'll be good for a while. I've got bagels, protein shakes, and oatmeal if you get hungry," Lucky told her.

She scrunched her nose. "No doughnuts?" she asked.

Lucky didn't know if she was kidding or not, but he made a mental note to pick some up the next time he went to the store. "No, sorry."

"It's okay," she said, her voice slurring.

Lucky could wake up like this every day for the rest of his life and be content. A sleepy Devyn was cute as hell and climbing out of bed was extremely difficult.

He took Angel and Whiskers outside and was glad to see that whatever had bothered Angel's digestive system seemed to have worked itself out. Both animals peed and he put food in their bowls as he headed back upstairs to get changed.

By the time he came back downstairs, both animals had finished their breakfasts. Angel was curled up in one of the four dog beds he'd bought recently, Whiskers contentedly by her side. Not wanting to traumatize the dog any more than she already was, Lucky had done the best he could to very gently get the mats out of her hair during last night's bath, and while she still looked pretty pathetic, at least her hair was shiny and clean.

Whiskers didn't take to grooming as well as Angel, but he'd cut out the mats in her coat as well. Since both animals had light brown fur with white patches, when they were curled up together, it was hard to tell where one stopped and the other started.

Deciding to take the chance and leave them out of the bathroom, Lucky gave them both one last pet, pleased when neither flinched. At the last minute, he turned back and grabbed a piece of paper and scrawled out a short note for Devyn...just in case she came downstairs before he got back. Then he left in an extremely good mood.

He and Dev still needed to talk, and she needed to get whatever big secret she was keeping off her chest for her own mental well-being, but it had been pretty damn amazing to wake up with her in his arms. He could do that for the rest of his life and be perfectly happy.

That thought should've stopped Lucky in his tracks, but instead, it just made him smile. Somewhere in the last several months, he'd fallen in love with Devyn. Maybe even upon first sight. And it *had* to be love. He'd never felt this way about another woman before. Ever.

When he arrived on post and joined up with the team in front of the motor pool, he was still smiling.

"Oh, shit, what's that grin for?" Doc asked.

"Nothing. I'm just in a good mood this morning," Lucky told him.

"We're about to run ten miles and you're in a good mood?" Oz asked.

"Well, yeah. We aren't running with our packs, so this'll be a piece of cake," Lucky said.

"I'll never understand people who *like* to run," Brain muttered under his breath.

While his teammates stretched and argued good-naturedly about working out in general, Lucky managed to pull Grover and Trigger aside.

"I need some time off today. We don't have any planning meetings, do we?" Lucky asked.

"No...unless something comes up this afternoon, which could be possible. It looks like we're going to get to do Olympic duty this year, so soon we'll have to start coordinating that with the other teams around the country who were picked," Trigger said.

"Really? Cool. It's one of the very few missions I look forward to," Lucky said. That was somewhat of an understatement. While the chance that some crazed terrorists would target the Olympians who gathered to compete for their country was always a possibility, guarding the athletes was considered a perk in special forces circles.

Deciding to get to the matter at hand, Lucky turned to Grover. "Dev spent the night at my place last night," he said without preamble.

To Grover's credit, his facial expression didn't change. "And?" he asked. "I know you aren't telling me you're sleeping with my sister to try to get a rise out of me."

"I *did* sleep with her, but that's all we did," Lucky said quickly. "I went over to her place last night because she'd been avoiding me. Avoiding all of us, as you know. She looked rough, man. Like the weight of the world is on her shoulders. I fed her—something better than the crap she admitted she's been eating—and brought her home with me. Angel had some digestive issues, and by the time I dealt with that, Dev was out like a light. I'm telling you this because I need the time off so I can talk to her. And I promised what she told me would stay between the two of us."

Grover frowned.

Lucky went on. "She swore that it wasn't that she was sick again or that her life was in danger. As I told you before, I'd never keep either of those things from you."

Grover's shoulders relaxed. "I appreciate that. And I trust you. As much as I worry about Devyn, she's an adult. I wouldn't want to stand in the way of you forming a tight bond with her."

"I love her," Lucky blurted.

He must've said it loud enough for everyone to hear, because the other teammates around them got quiet.

"Shit," Lucky muttered.

"Please tell me you've told *her* that before you just blurted it out to all of us," Lefty said.

"Because if you're telling us you love Devyn before you tell her, that's fucked up," Brain added.

"*You're* going to talk about fucked up?" Oz said, smacking the back of Brain's head.

"Fuck off," Brain told his friend.

Lucky couldn't help but smile. God, he loved these guys. They were uncouth at times, but their hearts were always in the right place. "I'm not sure it's that big of a surprise to you guys that I love Devyn."

"True," Trigger mused. "You've been giving her moony eyes for a long time now."

"Moony eyes?" Doc asked. "What the hell is that?"

"You'll know when you meet the woman who's perfect for you," Lefty told him.

"It's when no matter what she does, you think it's damn adorable," Brain said. "Even when other people think she's being ridiculous or menstrual, you can't get enough of it."

"I haven't looked at *any* woman like that, and I doubt I ever will," Doc admitted.

"Oh, yeah, famous last words," Lefty teased.

"Anyway, we all know that you're head over heels for her," Trigger said. "And if you can figure out what's bothering her, we'd all appreciate it. I know Gillian has been worried for weeks about her, and I hate seeing her so worked up about one of her friends."

"Same with Kinley," Lefty said.

"Aspen too. She and Riley talked for at least twenty minutes the other night about what they could do to try to make Devyn comfortable enough to confide in them," Brain added.

"If it's okay with Trigger and the commander, I'm gonna take some time off today and see if I can figure out what's been on her mind," Lucky admitted.

"Good," Doc said.

"You'll let us know if we can do anything?" Trigger asked.

"We're here if you need us," Oz said.

Lucky appreciated his friends more than he could say. Their unwavering support was something he would never take for granted. "You know I will," he told them.

"And you might consider telling *her* that you love her," Brain said. "Women like to hear that kind of thing."

"And if she finds out you told us before you told her, you might be sleeping on the couch instead of in your nice comfy bed next to her," Trigger said with a chuckle.

It was way too early to be telling Devyn that he loved her, but Lucky knew his friends had a point. He nodded noncommittally.

"I hear Logan's been kicking butt in his baseball league," Lefty said to Oz, effectively changing the topic.

As the team started out on their long run that morning, Lucky listened as Oz talked about his nephew and how well he was doing. He bragged that he was one of the best players on his team, even though he'd just started playing. His niece, Bria, was also blossoming. She was about to finish the first grade and was going to take classes in the summer to make sure she was caught up with her peers before she started second grade in the fall. The past year had been rough on her, and her psychologist suggested that keeping her on a schedule would be best.

Brain and Oz talked about their upcoming babies, which would be born only a few months apart. Aspen should be giving birth within two months, and Riley wouldn't be too far behind.

Their lives were changing faster than Lucky would've imagined, but everyone seemed more than content. When their friends on another Delta team stationed on the base had all gotten married and started having children, Lucky'd had a hard time understanding how they'd manage to juggle their personal lives with the demands of their job. But he got it now. It wasn't an either/or kind of thing. They could be fathers and husbands, *and* be kick-ass Delta Force soldiers. Loving someone didn't make them weaker; in a lot of ways, it made them better at their job.

He'd seen it firsthand with his own team. Trigger and the others were more cautious now, perhaps, but that wasn't a bad thing. They worked harder at digging up as much information as they could get before they left on a mission, and their actions while deployed were more purposeful. They didn't rush into situations and were very careful with both their own lives, and the lives of everyone else on the team.

Wanted to come home to Devyn after a mission. Wanted to build a life with her. Wanted to watch her blossom, and possibly even have kids with her. It was a strange thought for a man who'd never considered having children before. He'd previously felt young at thirty-one, but all of a sudden it seemed as if his life was passing him by. Lucky saw daily how happy Oz was with his niece and nephew, and how excited he and Brain were to have babies on the way...

He found himself thinking about what his and Devyn's kids would look like. They'd be tall, and he hoped they'd inherit her blonde locks rather than his dark hair.

Those thoughts were insane...yet, they felt right.

But deep down, Lucky had a feeling things with Devyn

wouldn't be as easy as he was hoping. It seemed as if all his friends had had to go through a trial by fire. He wasn't conceited enough to think his relationship with Devyn would be any different. But, on the flip side, the shit his friends had been through had only made their relationships stronger.

Lucky absolutely didn't want anything to happen to him or to Devyn. Nothing like what his friends had gone through. As far as he knew, she had no ex-boyfriends who could suddenly appear and want to do her harm. She hadn't been in a hijacked plane with a bunch of terrorists, and hadn't worked for an unknown serial killer. But he knew as well as anyone that sometimes evil appeared out of nowhere.

His first step would be to find out what was pressing on her mind. Once they dealt with that, he'd make sure she knew how much he loved her...and that he'd do whatever it took to keep her happy and protected.

* * *

Devyn woke up about an hour after Lucky had left. She had a slight headache but otherwise felt surprisingly good. She'd made a decision last night to talk to Lucky, and with that choice, it felt as if a huge weight had been lifted off her shoulders.

She'd been ridiculous the last few days, including when Lucky had shown up at her door. Acting like a teenager. All this angst wasn't her. She was a "tell it like it is" kind of person. Had learned to be so after all her time in hospitals. Even as a kid, she'd much preferred the doctors and nurses who hadn't been wishy-washy with bad news. The ones who told her what was happening and then how to deal with it.

But in the year-plus since arriving in Killeen, keeping the secret about Spencer's addiction had completely messed with her head. She might not be ready to tell the rest of her family about Spence, but she knew without a doubt she could trust Lucky. And the fact that he'd said he'd keep whatever she told him from Fred meant the world to her.

She wasn't an idiot; she knew how close Lucky was with his teammates. He had to be. They had each other's backs and kept each other alive on missions. Forcing Lucky to keep her secret could hurt that closeness, but before that happened, she had to hope that Spencer would finally pull his head out of his ass and get the help he needed.

But thinking about the latest chat she'd had with him, she wasn't so sure. It was hard to believe he owed some loan shark fifty thousand dollars. And the fact that he thought he could get five grand from her and turn it into fifty was completely ridiculous. Devyn hated the thought of her brother being hurt by someone if he didn't pay back the money he'd borrowed...but a small part of her couldn't help but think that maybe this situation would be the push Spencer needed to finally get serious about his addiction.

Stretching, Devyn climbed out of Lucky's very comfortable bed and went into his bathroom. She brushed her teeth and hair, then wandered out of the room and down the stairs. She hadn't bothered to get dressed, feeling comfortable in her sweats and tank top. She'd never had to worry about not wearing a bra, as she was only a B cup on a good day, *and* with a quality push-up bra. She'd always lamented her lack of any kind of boobs, but remembering how Lucky's eyes had practically devoured her when she'd come out of the bathroom dressed for bed made her feel a lot better about her attributes.

Angel and Whiskers were sleeping on one of the dog beds Lucky had bought in the last week. He'd decided that the one bed she'd picked up that first night wasn't enough, and he'd made sure there was a soft place for his new pets to sleep in every room. Angel and Whiskers were going to be the most spoiled dog and cat in the history of the world, but she didn't think Lucky, or the animals, were worried about it.

Angel lifted her head when Devyn came into sight, and then promptly put it right back down. Devyn was thrilled. In the first few days after the adoption, Angel—and of course Whiskers—would leave the room when she entered, unless Lucky was with her. So she was chalking it up as a huge win when they didn't bolt.

"Good morning, girls," Devyn said in a cheerful tone. "Did Daddy take you out already? He said he would. And I'm sure you've eaten. You might be scared of people, but you know better than to turn up your nose at food, don't you? Smart. I think you're the most smartest pets in the world." She knew she was talking nonsense, but she wanted the pair to get used to her voice.

Devyn padded into the kitchen to make some coffee, only to realize that Lucky had already done so. She poured herself a cup and stilled with the mug halfway to her lips when she saw the note on the counter.

She reached for it, putting down her coffee and smiling at seeing Lucky's messy, masculine handwriting.

Coffee's ready to go. The kids have been out and fed. I bought brown sugar yesterday because I know you like your oatmeal sweet. If you're good and eat something healthy, I'll stop and get some doughnuts on my way home.

-Lucky

PS. I liked having you in my bed last night...and this morning. I think we need to make this a habit.

. . .

Devyn read the note three times before closing her eyes and sighing in contentment. It was such a Lucky kind of note. Short and to the point.

Who knew Lucky could be so sweet? If someone had told her when she first came to town that she'd be here right now, standing in Lucky's kitchen in her pajamas, reading a note from him about their "kids" and how he liked having her in his bed...she wouldn't've believed it.

But it felt so right.

Shit...

She loved the man.

Which was why she was here, admittedly. Lucky didn't need her help with Angel and Whiskers. From what she'd seen, he had everything under control as far as helping them assimilate and be socialized. He was patient and kind and never got upset, as evidenced by his barely blinking when he'd seen his bathroom covered in shit.

And she'd felt perfectly safe falling asleep in his bed. Devyn had had no fears that he'd take advantage of her. And she'd been right. Not only that, but he'd made her coffee and was going to get her doughnuts. Could the man be any more perfect?

She couldn't wait for him to get home. So she could talk to him. It would feel good to have a sounding board about Spencer. She loved her brother, which was part of the reason she'd been so messed up in the head about his actions. She wanted to help him, but she also knew he needed to want to help *himself* before anything would change.

Devyn picked up the note and headed for the stairs. She needed to put it somewhere safe. It was her first note from Lucky, and she wanted to cherish it forever.

Now she was acting like a silly teenager again...but Devyn didn't care. She hoped Lucky wrote her a thousand more notes, but as this was the first, it was special.

Then she went back downstairs, picked up her coffee, settled on the couch, and waited for Lucky to get home so they could have their talk.

CHAPTER EIGHT

Lucky opened his door and smiled at the sight that greeted him. Devyn was sitting on the floor next to a dog bed, with her back resting against the couch. Angel had her head resting on Devyn's knee and Whiskers was on her back in the bed, with Devyn petting her belly.

The smile Devyn gave him warmed him from the inside out.

"They like me...well, they like me this morning," she said.

"I see," he told her, moving slowly toward the trio so as not to scare the animals. He crouched down in front of them, and the tip of Angel's tail began to move back and forth. It was the first time he'd seen that kind of reaction from her since the Humane Society, and it thrilled him.

"You guys have a good morning?" he asked rhetorically. "I see you've got Dev in the palm of your hand, don't you? What a good dog. And cat. The bestest animals in the world," he crooned.

Devyn chuckled softly. "I'm glad I'm not the only one who baby talks to them."

Lucky turned his head to smile and realized his face was inches from Devyn's. "Morning, beautiful."

"Morning," she returned, blushing a bit.

"Sleep okay?" he asked.

"Extremely. You?"

"Best I've slept in a hell of a long time, if you really want to know. Must've been the human pillow curled up against me," he said with a smile.

Her eyes dropped to the bag in his hand. "Are those doughnuts?"

"Depends. Did you eat something healthy this morning?" he teased.

Devyn pouted. "Seriously?"

"Yup. You were the one who admitted you'd eaten fourteen damn cheese sticks yesterday."

"Cheese is good for you," she protested.

"Maybe, but you have to eat other stuff along with it. Like vegetables and fruit. And protein. Pop-Tarts and peanut butter eggs don't fit into any of those categories."

"Are you seriously going to keep those doughnuts from me until I eat something you deem worthy first?"

"Yup," Lucky said, not feeling bad about it for a second.

"Well, then, it's a good thing I had a bowl of oatmeal already, isn't it?" she crowed.

Lucky laughed, startling Angel and sending her scurrying backward.

"Sorry, girl," he told her softly. "Didn't mean to scare you. Dev's being silly this morning. Did she really eat oatmeal, or is she just saying that to get her hands on one of my doughnuts? Maybe she fed *you* guys the oatmeal to get me to think she ate it. Huh? Did you get a second breakfast this morning?"

"Step away from the doughnuts and no one will get hurt," Devyn warned in a fake serious tone.

God, Lucky loved this. Bantering back and forth with Devyn. Teasing her.

He moved without thought, putting his lips on hers.

They both froze in surprise for a heartbeat, before Devyn sighed and brought a hand up, clutching the front of his T-shirt in her hand.

The kiss went from light and teasing to deep and serious in seconds. She tasted like brown sugar and coffee, and Lucky couldn't get enough.

He hadn't meant to do this. Not right now. But since he was, Lucky was going to enjoy every second. He reached out and put a hand behind Devyn's neck, increasing the intimacy of the moment. Their tongues moved together, learning the taste and feel of each other.

After what felt like minutes, but was probably only fifteen seconds or so, Lucky felt a nudge on his knee. He pulled back, licking his lips and staring at Devyn, trying to decide whether to throw her onto the couch right behind them, or put her over his shoulder and take her upstairs to his bed.

But a small sound caught his attention, and Lucky looked down.

Angel was standing next to him, and when she saw him looking at her, she put a paw up on his knee and whined.

Lucky hadn't taken his hand from Devyn's nape, and he felt as much as he heard her chuckle. "I think she's jealous."

Moving slowly, Lucky reached out with his free hand. "Is that it, girl? You jealous? No need. You'll always be number one with me. But Dev here is gonna be around a lot. And I'm gonna kiss her again too. So you'll need to be okay with that. But me kissing her doesn't mean you're any less important. Nope, you're my pretty girl. You and Whiskers." Lucky knew he was talking nonsense, but he couldn't deny he freaking loved that the dog had reached out to him. It was the first time for a lot of things this morning, and he couldn't be happier.

Lucky gently petted Angel's head and rubbed her ears as he looked back at Devyn. "That was..." He was suddenly at a loss for words.

"Amazing? Wonderful? Pretty damn awesome?" Devyn said with a smile.

"Yeah. That," Lucky agreed.

Angel was apparently done showing affection, and she turned and went back to her dog bed, curling up around Whiskers, who immediately started purring.

Her quick movement stirred the air around him, and Lucky realized for the first time that he stunk. He wrinkled his nose. "I need a shower."

Devyn smiled. "Yeah. You do. Did you run a marathon this morning or what?"

"Only ten miles. Well, twelve, since Brain said something to irritate Trigger and he made us keep going."

"Oh, only twelve. Slacker," Devyn joked.

Lucky shook his head and stood.

"Hey!" Devyn said, reaching out and grabbing the hem of his shorts.

Lucky's brain almost short-circuited, seeing her fingers so close to his cock. He managed to control his reaction so he didn't freak her out by popping a woody in her face.

"Yeah?" he asked.

"Gimme my doughnuts," she ordered, holding out her hand and wiggling her fingers.

Lucky burst out laughing again. He'd smiled more this morning than he could remember doing so in the recent past. "Right, sorry. Here they are," he said, holding out the bag as if it contained a bomb that might go off with the least amount of movement.

Devyn beamed and snatched it, immediately looking inside.

"I didn't know what you liked. So I got a plain glazed, a cream-filled chocolate one, a cinnamon twist, and a cake one."

"I like 'em all," Devyn said with a smile. "Which is your favorite?"

"I don't usually eat doughnuts," Lucky told her honestly.

"If I held a gun to your head and told you that you had to eat one, which would it be?" she asked, still smiling.

"The cinnamon twist."

"Okay. I'll save it for you," Devyn said. "But if you take ten years in the shower, I can't guarantee it'll still be here when you get out."

"I'm not going to take ten years," Lucky told her. "And if you want to eat them all, go for it. I can get more."

"Not sure my ass needs four doughnuts added to it. Probably doesn't even need one," she mumbled.

Lucky reached down and put his finger under her chin so she had to look up at him. When he was sure she was paying attention, he said, "I think I proved earlier that I like you exactly how you are. It wouldn't matter to me if you put on a hundred pounds, or lost fifty. Neither would exactly be healthy, but it wouldn't make me like you or want you any less. I don't care if you don't like to work out, or if you do yoga for an hour every night. I want you to be healthy because I want you to be around for a very long time. But anything you want, I'll bend over backward to get for you because most of all, I want you to be happy. Okay?"

She swallowed hard before nodding. "Okay."

He backed up and headed for the stairs without taking his gaze from hers.

When he reached the first step, Lucky looked back and said, "That was the best kiss I've had in my life. And I'm not just saying that. We're gonna work, Dev. I'm gonna do everything in my power to help figure out what's mucking up your head, and we'll get through it. You know what I do, what my job is, and if you can handle that, we can handle *anything*. Literally.

"I'll be back after I get cleaned up and we'll talk. Then we'll take the girls out and see if we can't get them to take a short walk. I haven't done that yet, just tried walking them in the yard, so I don't know how it'll go. But we'll give it a shot. And I know you have to work this afternoon, but I can drop you off and head to post, then pick you up when your shift is over and bring you back here for dinner. We'll play the rest of the evening by ear. That all right with you?"

"Yes," she said softly.

"Good."

There was a lot more Lucky wanted to say. He wanted to tell her that he loved her, and if she ultimately decided she didn't want to be with him, it would devastate him.

But instead, he turned and headed up the stairs to his bedroom. He knew this would be the quickest shower he'd taken in quite a while. He wanted to spend as much time as possible with Devyn. He liked being around her. Bantering back and forth. And he couldn't help but admit he was dying of curiosity to know what was on her mind.

* * *

Devyn fell back against the couch and let out the breath she'd been holding with a long whoosh. Good God, the man was lethal. He was a master at kissing. She'd never gotten goose bumps from kissing someone before. But the second his tongue wrapped around hers, she was a goner. Then when he'd palmed the back of her neck? *Goo.*

She sat up and looked down at the animals. "Your dad is

lethal," she whispered. Neither Angel nor Whiskers responded, they just gazed up at her cautiously.

Moving slowly, Devyn stood and brought the bag of doughnuts into the kitchen. She might've exaggerated her obsession with the tasty treats, but that didn't mean she wasn't going to enjoy the hell out of them. She wasn't picky when it came to her favorite. She ate just about anything... except strawberry icing. It was just fundamentally wrong to put fruit icing on a doughnut.

By the time Lucky came back down the stairs, she'd eaten the glazed doughnut and half of the cake one. She was saving the cream-filled one to torture Lucky a bit. She wanted to drive him as crazy as *she* felt every time she was around him. And if using the cream to make him think of sex might actually work—and made him kiss her again—she was all for it.

Devyn supposed she should feel a wee bit ashamed about being so blatant, but she wasn't. She'd waited months to see what Lucky was packing in his shorts, and she was going to go after what she wanted. She'd loved sleeping in his bed, being held by him all night, but tonight she was going to get more than a cuddle. It had been a hell of a long time since she'd had an orgasm she hadn't given herself. Tonight was going to be her night. *Their* night.

She'd get through their talk, work a shift, then after dinner, she'd take Lucky's hand and lead him up his stairs and—

"I'm surprised you haven't eaten them all yet."

Devyn jerked in surprise and turned around to see Lucky coming toward her. He made a detour to pet Angel and Whiskers, then came over to where she was sitting at the table and leaned down and kissed the top of her head. Finally, he went to the cabinet and got a mug down to pour himself a cup of coffee. He joined her at the table and reached for the cinnamon twist.

He smelled divine. Whatever soap or body wash he used made her want to crawl into his lap and latch on and never let go. It wasn't fruity, nor was it overpowering or fake-scented. It was fresh and light. She'd loved it when she'd first smelled it, and now she loved it even more.

She self-consciously looked down at herself. She'd brushed her hair this morning, but she was still in her pajamas, while he had on a pair of cargo pants with his army-green T-shirt tucked in. His biceps bulged with each movement...and suddenly she felt like the biggest frump that ever lived. She should've showered and put on some makeup before he got home. But she'd been overwhelmed with the sweetness of the note he'd left for her, and then Angel and Whiskers had been super cute and she'd wanted to get them to trust her more.

"What's wrong?" Lucky asked. It seemed that he was always in tune to her feelings.

"I'm a little underdressed," she said with a wrinkle of her nose.

"If you ask me, you're overdressed, but that's neither here nor there. You look fine, Dev."

Well. All right then. At least they were on the same page when it came to what was hopefully going to happen tonight.

Without thinking, Devyn reached for the cream-filled doughnut and took a healthy bite. Predictably, cream oozed out the side of the confection, and she used her tongue to keep the filling from falling onto the table or floor.

She looked up—and would've laughed at the look on Lucky's face if her mouth hadn't been full. Distracted by his looks, she'd forgotten all about trying to seduce him by eating the doughnut as sexily as she could, but it seemed she'd done just that without even trying.

Taking her time, she licked the cream and frosting that had gotten onto her fingers, knowing she was torturing Lucky in the process.

"Have pity on me, woman," Lucky said in a low, gruff tone.

This time she *did* laugh. "You have to admit, you opened that door for me to walk right through by buying a cream-filled doughnut."

"I wasn't expecting you to torture me with it," Lucky complained as he reached for her hand. He plucked the doughnut out of her fingers and dropped it on the plate in front of her. Then he shocked the hell out of Devyn by bringing her hand to his mouth. His lips wrapped around her finger, sucking off some white cream she'd missed. Then he ran his tongue down the digit to the webbing between her fingers and licked.

The action was so damn sensual, Devyn pressed her thighs together, trying to control her arousal. "Lucky..." she complained.

"Turnabout's fair play," he said as he continued to practically make love to her hand. He stopped long before she was ready and sat back. They stared at each other for a long moment.

"That almost got out of hand," he finally said.

"You think?" she deadpanned.

They both chuckled.

"Right. Go wash your hands, Dev. I'll clean this up. Then we'll talk. Yeah?"

"Yeah," she said. She didn't really want to have this talk, but at the same time, she needed it done. Needed it behind her. She knew she'd feel better if she didn't have to bear the burden of Spencer's secret all on her shoulders, but she didn't know how Lucky would react. He could wonder what in the world she was so upset about, or he could be pissed, or he might even want to have a talk with Spencer himself.

But the bottom line was that she knew, without any

doubt, that Lucky would do whatever he could to make her feel better about the situation. No matter what that took.

It was that thought that had her getting up and heading to the kitchen sink.

It was time. She was glad he'd pushed the issue. She was sick of having all this angst bottled up inside. She needed to be an adult and discuss her worries. And she couldn't think of anyone better to talk to than Lucky.

They worked in tandem to straighten up the kitchen. He put their coffee mugs in the sink and got out two bottles of water. She tossed the bag the doughnuts had come in and wrapped up the leftovers. She wasn't going to let good dough-nuts go to waste. She thought they made a pretty good team, and she loved intentionally brushing up against Lucky as they moved around his huge kitchen.

He then took her hand and led her back to the sofa. She sat in the middle, not surprised when Lucky settled next to her. He turned so his knee brushed against her thigh. He opened his mouth to start, but Devyn beat him to it.

"I think Spencer's a gambling addict." She just blurted it out, deciding it was better to say it quickly than to stew over the best way to bring it up.

Lucky blinked, but didn't otherwise react. "Why don't you start at the beginning?" he suggested.

She appreciated his non-reaction, though she could tell he wasn't exactly happy.

"I didn't think anything of him asking me for money at first. He'd come over, have dinner with me, then he'd ask if he could borrow twenty bucks, fifty, a hundred bucks, until his next pay day. Of course I said yes. But after the third time, I questioned him about it. He admitted that he was having some money issues. I felt horrible for him, so I gave him a bit extra because he said he was having a hard time paying his rent."

"Let me guess—that wasn't the end of him asking for money," Lucky said dryly.

"No. It eventually got to the point where he'd borrowed too much, and I was trying to avoid him, which made me feel really guilty. My mom called one day and said Spence told her I was acting weird toward him, and he was upset about it. The guilt trip from my mom didn't exactly make me feel better, so the next time Spencer asked if he could come over, I said yes. He acted normal, and I was relieved. But after he left...I realized that several things were missing from my apartment."

"He *stole* from you?" Lucky asked incredulously.

"Yeah. Nothing huge, some costume jewelry that he probably thought was worth more than it was and about forty bucks in bills I'd stuffed into a jar of coins," Devyn said.

"What an asshole," Lucky muttered under his breath.

Devyn looked down at her lap and tried not to cry. She shouldn't be this upset about everything that had happened what seemed like forever ago. But she was. "I immediately confronted him about it, but he denied everything. Said I had probably spent the money and forgot, and that I'd just misplaced the jewelry. He tried to turn everything around on me, saying I was trying to get him in trouble with Mom and Dad and that I was a spoiled brat. It actually surprised me how quickly he turned on me."

"He's the reason why you left Missouri, isn't he?" Lucky asked. He picked up her hand and gently rubbed the back of it with his thumb.

Devyn nodded.

Several moments went by as she tried to think of how best to tell Lucky this next part. She knew he wasn't going to take it well. And as much as Spencer had done to hurt her feelings, she still felt like she was betraying him.

But Lucky didn't rush her. Didn't interrupt her thoughts.

He let her think things through and determine when and how to continue her story. Deciding it was best to be as straightforward as she'd been about everything else, Devyn took a deep breath and continued.

"After that, I didn't see Spencer for a couple months. But then one day, I came home from work and he was in my apartment. I'd forgotten I had given him a key in case of an emergency. He had a big box and was filling it with anything from my apartment he thought he could sell. I was *so* mad... but also worried about him. I flat-out asked him if he was a drug addict. He'd never really told me what he needed all the money for, and that was the only thing I could think of.

"He genuinely looked shocked and denied it. He showed me his arms, and there weren't any bruises or anything on them. Now, I know people can shoot up in other places—between their toes, things like that—but I believed him. He didn't act like he was high or otherwise on any kind of drug. Eventually I got him to admit that he was gambling the money away. But he quickly reassured me that he wasn't an addict. That he could stop at any point. I laughed at that, and it really irritated him.

"He swore he was fine, that he was going to pay me back for the stuff he was stealing. Then insisted he'd score big one day, and I'd regret laughing. He'd have millions of dollars and he wouldn't give me a dime. I told him that I didn't *want* his money. That I just wanted to spend some time with him without having to worry if he was going to rob me blind!"

Remembering what happened next made the first tear leak out of her eye. It was nearly impossible to believe what was happening *then*, in the middle of their fight, and now, over a year later, it was still hard.

As Devyn was trying to get herself under control and not become a sobbing mess, she jerked in surprise when Angel hopped up onto the couch next to her. The scruffy dog nuzzled her hand, and dutifully, Devyn petted her head. Angel plopped her butt down and stretched out, resting her head on Devyn's leg.

Looking up at Lucky, she whispered, "Has she done this before?"

"No," Lucky said softly. "She's never demanded pets like that with me before."

Devyn looked back down at the dog practically sitting in her lap. Her fur was still a mess, she looked like she'd just woken up from a particularly hard nap, with hair sticking up all over her head. But her soulful brown eyes looked into her own, and Devyn wanted to melt. She petted the dog with one hand while Lucky still held the other.

"I don't think she likes it that you're upset," Lucky said. "Can't say I do either."

Whiskers was sitting on the floor in front of the couch, looking up at her protector with concerned eyes. It was obvious she was trying to decide what to do. In the end, she hopped up onto the couch and settled in next to Angel.

"Now you're all sandwiched in," Lucky said with a smile.

Devyn nodded and took a deep breath. She wiped away her tears and continued with her story. "Right. So, Spencer thought the next big win was just around the corner. He had the balls to ask me for a thousand bucks. The box of my shit —which he was going to *steal*—was sitting on the floor next to him, and he wanted to borrow money. I laughed again. I couldn't help it. Told him that even if I had that kind of money, I wouldn't give it to him to throw away.

"He didn't like that. Said I was selfish and always had been. Ranted about how I *owed* him, that I took away his childhood, since Mom and Dad were always with me in the hospital. We got into a big fight, screaming at each other. I said things I regret now, and I'd like to think he regretted saying what he did too. At one point, I tried to push him toward my door, to get him to leave, and he shoved me back. Hard. I stumbled and lost my footing, and I fell against my table. That's how I *really* got that nasty bruise Kinley saw when you guys were helping me move into my apartment."

When Lucky didn't say anything, Devyn risked looking up at him.

Shit. He looked absolutely furious.

"Your brother put his *hands* on you? He hurt you?"

Devyn shook her head. "It was an accident. He didn't mean to push me so hard." She wasn't sure why she was trying to protect her brother. She knew in her gut his push was intentional.

"Bullshit. He knew what he was doing." Lucky said, his tone tense. "I wouldn't care if you guys were twins, it's *never* okay to put your hands on someone else."

Devyn couldn't deny that Lucky's anger on her behalf, and his support, felt damn good. "Anyway," she said. "I fell, and he left without another word. I knew I couldn't stay in Missouri after that."

"Because you were afraid he'd hurt you again," Lucky interrupted.

"No. Because I knew he'd never stop asking me for money. He was desperate, Lucky, I could see it in his eyes, and sneaking into my place and trying to steal my shit made it abundantly clear. I called him later that night and begged him to get some help. To go to Gamblers Anonymous or something. But once again he denied that he had a problem. Told me that if I wouldn't help him, he'd find the money somewhere else. I didn't like the sound of that, but was kind of relieved I wouldn't have to worry about it anymore. Still...I made up the story about my boss hitting on me and left within a few days. I didn't want Mom and Dad to know about Spencer."

"Why not?" Lucky asked.

"Because it would devastate them. He's always tried so hard to get their approval. I think because he felt somewhat lost in the shuffle growing up. I had their attention because of the leukemia, my sisters were older, and so they had plenty of attention from their friends and boys, and Fred honestly didn't care one way or another. But Spencer *always* cared. He craved their approval. I didn't want to tell Mom and Dad about my suspicions because they'd be disappointed in him. They'd already almost divorced because of the stress over me being sick, and I don't want to add any further stress to their lives."

"Why not tell Grover all this when you got here?"

"Because he'd get really mad at Spencer, and I didn't want *that* either. They've always had somewhat of a competitive thing between them, more on Spence's part than Fred's. He was always trying to live up to his big brother's sterling reputation...and falling flat.

"Don't you get it, Lucky? I don't want to be the reason my family splinters," Devyn said, finally admitting her deepest fear. "And if Fred knew Spencer was on my case about money, he'd lose his shit. He'd tell Mom and Dad, they'd be upset, my sisters would hear about it and yell at Spencer...it would be a disaster."

"So you're trying to deal with it on your own," Lucky said. "Upending your entire life to protect your brother."

Devyn shrugged. "Yeah."

"And now he's calling you again. I'm guessing he's harassing you for more money."

Devyn nodded and refused to look up at Lucky. She didn't know why she felt ashamed, when Spencer was the one who should feel bad.

"Look at me, Dev."

Taking a big breath, she did.

"Thank you for telling me. I know that couldn't have been easy."

"You can't tell Fred," she said, biting her lip.

Lucky pulled her lip out of her teeth with his thumb, then palmed the side of her neck with his huge hand. "I won't. As long as Spencer doesn't do anything dumb, like break into your apartment, steal from you again, or put his hands on you."

"He's still in Missouri, he can't do any of those things."

"I know. Even still. You know you can't help someone until they truly want to help themselves, right?"

"I know. But...he's gotten worse," Devyn admitted.

"How so?"

"He called me recently and said he needed fifty thousand dollars," Devyn said.

Lucky shook his head and blew out a breath. "That's a lot of money."

"I know. He begged me to help him. Said he was in trouble. That if I could give him five thousand, he knew he could turn that into the fifty he needed."

"You know the odds of him being able to do that are extremely low, especially considering his track record," Lucky said.

"I know. He said more nasty things, then told me that when his dead body turned up in a cornfield somewhere, it would be all my fault."

"Come here," Lucky said, reaching for her.

Devyn ended up sitting across Lucky's lap, with Angel pressed against her legs resting on the couch cushions. She lay her head on Lucky's chest and held on to him as tightly as she could. His arms around her felt amazing. Safe.

"I'm sorry, Dev. It must've been so hard keeping all this bottled up inside."

She nodded.

"You can always use me as a sounding board. I might not like everything you say, but that doesn't mean I won't listen, or won't do everything I can to help solve whatever you're worried over. Okay?"

"Okay," she said softly.

"It sounds like your brother borrowed money from the wrong people."

She nodded again.

"Do you think he was bluffing?"

"I don't know. It's possible. I think he'd do or say anything to get money to gamble with. It really is an addiction, like drugs. I don't think he can help himself. He truly believes he's just one bet away from hitting it big."

"What do you want to do?" Lucky asked.

Devyn appreciated him asking more than he could know. He didn't try to take over, tell her what she needed to do, or tell her that Spencer was a lost cause and she should write him off. She was upset with her brother and couldn't believe he'd gotten himself into the situation he had, but she was still worried for him. "Honestly? I want to give him fifty thousand dollars then force him to go to rehab. But one, I don't have that kind of money, and two, like you said earlier, if he doesn't want to get help, it won't do any good."

"What do you need from me?" Lucky asked.

"This," Devyn said immediately. "Holding me when I'm sad. Letting me borrow your amazing pets to make me feel better. And supporting me without being judgmental or trying to take over."

"I have to admit, I'm not doing very well in the judgmental category," Lucky said into her hair. "But I'm trying. Like you said, I don't have any siblings, so it's hard for me to be as easygoing about this."

Devyn looked up at Lucky. "You really aren't going to tell Fred?"

He sighed. "No. Not at this point. I don't like how much money we're talking about here. If Spencer wasn't lying, fifty G's is a lot of cash and a loan shark may very well resort to violence to get it from him. But as I promised you, unless *your* life is in danger, or you're sick, what we talk about stays between the two of us."

"I'm sorry," Devyn blurted.

Lucky frowned. "About what?"

"About you having to keep this from Fred. I know you guys are super close and your first instinct is to talk to him about it, but...I don't want to hurt my family."

Lucky kissed her forehead. "Your compassion is one of many things I love about you. Your compassion for animals, for your friends, and your family."

Devyn's heart stopped beating in her chest for a moment. Had he said what she thought he'd said? She was too chicken to ask him to say it again, so she just burrowed her head back into his chest and held on tight.

Could he really love her? They hadn't even been dating very long. But it wasn't as if they'd just met. She knew a lot about the man whose lap she was sitting on, simply from hanging out with Fred and his friends for so many months.

They were friends long before they'd started dating, which was why she knew without a doubt that she'd have a hard time finding someone more amazing than Lucky. He was one of the biggest reasons why she hadn't left town to start over somewhere new.

Devyn loved this man. She did. And she couldn't imagine not seeing or talking to him every day. She'd already been planning on making love with him, but now with him all but admitting he loved her back? She couldn't wait for this evening.

After a few minutes, he asked, "You okay?"

Devyn nodded.

"If he calls again, you'll let me know?"

"Yeah. But I'm not planning on taking his call if he *does* try to get in touch with me. Spencer is an adult, and I can't bail him out this time. It'll kill me if he gets hurt...but maybe this is the push he needs to straighten his life out. I feel horrible saying that, and I'll drown in guilt if something actually happens to him, but I'm done."

"I'm proud of you," Lucky said. "How about we take Angel and Whiskers for a walk? Or at least attempt to. I'm not sure how it'll go. Then you need to shower and get ready for work. I can make lunch before we have to go."

"How'd I get so lucky?" Devyn asked.

Lucky grinned. "Did you mean that as a pun?" he asked.

Devyn laughed. "Actually, no, but if the shoe fits."

"You got me because you're cute, and compassionate, and because I blatantly used Angel and Whiskers to lure you into my lair," he said.

"You think a guy hasn't tried to use a pet to pick me up before?" Devyn asked.

Lucky scowled. "They have?"

"Down, boy," Devyn said, patting Lucky's chest. "And of course they have. They bring cute little puppies into the clinic and then proceed to flirt their asses off as I'm doing the pre-exam on their pets. The looks of devastation when they strike out are so amusing."

"You're a hard woman," Lucky teased.

"Eh. It's not hard to figure out the owners who are genuinely in love with their animals, and those who are using them to try to get laid."

"I'm almost afraid to ask where I fit in that crowd."

Devyn smirked, feeling so much lighter now that she'd told Lucky everything. It was amazing how talking about your feelings and shame somehow made that burden lessen. "You love Angel and Whiskers, that's easy to see, but I have to admit...you're totally gonna get laid as well." Then before he could respond, she scooted off his lap and stood. "Let me get some real clothes on, then I'll go get their harnesses."

"Shit, woman, that was cruel," Lucky said.

But he was smiling as he said it, so Devyn wasn't too worried. "Cruel would be using *you* for your adorable animals, but since we're both gonna get what we want, I think we're both gonna come out on top in the end."

"Oh, we're both gonna come, all right," Lucky muttered as he stood.

Devyn couldn't keep the smile off her face as she headed for the bedroom to put on something other than her pajamas.

CHAPTER NINE

"You talk to Devyn? Find out what's up with her?" Grover asked as soon as Lucky walked into the conference room later that afternoon. He'd dropped Devyn off at the vet clinic and they'd shared another very hot, intense kiss in his truck. The chemistry between them had shifted. Neither of them were tiptoeing around their attraction anymore, and it felt damn good.

He was all for showing Devyn how great things between them could be in bed, later that evening, and it seemed as if she was on the same page. It was refreshing not to have to wonder what she thought in regard to moving their relationship to the next level. She'd flat-out told him she wanted to make love, and he was one hundred percent on board with that.

Lucky also knew going that next step would bring them closer together, rather than make things awkward between them. Sleeping with your best friend's sister was frowned upon by a lot of people, but Lucky had already gotten Grover's blessing to be with Devyn, and it felt great.

But before he could move his relationship with Devyn to

the next level, he needed to get through the afternoon. And it wasn't as if he could jump on her the second he brought her back to his townhouse either. They'd need to eat, the animals would need to be tended to, but then—

"Lucky? Did you talk to her or not?" Grover asked, interrupting his thoughts.

"Yeah. We talked."

"And?" Grover asked.

Lucky tensed. He'd hoped after his conversation with Grover that morning, his friend wouldn't question him about his sister. But it looked like it was happening, after all.

"She's not in danger and she's not sick," Lucky said, keeping all emotion from his face.

"Ouch, man, looks like you've been left out in the cold," Doc said with a chuckle.

But no one else laughed.

"You seriously aren't going to tell me, are you?" Grover asked.

"We talked about this," Lucky said.

Grover sighed. "I know. But it's harder than I thought it would be to have both you *and* my baby sister keeping secrets from me."

"Do you tell her everything that's going on with your life?" Lucky countered.

The two men stared at each other for a long moment before Grover said, "You know I don't."

"She know about Sierra? About how you were interested in a contract employee you met in Afghanistan, and how upset you were when she didn't respond to any of your emails?" Lucky pushed.

"No."

"Or about the time you totally forgot Dev's birthday and covered by sending that singing telegram guy to her office, but you didn't pay attention, and instead of singing happy birthday, he thought she was celebrating her last day of being single?"

Grover laughed. "Uh, no. And if she ever finds out it wasn't just a prank, and I'd forgotten her birthday, you're dead meat."

"Right. She's an adult, Grover. Twenty-nine years old. There's a lot you don't know about her either. But she's okay. We talked, and we'll deal with what's been bothering her together. I wish I could tell you. It's killing me to keep stuff from you. But I gave her my word, and the last thing I want is to lose her over this."

Grover strode over to Lucky and put a hand on his shoulder. "I get it. It sucks, but *nothing* will come between us. I trust you with my sister's life. That means her actual life, and her emotional well-being, as well. Forgive me if I get nosey in the future, I just love her, and I want the best for her. If I could wrap her in a protective bubble, I would."

"I know," Lucky said. And he did. He felt the same way, though his love was a lot different than Grover's love for a sister.

"Right, so with that done and out of the way, can we get on with the meeting?" Grover asked. "I, for one, am looking forward to this Olympic assignment. While we're there to protect the US athletes, we can put in requests for three competitions we want tickets to. I'm thinking basketball, baseball, or beach volleyball." His eyebrows went up suggestively. "You know...hot women in bikinis jumping around on the beach? Sounds like a winner to me."

Everyone laughed as they took their seats. "We're allowed to put in our top three requests, but there's no guarantee we'll get them," Trigger reminded him.

Lucky listened intently as they discussed the pros and cons of protecting the athletes from the different sports, and the logistics of how the Olympic Village would be set up. The competition venues were fairly spread out, due to the nature of the different sports, and it would be a challenge to come up with a plan to protect them all. Even though there were several special forces teams being deployed as security, in addition to the hosting country's own police and security, it was a huge task.

It sucked that special forces had to be used at such a prestigious event as the Olympics, but as had been proven in the past, terrorists would take any opportunity to get publicity for their cause, and to spread fear and terror.

By the end of the meeting, the team had decided to put shooting, diving, and boxing down as their requested sports to watch during their time off. They all knew it was a crap-shoot as to whether they'd actually get any of those sports, but it was worth a shot.

The team had worked the winter Olympics a couple years ago, and it had been educational as well as exciting. Much different from their usual missions.

"Now that we're done talking about fun shit...we need to talk about Shahzada," Trigger said. "Another contractor has disappeared. This is no longer a simple possibility of people getting sick of their job and walking out, like it's been suggested."

"Seriously?" Grover asked. "People think workers out in the middle of Afghanistan suddenly decided they didn't like their jobs and just up and left?"

"Yeah, that's exactly what they think. Especially when all their stuff disappears with them," Trigger said grimly.

"It's such bullshit," Brain said.

"What are they doing about it?" Oz asked. "Leaving without their stuff and without saying anything to anyone isn't normal. And more than one person? It's all fishy as hell."

"I agree. As does the commander. He's in talks now with the general of the base and they're trying to work with the private investigators the contractor companies hired to try to find their missing employees," Trigger said.

"Fuck," Brain said in frustration. "And we're sure this ties back to Shahzada?"

"Unfortunately, yes. Intelligence is saying he's planning something big. And that the contractors who have gone missing were specifically targeted."

"Why?" Grover asked.

"That's the big question. No one's sure. But what they *are* sure about is that Shahzada's followers have gotten more aggressive and vocal over the months since we were last there. The base general has forbidden the soldiers to go into the nearby town because it's simply not safe. They're fortifying the base as best they can, but it's hard to know exactly what Shahzada has planned, especially when there's no clear pictures of the man," Trigger said with a concerned expression.

Lucky heard Grover inhale sharply. "What?" he asked his friend.

"He's got Sierra," Grover said.

"You don't know that," Oz said.

"I think we *all* know that," Grover countered heatedly.

"She's been gone a while," Lefty agreed cautiously.

"And she's a woman," Doc added.

"Exactly," Grover bit out.

Sierra had fallen off the radar months ago. They all knew the odds of the petite redhead being found alive were slim to none if she'd been kidnapped by Shahzada.

The team was quiet for a moment before Trigger continued on with the briefing, discussing the area of Afghanistan and what intelligence had discovered about Shahzada.

As much as Lucky tried to fully concentrate on the briefing, the reminder of Sierra missing made his mind return to Devyn.

He wanted to kill Spencer for putting his hands on her. Intellectually, he could understand what Devyn had said about brothers and sisters fighting and not thinking anything about it, but the fact that *she* was the one who'd ended up with a horrible bruise made her point moot in his eyes.

He was also very aware that Devyn loved her brother. And that she was worried about him. Lucky was worried too. If Spencer had gotten himself involved with a loan shark who wouldn't think twice about setting an example to other clients who didn't pay him back, Spencer could be in big trouble.

As long as the man didn't drag Devyn down with him, there wasn't much Lucky could do. He'd be there to support Dev however she needed him.

But if Spencer ever laid a hand on her again, he'd regret it.

The day seemed to drag, but finally their meetings were over and it was time to go home. Grover caught up to Lucky on his way out the door. "Can I have a sec?"

Lucky said goodbye to his other teammates and turned to Grover. "What's up?"

"I know whatever's bothering Devyn has to do with Spencer. I also know she's been avoiding him, and after she got that call from him at Oz's place, nothing's gotten better. I still can't get ahold of my brother, so I don't know what he's done...but I want you to know that I'm not going to take sides, no matter what Devyn might think."

Lucky had promised Devyn he wouldn't interfere, so he nodded. "Good to know. I don't have any flesh-and-blood brothers or sisters, but I'm fairly certain if I did, I'd be protective of them."

"Exactly. Devyn was vulnerable for so long. Physically and mentally, I think. Everyone thought she was doing great when she started indulging in all those crazy things like bungee jumping and skydiving, but to me, it seemed as if she wanted to spit in death's face. I'm not even convinced she actually enjoyed doing them, so much as she was being extra reckless just to try to prove she wasn't the sickly kid we all saw her as."

Lucky thought Grover had an extremely good point. He simply nodded again.

"Even though Spencer is between me and Dev in age, he always seemed more immature. Wanting all of Mom and Dad's attention when they were home, even physically pushing Devyn out of the way when he needed to. I just...if they're fighting, it wouldn't surprise me. I'm not going to take sides, and if that's what Devyn's worried about...she doesn't need to."

"I'll let her know."

Grover eyed Lucky. "Am I even close?" he asked.

Lucky sighed. "Yeah. Family dynamics are always weird, and I imagine they're even more so in your circle because of how sick Dev was. But she loves you and wouldn't do anything to hurt you, I think you know that."

"I do. But I don't want her not hurting me to actually hurt *her*. If that makes any sense."

"It does," Lucky told him. "I'm gonna keep my eye on things. In the meantime, I think she just needs to feel as normal as possible. Hang out with everyone, get some girl time in, that sort of thing."

"Is she going to start working full time?" Grover asked.

"I'm not sure."

Grover sighed. "Right. I want her to, because that would mean she's gonna stay. For a while there I thought she was gonna bolt at any second. Anyway, I'll see you in the morning," Grover said. "Tell Dev I love her."

"Sure thing. See ya tomorrow."

Lucky headed for his truck with a spring in his step. He had no idea what he and Dev were going to do for dinner, but they'd figure something out. It didn't matter if they had hotdogs or filet mignon, he'd be spending time with her, and that was enough to make it the perfect ending to the day.

For the first time in his life, he wasn't overanalyzing how he wanted something to go. If he and Devyn made love, great. If she'd had a hard day at work and just wanted to talk and sleep in his arms, fine.

That was how Lucky knew this was love. He didn't feel an urge to move things along simply to get his rocks off. He loved Dev, and whatever pace she wanted to move at was perfectly all right with him. As long as he got to spend time with her, he'd be satisfied.

That feeling of satisfaction was bone deep every time he saw Devyn. He hadn't realized what it was until recently, and he hoped she felt the same. Because if she didn't, if he was a casual fling for her, it would devastate him. Lucky couldn't continue to see her at get-togethers with the team if she broke up with him. It would kill him.

He had to do everything in his power to make sure Devyn knew how much she meant to him. How much she was appreciated. It wouldn't be a hardship. She deserved the world, and he was prepared to give it to her.

CHAPTER TEN

"See you tomorrow!" Margaret, one of the other vet techs, called out, as Devyn headed out the door. She waved back at her but kept her eyes on Lucky. He'd pulled into a space outside the clinic and had texted her to let her know he was there.

She hadn't yet told the veterinarian that she wanted to work full time. Devyn wasn't sure why she was hesitating. She supposed it was because she wasn't yet fully convinced things with her and Lucky would work out.

Oh, she *wanted* them to work out. But somehow, in her life, something always seemed to go sour right when she thought things were fine. The last thing she wanted was to put her coworkers and the vet in a lurch if things got weird between her and Lucky. She wouldn't be able to stay and see him all the time. She absolutely couldn't stomach seeing him dating someone else.

So, she was hesitating. It was cowardly of her, but she wasn't comfortable enough with everything to go all in...yet. Devyn hoped tonight might change her feelings. Going that final step might solidify in her mind that they really were a serious couple, and she could commit to staying in Texas.

"Hey," Lucky said in that low, rumbly tone that always got her all hot and bothered.

"Hi," she returned as she climbed into his truck.

"Have a good day today?"

"Yeah. I got to cuddle a litter of the cutest kittens. Oh! And I got to hold a greyhound puppy. They're like unicorns."

"Yeah?"

"Uh-huh. There aren't many around. I mean, there are, but not many that are brought in to regular family vets. Because of the racing circuit, most are raised with their litter-mates for over a year, and outside of racing, most are bred as show dogs."

"So there aren't any puppies outside of racing?" Lucky asked.

That was another thing she loved about him. He always seemed very interested in whatever she had to say. He never brushed her off. "No, of course there are. There will always be backyard-bred puppies of every breed, someone wanting to make a quick buck. Greyhounds aren't exactly in high demand as far as family pets go, so there are fewer puppies. But you should've seen this little guy. He looked a lot like any other kind of puppy, so it's hard to believe they grow up to be as big as they do, and with such long legs."

"You love what you do," Lucky said.

"What?" Devyn asked in surprise.

"You love what you do," he repeated. "It's obvious. You light up when talking about the animals and you have so much compassion for them. I could listen to you talk about your four-legged clients all day."

Devyn knew she was blushing, but couldn't help it. "I just...animals have such a huge capacity for love and forgiveness. I've seen the most abused and neglected pets lick and cuddle up to the very people who've beaten them. And you've seen it yourself with Angel and Whiskers. People don't trust as easily when they've been hurt."

"What about you?" Lucky asked.

"Me?" Devyn asked, feigning confusion and stalling for time.

"Yeah, you. You didn't say it this morning, but I know your brother targeting you for money for his gambling addiction has to hurt. Has it made you less trusting? More wary of people in general? I'm only asking because I didn't know you before you got to Texas, and I'm trying to figure out what makes you tick...and how hard I'm gonna have to work to get you to trust me."

"I do trust you," Devyn said, and she meant that one hundred percent. "I wouldn't have told you about Spencer if I didn't."

"That means the world to me, sweetheart," Lucky said, reaching over and taking her hand in his. He rested their clasped hands on the console between them and rubbed his thumb over her skin soothingly.

"And to answer your question, not really," Devyn said. "I'm an optimist at heart. I have a tendency to think people are generally good...unless they show me otherwise. I'm sure that's not very smart, and I should probably protect my heart better, but I don't think I want to go around thinking everyone is out to get me, or is a liar and a cheat."

"How about I be the cynical one in this relationship? I'll be the one who thinks that, and I'll have your back when necessary. You can be the light, happy-go-lucky half, and I'll be the sulky brooding half."

Devyn got goose bumps hearing him talk about them as a couple. But she laughed. "You aren't broody or sulky. And I'm not sure that's even a word."

Lucky smiled over at her. "I like you exactly how you are,

Dev. I don't want you to change. I'm sorry your brother's been on your case, and I'll do whatever you need me to in order to get him to back off. And I'll even try to convince him to get some professional help, if only because I know it'll put your mind at ease."

"Thanks," Devyn whispered. This man...gah...he was killing her. But he was also making the decision to sleep with him very easy.

She wanted him. Wanted to experience his focused attention in bed, because she knew it would be just as potent as when they were simply having a conversation, like now.

"What do you feel like for dinner?"

Food? She couldn't think about anything other than finally being able to check out the tattoo he had on his right shoulder, up close and in person. She'd seen it when they'd all gathered at Grover's new farmhouse a while ago. He'd taken off his shirt because it had been warm, and he and the rest of the guys were tearing down an old barn on the property. She knew it was black, but not exactly what it looked like.

Devyn's mouth almost watered at the thought of exploring Lucky's body. She might not be all that confident in her own sex appeal, but she had a feeling when she felt Lucky's skin against her own, she'd forget all about what *she* looked like.

"Dev?" he asked with a knowing smirk on his face. "Dinner?"

"I don't care," she said. "Anything."

"Anything?" he asked, the shit-eating grin growing.

Devyn did her best to get her libido under control. She couldn't exactly jump him the second they were inside his townhouse. Angel and Whiskers would need to be tended to, fed, and she needed to shower and change. She had dog and cat hair all over her scrubs and probably smelled like the inside of a dog kennel.

"I don't know what you have. I'm not super hungry though. What about stir-fry?"

"I think I've got enough veggies to swing that. Rice?"

"Absolutely. I know the trend is anti-carbohydrates right now, but I love me some carbs. Besides, I could use some more padding anyway." Devyn gestured to her chest self-consciously.

"You aren't seriously putting yourself down, are you?" Lucky asked.

Devyn shrugged. "I'm not exactly Dolly Parton."

"Thank fuck," Lucky said, squeezing her hand. "I've already told you this, but you've obviously forgotten. I like you exactly how you are, Dev. You're tall and willowy, and you turn me on so much, my cock's been hard for what seems like months. You move like you're totally in tune with your body. Not only that, but you laugh when something's funny, you get emotional when you see one of those ads for the ASPCA and they show abused animals. If your tits were bigger, you'd be top heavy. You're fucking perfect, Devyn, so don't you go thinking I want anything different. I can't wait to see what I've been dreaming about for months, up close and personal. And I know without a doubt you're going to blow every one of my fantasies out of the water. So if you want rice, that's what you'll get."

Devyn released a long breath. She wished she had a recorder going, so she could replay what he'd just said in the future, when she felt insecure about her body. "Okay." It was all she could think to say.

"Okay," Lucky agreed. "You *are* staying the night tonight, right?"

"If that's all right," she said shyly.

"It's more than all right," he told her immediately. "And just to get this awkward part out of the way, I've got condoms. Bought them two days ago. Not to rush you in any way, but because I wanted to be prepared so I could keep you safe."

"I'm on the shot. The birth control injection that's good for three months at a time," Devyn told him. She was just slightly embarrassed by the topic, but still relieved that he was bringing it up now.

"You okay?" he asked.

Devyn frowned in confusion. "Okay?"

"Yeah. I know you aren't dating anyone, and some women go on birth control to control heavy periods or because of extreme cramps and stuff, or because of ovarian cysts. So are you okay?" he asked again.

"I'm fine. I started on it in my mid-twenties because it seemed like the responsible thing to do for someone my age, who was actively dating. The last thing I needed was an unwanted pregnancy. I like knowing when I'm going to get my period and how long it'll last. It just became part of my routine."

Lucky squeezed her hand. "Right. I haven't been with a woman since months before you arrived. I'm clean; we get tested by the Army regularly. I can show you my latest test results."

Devyn squeezed his hand. "I don't need to see them. I trust you."

He smiled over at her. "That means the world to me. But I'm gonna show them to you anyway."

"I'm clean too. I need to find a new doctor here in Texas, but I get a yearly exam."

"That's good."

Devyn debated what she was about to say, but finally decided just to go for it. "So...if I'm clean, and you are too... And I'm on birth control...are the condoms necessary?"

When he didn't immediately answer, she felt stupid. "Yeah, it's probably for the best. I mean, no birth control is one hundred perfect effective, and it's just smarter if we play it safe."

They'd arrived back at his townhouse by now, and Lucky pulled into a parking spot in front of his door. He turned off the engine and immediately turned to her. He reached out and pulled her toward him with a hand behind her neck. Without a word, he kissed her.

It was a possessive move, and he took complete control of the kiss.

Her head spun, and all she could do was hang on as Lucky took her mouth. When he finally pulled back, the intense look he gave her made Devyn shiver.

"I've never made love without a condom before," he said, shocking the hell out of her.

"Never?" she whispered.

"No. Never trusted a woman enough to do that. And honestly, haven't really felt the *need* to. But with you? I'd kill to get inside you bare. But I don't want you to offer that unless you're sure you want a long-term relationship with me. Because I already know you're going to ruin me for all other women, Devyn."

God. He was killing her. "I want that," she said softly. "I want you. Just you."

Lucky shut his eyes as if he were in pain. Then they immediately opened once more. "You've got me. Come on, we need to let Angel and Whiskers out, then I need to feed you. And if I don't get out of the truck in the next ten seconds, I'm gonna take you right here."

Devyn giggled. "I've never done it in a car before," she teased.

"Fuck, you're killing me. Have mercy, woman." Lucky leaned forward and kissed her once more, a fast, hard kiss that wasn't meant to entice, before he turned to climb out of the truck.

Devyn hopped out on her side with a huge smile on her face. Being with someone had never been as easy as it was with Lucky. She couldn't deny she felt more at ease now that they'd had the birth control talk. She hadn't mentioned she'd never been with a guy who hadn't worn a condom. Granted, she hadn't slept with all that many men in the first place, but she had a feeling Lucky wouldn't want to hear anything about that.

He was a typical alpha male in that sense. But that was all right, Devyn was perfectly happy not knowing about his previous love life either.

A part of her couldn't believe this moment was actually here. She'd wanted Lucky from the first time she'd met him; she'd just kept those feelings to herself.

But tonight, he'd finally be hers. Or would she be his? She didn't know, but in the end, it didn't matter. How this would turn out, she also had no idea, but she'd do whatever it took to hold on to him. She knew a good man when she saw one, and Lucky was one of the best.

Smiling to herself, she took Lucky's hand when he held it out, and they walked hand-in-hand to his front door.

CHAPTER ELEVEN

Lucky couldn't stop staring at Devyn. He knew he was being a little creepy, but he couldn't help it. She was going to be his tonight. And every night from here on out.

He'd been half hard all evening. Through their short walk with Angel and Whiskers, while laughing together as they made dinner. As they sat on the couch and watched the news. He knew the second he let go of his control, he'd be hard as a pike and ready to go.

But he liked this. Hanging out with Devyn. Talking about the people she worked with. About the animals she'd seen that day. Discussing what he could about his job. He didn't have to explain how close he was to Trigger, her brother, and the other guys. She knew.

They talked about Aspen and Riley's pregnancies and joked about how many kids they'd end up with. Oz had made no secret of the fact that he wanted a big family. It was as if once he'd gotten guardianship of his niece and nephew, he'd realized firsthand how awesome children were and wanted as many as he could get...as fast as he could get them.

It was obvious Riley was going to have to rein him in, and

Lucky loved how easily he could joke about the situation with Devyn. She fit in with their crew as if she'd been there all along.

"Grover's thrilled that you're here," Lucky told her.

Devyn snuggled into his side and nodded. "I know. I kinda sprung myself on him, and he could've been resentful that I basically shoved my way into his inner circle, but he welcomed me with open arms. When we were kids, he never minded if I tagged along with him when he hung out with his friends. I know he got shit for it from them, but he didn't care. I love him so much, and I just want him to find a woman who can appreciate him for who he is."

"And who you can be friends with," Lucky said.

She sighed. "Yeah. I would hate for him to end up with someone who doesn't like me. Or you guys, for that matter. I mean, I don't think he'd put up with that, but love can make people do weird things."

"I have faith in him. He knows what he wants," Lucky said.

"And what's that?" Devyn asked, tilting her head up to look at him.

"Someone who will support him no matter what. Someone who looks at him as if the sun rises and sets with him, but at the same time, knows her own worth. A woman who's independent and can fend for herself and their kids, if they have them, when he gets deployed. She should have a sense of humor and not take herself too seriously. But most of all, I think Grover needs someone strong. Outgoing. Who isn't afraid to stand up to him or anyone else who might think they can give her shit."

Devyn nodded. "You're right. He can get pretty bossy, and if he doesn't find someone who can go toe-to-toe with him, he'll run roughshod over her in no time."

"Exactly. And he's good at what he does, but he has a tendency to think about work all the time."

Devyn nodded. "You think he'll find her?"

"Yes."

She chuckled. "You said that really fast."

"I think we were all just coasting along. Happy to date casually. Then Ghost and his crew—that's another Delta team on post—started falling one by one. We attended Truck and Mary's wedding and saw how deliriously happy they all were. And that they were making it work...relationships *and* their job. I have a feeling we all just assumed we couldn't have a wife while being Delta. So that wedding opened our eyes. And we realized that we weren't getting any younger."

"Then Trigger met Gillian," Devyn said.

"Yes. And it's been a domino effect," Lucky said with a smile.

"Do you think their relationships have worked because of the situations Gillian and the others got into?" Devyn asked.

"What do you mean?"

"Just that. Gillian and Trigger met under extreme circumstances. And Kinley and Lefty got through her witness protection thing, and Aspen and Brain actually were on an op together and she's damn badass. And of course, they went through Brain's attack. Then Riley and Oz had that drama with his niece and nephew. My life is downright boring compared to theirs, and what they've been through." She shrugged.

Lucky checked on the animals, and saw they were both snoring in the fluffy bed in the corner of the room. He stood, pulling Devyn up with him.

"Lucky?" she said, but he didn't respond. He checked the front door to make sure it was locked before leading her up the stairs. He pulled Devyn into his room, then sat on the bed, pulled her closer, and urged her to straddle his lap.

Her face was now level with his own, and he cradled her head in his hands. "Listen to me, Dev. I don't give a rat's ass how my friends met their women, I'm just glad they did. I didn't need some big drama to know I wanted you. I don't need you to be in a shootout, or to have some crazy terrorist try to shank you. I don't need some huge life event to happen to either of us to know that I love you. I just do. Because you're *you*. You play things close to the vest, and it's been hell trying to go slow with my attraction to you. I wanted you to get to know me, to see that I'm not going to take over your life, I'm not going to be all crazy possessive. You're a grown woman who's been managing her life perfectly fine without me. I'm okay with our lives being boring as fuck. It won't change how I feel about you."

He watched her swallow hard and bite her lip. "You love me?" she whispered.

Lucky grinned. He should probably be a little concerned that he'd just blurted that, but since she hadn't jerked out of his embrace and didn't look horrified by his declaration, something inside him settled.

"Yeah, Dev. I do. How could I not? I'd be as lucky as my nickname implies if you could find it in your heart to like me back even a fraction of how much I love you."

"I love you too," she whispered, as if she was terrified to say it out loud.

Lucky knew he was smiling like a crazy person, but he couldn't help it. "I'm sorry, I couldn't quite hear you. Can you repeat that?"

Devyn frowned. "You heard me."

"Nope. I think you need to say it again. I mean, I *am* older than you and I've been through a few explosions. My hearing isn't what it used to be."

"You heard Angel whining the other day from two rooms away. You rushed in there to see what the issue was and realized that the treat you'd given her had somehow been pushed under the couch and she couldn't reach it," Devyn accused.

"Hmmmm, you must be mistaken, I couldn't have heard that," Lucky told her, still smiling.

Devyn wrinkled her nose at him, and instead of saying what he wanted—no, *needed*—to hear again, she dug her fingers into his sides, tickling him.

Lucky let out a downright girly screech and immediately began to laugh. He was extremely ticklish, something he'd never told anyone, and yet somehow his woman knew exactly where to touch him to render him completely helpless.

He tried to squirm away, but Devyn didn't let up, kept tickling him mercilessly.

"Uncle!" Lucky shouted, trying to wiggle away from her fingers with no luck. "I give up!"

"You gonna admit that your hearing is fine?" she asked, her fingers slipping under his shirt to increase the torture factor of her tickling.

"Yes! Anything! Please, for the love of God, stop!"

"Holy crap, you call yourself a Delta soldier?" she asked as her fingers finally stilled.

Lucky closed his eyes in relief. He was on his back and Devyn was still straddling his hips, but she hadn't yet moved her fingers out from under his shirt.

"Tickling wasn't a part of torture-endurance training," he said weakly.

Devyn chuckled. Then she laughed. Then she was guffawing uncontrollably. Lucky took the opportunity to roll over and trap her body under his. But she still didn't stop laughing. He didn't mind he was the butt of the joke. Who ever heard of a special forces operative being brought down by less than a minute of playful tickling?

He could watch her laugh without reservation for hours.

When she finally had herself under control, she looked up at him with tears in her eyes. "That was priceless," she said.

"I love you," Lucky said quietly. "You bring joy to my life, and that's not something any other woman has done. I've been happy and content and I told myself I wasn't lonely in the least. Then you moved here, and I realized how boring my life really was. I can't lose you, Dev. If I screw up, tell me immediately so I can apologize and fix whatever it was I fucked up. If I don't spend enough time with you, or you feel ignored, for the love of God, tell me. Please. I couldn't stand it if you left me because of something I could fix."

"I love you back," she said. "And the same goes for me. I try not to get sucked down into drama, but if I do, call me on it. I never want you to feel as if you're second fiddle in our relationship. If I talk too much about work, or don't take enough time off, you have my permission to kidnap me."

"No one's kidnapping anyone," Lucky said, then he brushed a lock of hair off her forehead. "Will you let me make love to you? Show you how much you mean to me?"

"*Let* you? No. I'm gonna have to beg you to please hurry the hell up and fuck me already."

Lucky grinned. Damn, this woman was perfect for him. "You like it fast and hard?" he asked, rocking his hips against her.

"With you, I have a feeling I'll like it however you want to give it to me."

"Good answer," Lucky said with a chuckle. "How about we play it by ear?"

"Sounds like a plan. But...I need to brush my teeth first. And pee. And maybe take off some clothes."

"So practical," he teased.

Devyn shrugged. "I've never understood how people in romance books and movies manage to get naked while hori-

124

zontal. It's way more complicated than they make it seem. It's just easier to take everything off before getting into bed."

"Right," Lucky agreed. "Although later, I'm gonna want to peel your clothes off item by item. There's something sexy as hell about revealing your prize inch by inch."

"Deal. As long as I can return the favor."

Lucky stared at her for a long moment without a word.

"What?" she asked a little self-consciously.

"I'm just memorizing this moment," Lucky told her.

Devyn smiled tenderly. Then said, "If you don't move, I'm gonna tickle you again."

Lucky immediately rolled off her. "Sadist," he grumbled.

She laughed. "I want to kiss you and see you naked, but I don't wanna have fish-head mouth when we make love for the first time."

"You don't have fish-head mouth," he told her.

She raised an eyebrow at him.

"Wait, do *I* have fish-head mouth?" he asked in horror.

She didn't reply, just smirked and headed for the bathroom.

Lucky shook his head as she disappeared inside, but he hurried to the guest bathroom in the hall to brush his own teeth. It was obvious he was going to have to keep his head about him when she was around. She liked to joke, and he freaking loved that. He'd never smiled so much around a woman as he did around her.

Within two minutes, he was back in his bedroom. He'd stripped off his T-shirt and cargo pants and was standing awkwardly by his bed waiting for Devyn to return. Maybe this was why people usually took off their clothes while lying in bed. It was uncomfortable standing there nearly naked, waiting for her.

Then she was there.

And she shocked the shit out of him by walking out of his bathroom completely nude.

He'd expected her to wear a towel, or to have kept her bra and panties on. But she strode toward him naked as the day she was born...and his mouth literally watered.

Her cheeks flushed from the blush that started at her chest and worked its way upward, probably from his staring, but he couldn't take his gaze from her body. Her tits were small, but topped with mouthwatering nipples that were already rock hard. Her blonde hair brushed the tops of her breasts, making him want to feel the strands against his own body when she straddled him. Even though she was slender, her stomach had a small pooch, which was sexy as hell to him. Her legs seemed to go on forever, and Lucky couldn't help but imagine how they'd feel wrapped around him, her heels pushing into his ass as he stroked deep inside her.

Thinking about stroking had him remembering that he was going to be able to take her bare, which made his cock grow inside his boxer briefs. Distractedly, Lucky shoved his underwear down his legs, freeing his dick. He felt it bob up and down as if in greeting.

The relieved smile on her face made any discomfort he'd felt about standing around naked well worth it. "Come here," he said, holding out a hand.

Devyn immediately walked toward him, taking hold of his fingers as if they were a life line. He wanted to be that for her. Always.

"So fucking brave," he told her.

"I'm actually not," she said. "But I thought it would be even more weird to come out with a towel on...especially after all my bravado earlier."

"Nothing would be weird between us," Lucky told her. "You do what you feel like doing. Always." Then he pulled her into his body. The overhead light in the room was still on and

Lucky was thankful for it. He wanted to see every inch of Devyn as he took her.

As he held her to him skin-to-skin for the first time, any nervousness about what was about to happen disappeared. She felt so very right against him. He ran his hand up and down her back, loving how soft and silky her skin felt. She was so different from him. He was all hard angles and calluses. She was soft and sleek.

"It's a skull," Devyn said in surprise.

Lucky saw that her eyes were glued to the tattoo on his shoulder. "Yeah."

"I couldn't really see what it was before. I thought it was something tribal," Devyn told him.

"I got it after I joined Delta. It seemed appropriate. Skulls represent mortality, and it's a reminder to myself that I'm not immortal. I might be a Delta, but I'm not invincible. It reminds me to always to stay on alert, otherwise I can end up just like the terrorists we hunt. It's a bit ghoulish though, so I don't show it off much."

"I like it. It fits you," Devyn said, running her fingers over the design.

It shouldn't have been such a relief that she didn't hate his ink, but Lucky couldn't help recalling the horrified reaction of another woman who'd seen it. It wasn't someone he'd been dating; it had been at a volleyball game on post. He'd over-heard her telling her friends how awful it was. How she couldn't believe he'd ruin his body by getting something so horrible tattooed on it.

He'd been extremely cautious about who he took off his shirt in front of after that, but knowing Devyn wasn't repulsed by it—and, if the way she was licking her lips as she examined it, might actually be turned on by his tattoo—went a long way toward making the other woman's words fade into nothingness.

"You gonna stare at my shoulder all night or are we gonna do this?" he teased.

Her gaze came up to meet his own. "You in a hurry?"

"As a matter of fact, yeah," he told her, pushing his hips against her. His cock was weeping precome, and he knew she could feel it against her lower stomach. He was happy that he wouldn't have to contort his body in order to make love with her. They were almost perfectly aligned. It wouldn't be hard to take her standing up, against the wall, in the shower...He groaned as each carnal image flashed through his brain.

As if she knew what he was thinking, Devyn smiled and lifted one leg, curling it around his thigh and opening herself to him.

"That's it. Bed," Lucky declared, spinning them around and lifting her and practically throwing her back onto the mattress.

Devyn laughed and immediately scooted backward, giving him room to join her. Lucky crawled toward her on his hands and knees, not stopping until he was hovering over her. "I wanted to go down on you first," he said seriously. "But I don't think I can wait."

Her hand snaked between them and circled his cock. Lucky inhaled sharply as she stroked him. "I could give you a blow job," she offered.

The thought of her lips around him made Lucky groan. He came up on his knees and reached down and brushed her hand off his cock, then took hold of himself with a firm grip at the base, preventing himself from coming right then and there. "Holy shit, woman. You can't do that to me."

"What? Offer to suck you off?" Devyn teased.

"Yes. At least not before I get off inside you a few times. Maybe I'll have more control then, but I'm guessing I'll always have a hair trigger with you," he told her honestly.

"If that's supposed to turn me off, it doesn't," she

informed him. "I don't know why guys are so worried about lasting for hours. Frankly, after a while, all that pumping in and out hurts. Give me a nice quick fuck any day."

"You come easily?" Lucky asked, desperate for as much information as he could get from her so he could make this good for them both.

The blush returned to her cheeks, but she nodded. "I usually use a pretty strong vibrator. I can come within a minute if I don't tease myself."

"I wanna see that," Lucky declared.

"Well, not tonight, since I didn't pack my vibe," she told him.

He could deal with that. He spread her legs apart as he inched forward.

She grinned up at him. Loving the lust he saw in her eyes, Lucky reached between her legs. He might not have the patience to be able to eat her out right this second, but he could definitely make sure she came before he took her.

Using his thumb, he went right for her clit. He watched her reactions as he learned what kind of touch turned her on.

"Oh, yeah, harder," she coaxed.

Lucky knew he had a stupid grin on his face, but he couldn't help it. He could smell her arousal and it made this moment even more carnal. The bright light overhead allowed him to see how pink her inner folds were, and he used her own wetness to lube his finger as he continued to stroke her clit.

Her hips began to subtly thrust upward toward him as he brought her closer and closer to orgasm. With his other hand, he gently inserted a finger into her body, going even harder when she immediately clamped down on it and began to fuck herself on his hand.

"I'm close!" she gasped.

He didn't need the warning. He could tell by the way her

chest flushed and how her thighs began to tremble. She was so fucking beautiful like this. Spread out in front of him in the throes of desire. *He* was giving this to her. And it made him feel ten feet tall. Lucky wanted to lean down and take one of her nipples in his mouth. Wanted to kiss her. He wanted it all, but he needed to see her go over the edge this time. Wanted to watch as he gave her pleasure.

"Come for me, love," he rasped as her legs tried to spread even wider, as she tried to impale herself on his finger harder.

"Ungh!"

The noise she made as she went over was cute as hell. Without giving her any warning, Lucky took hold of his cock and slipped the head just inside her body as she shook with her orgasm.

"More," she ordered, reaching down and grabbing hold of his ass, trying to pull him inside her.

The feel of her hot, wet body trying to strangle his cock was overwhelming. He'd never felt anything so amazing before. He pushed the rest of the way inside her quickly, without much thought to how it might feel for her. He couldn't wait. He needed more. More of this skin-on-skin contact. Lucky felt as if he was going to explode already.

His balls were tight up against his body and he knew he was going to lose the fight with his control way before he was ready. He wanted to stay inside her like this forever. Wanted to feel her inner walls squeezing and caressing the extremely sensitive skin of his cock. It was like he was a virgin all over again. He had no control. None.

"Gotta move," he croaked.

"Yes, more," Devyn breathed.

He meant to go slow. To savor every second of this gift she was giving him. Not only of her body, but by trusting him enough to let him inside her without protection. But again, he couldn't. The first time he pulled his hips back, any thought of slow and steady went out the window.

The way his cock slipped through her arousal was nothing like he'd ever felt before. He could feel her heat all the way to his bones.

Lucky slammed his cock back inside of her to feel it again. Devyn's small tits jiggled on her chest and he felt her Kegel muscles clamp down on his dick as he pulled his hips back.

He had no idea how many strokes he lasted; all he knew was that he was in fucking heaven. When he felt her thighs rise up and stroke against his own, then her heels digging into his ass...he was a goner.

He took her as if it was the last time he was ever going to be inside a woman. Hard, fast, and desperate. When her hand closed around one of his biceps and tightened so brutally, he knew he'd bear the marks of her fingernails, Lucky exploded.

One second he was thrusting like mad, and the next, he'd buried his dick as far inside her as he could get before letting loose.

He emptied what had to be the largest load of come *ever* inside her. He could feel his own juices mix with hers deep within her body, and it caused a second, less intense orgasm. His balls felt wet with their combined fluids, and even that was exciting and new.

"*Fuc*k," he whispered, his arms shaking as he did his best to hold himself above her and not flatten her with his weight.

But Devyn simply wrapped herself around him and said, "Lie down. You won't hurt me."

So he did. She kept her legs around his waist, and he stayed half hard inside her body. Lucky realized that he didn't need to immediately get up and take care of the condom so it wouldn't leak. There *was* no condom, and they were soaking wet already. It was seriously carnal and so very damn sexy. And messy. He grinned into her hair.

"What the hell are you laughing about?" she asked, sounding a little put out.

Lucky raised his head but kept the rest of his body glued to hers. "I was just thinking about how much laundry we're gonna have to do."

"Seriously? Laundry? What the hell's wrong with you?"

Lucky couldn't stop smiling. "We're making a mess," he told her, pushing his hips into hers, driving home his point.

"Oh!" she said.

"Yeah, oh," he repeated. "I never realized how messy this was."

"You think it's messy now, just wait until everything you put inside me comes out."

"It comes out?" Lucky asked.

Devyn burst out laughing. "Yes! What did you think it did? Got absorbed into my body?"

He shrugged uncertainly.

"News flash, buddy. That's not how it works. I'm not a freaking sponge. What goes in, eventually comes out. I mean, I haven't experienced it firsthand, because I've always used condoms, but I've heard enough talk about how messy quickies can be for women. For guys, it's wham, bam, thank you, ma'am, but women have to deal with leakage for quite a while afterward."

"I wanna see," Lucky demanded.

"What? No! Lucky, don't," Devyn complained as he slowly pulled out then kneeled up to look between her legs.

"Lord, this is so embarrassing," Devyn said as Lucky spread her legs and watched as his come leaked out of her body.

"It's not," he insisted. "It's sexy as fuck." He reached down and ran a finger between her folds, scooping up some of their combined juices. He then used that same finger to caress her clit. Devyn jerked.

"I can see we aren't going to need lube in the near future," he said with a grin.

"I'm not sleeping on the wet spot," Devyn declared.

"Agreed. So...how do you feel about trying this again, now that I've gotten the edge off?"

"Again?" she asked incredulously.

"Yup. Up. Hands and knees, Dev."

* * *

Devyn quickly turned over. She'd never been in this situation before. Hadn't ever had a man who could get it up twice in one night. Hell, she'd never orgasmed twice in one go before. But she had a feeling Lucky was going to be her first in many ways.

The second she got into position, Lucky groaned. "Holy shit, I wish you could see this."

"I think I'll pass," Devyn mumbled into the pillow. She could feel wetness dripping down her inner thighs. He'd obviously been *very* excited to take her bare, if the copious amount of come coating her thighs was any indication.

"I'm sorry, but this is so damn *sexy*," Lucky told her. A hand gripped her hip, then she felt the tip of his cock nudging against her swollen folds once more.

He felt even bigger in this position, and Devyn didn't bother to hold back her groan as he bottomed out inside her. When he pulled back, she could hear the squelch their bodies made.

She laughed, and it was Lucky's turn to groan.

"Man, I can feel it around my cock when you laugh."

And Devyn realized at that moment that she'd never really laughed during sex before. She liked it. "Just wait until I laugh with you in my mouth," she purred. Where this dirty talk was coming from, she had no idea.

"Fuck," he swore, and Devyn laughed again.

He began to do just that, fuck her hard. The sound of their skin slapping together was loud in the room. She bucked back against him as he took her, wanting more. Wanting everything.

"Touch yourself," Lucky ordered. "I want to feel you come around my dick."

Devyn immediately did as he asked, so turned on, she was desperate to come again. Her fingertips brushed against Lucky's dick as he pushed in and out of her body, and she loved hearing him moan in ecstasy.

Her thighs began to shake with the strain of keeping herself up, and she felt Lucky wrap an arm around her stomach to help her keep her balance.

"That's it, Dev. Almost there. I can feel you rippling against me. God, you feel so good, you have no idea! Get there, sweetheart. I can't hold out much longer."

Two more hard thrusts, and Devyn exploded. She made some sort of weird grunting, moaning noise and everything went white for a second. When she came to, she felt Lucky's groin tight against her ass, and he was coming inside her once again.

He held himself there for a long moment. Devyn could feel her heart beating out of her chest, and she had no energy to do anything but stay there, held up by Lucky's strength. She groaned when he slowly pulled out.

"Seriously...that's so damn hot," he said, before easing her down and spooning her from behind. One of his hands eased down her body and covered her pussy. His fingers lazily played in the wetness there, and she couldn't drum up the energy to be embarrassed about it.

"I love you," he said.

"Love you back."

"This is gonna work," he stated, as if daring her to contradict him.

"Okay," she mumbled.

"It is. I'm not letting you go, and it's not just because I'm addicted to your pussy. It's because I'm truly happy for the first time in my life. I get it now. I get what the fuss is about, having someone who you want to spend every minute of every day with."

His words felt good. Damn good. "I feel the same."

They shared a tender smile.

Then, a bit uneasy with the intensity of her feelings, she said, "I'm still not sleeping on the wet spot, no matter how much you butter me up."

She felt more than heard him chuckle against her back, then he was moving. Shifting them until he was on his back and she was using his shoulder as a pillow. Devyn hiked one leg over his thigh and put her arm around his belly.

"Better?" he asked.

"Yeah. I should get up and pee though; that will probably help with the mess in the morning."

"Later," he said. "I want to enjoy this."

So did she. "Lucky?"

"Yeah, love?"

"Thank you."

"For what?"

"For being you."

He chuckled. "You're welcome?"

Devyn knew she should adequately explain what she was feeling, but decided to let it go. Words could never make him fully understand how thankful she was that he was so amazing. She'd just have to do her best to *show* him how happy he made her.

She relaxed, more content than she'd been in months.

Lucky was everything she'd ever wanted in a man...and she wasn't going to let him go. She'd worried about her brother in the past, but this was different. If something happened to Lucky, she'd never recover. But he loved his job, was damn good at it, and she'd be the best damn partner he'd ever had. If Gillian, Kinley, Aspen, and Riley could deal with the uncertainty of dating a special forces man, she could too.

"Stop thinking so hard," Lucky said softly. "Sleep."

And she did.

* * *

Spencer paced the motel room he'd managed to scrape up enough money to pay for. He'd been evicted from his apartment last month, and ever since then, he'd been sleeping in his car or mooching from the few friends he had left. He'd stay a few nights on one of their couches, then move on to someone else's. He'd even stayed with his parents for a while, but he couldn't stand the disappointment and worry he saw on their faces every time they looked at him.

He hated that. Spencer wanted them to be proud of him. Like they were the rest of his siblings. And they would be. All he had to do was win big and they'd be over-the-moon excited for him. He would share some of his winnings so they could redo the basement like they kept saying they wanted to do.

But first he needed to pay off the loan he'd taken from Rocky.

He didn't know the man's real name, just what he went by on the streets. He'd been warned from several of his gambling acquaintances that the man wasn't one to fuck around with, but Spencer had been desperate for cash.

And now, when he needed help the most, he wasn't getting it. Devyn was the only one he could ask, and she was turning her back on him. Yeah, he'd made some mistakes in the past, stolen from her, but this was different. His *life* was on the line!

Hearing something outside, Spencer got up and cautiously peered around the curtain in his room. A man and a woman were walking through the dark parking lot, laughing, probably a prostitute and her next client. The motel wasn't exactly the Four Seasons. They rented rooms by the hour. It embarrassed Spencer that he'd had to resort to staying there.

All he needed was five thousand dollars. Was that too much for Devyn to give him to save his life? *He* didn't think it was. He had a line on a sure bet and a fast forty thousand bucks. He could give that to Rocky, then quickly make back the rest that he owed him.

But he *needed* that five grand.

Maybe if he asked Devyn in person, he could persuade her to help.

If she saw how desperate he really was, she'd give him the money he needed. He knew it. He'd have to make up an excuse as to why he was in town, but he could do that no problem. Fred would be glad to see him, would probably even let him stay at his new farmhouse.

Not to mention, getting out of town right now would be a good thing, since Rocky was looking for him and his money.

His decision made, Spencer felt as if a weight had been lifted off his shoulders.

He'd fix this. Get the money from Devyn, make enough to get Rocky off his back, then get on with his life. He wasn't an addict, like Devyn kept accusing. He could quit gambling whenever he wanted. But why quit when he *knew* he was on the verge of hitting it big? It would suck to quit now when the huge payout he'd been chasing for years was just around the corner.

He just needed to stick with it for a little while longer,

then he'd show everyone that he wasn't the loser they all thought he was.

Lying down on the bed, Spencer sighed in relief. Now that he had a plan, he could sleep. He needed to find some money for gas and food for his drive to Texas, then he'd be off. And... who knew? Maybe the gambling down south would be more profitable. He'd have to find some casinos or illegal gambling houses to try out.

Maybe he wouldn't need his little sister's help after all.

CHAPTER TWELVE

"I think I should get some sort of kickback on that bet you guys all made on me and Lucky," Devyn told the others a week later when they were all hanging out at Grover's house. He'd lured them over with the promise of margaritas for the non-pregnant ladies, and virgin drinks for those who were knocked up, and for Logan and Bria. While the ladies sat and talked on the porch, the guys—with the kids tailing along— were doing their best to build a new barn. It would end up being much smaller than the one that had been torn down, but they were loving the challenge.

"I knew it!" Aspen crowed in delight. "Was it awesome?"

Devyn sighed. "So awesome," she agreed.

"So...I have a confession," Aspen said.

"What?"

"I lied. There was no bet. That would be rude as hell. But I wanted to give you some incentive to get on that already."

"You're evil," Devyn said with a laugh.

"But if you want to thank me after I give birth to this bowling ball I'm carrying around, I'm happy to have you buy me a drink or two."

"Deal," Devyn told her.

"I can't believe you fell for that whole 'we made a bet thing,'" Gillian said with a laugh.

"Shut up," Devyn grumbled as she threw a balled-up napkin at the other woman.

Everyone laughed.

"But seriously, we're happy for you," Kinley said with a smile. "You guys have been eyeballin' each other for months, it's nice to see you actually do something about it."

"Are you dating or just seeing each other?" Riley asked.

"What's the difference?" Devyn asked, scrunching her nose in confusion.

"Seeing each other means you're not serious. You like each other, but you're open to seeing other people. Dating means you're exclusive. That you're going to see where this goes, and you'd even be all right with marrying him someday," Riley said matter-of-factly.

"I don't think that's a real thing," Gillian said. "Did you just make that up?"

"Maybe. But I still wanna know."

Devyn chuckled. God, she loved these women. "According to your definitions, we're definitely dating. I like him. A lot. It almost scares me."

All four of the other women beamed.

"What? Why do you all suddenly look like you've escaped from the looney bin?" Devyn asked.

"We're just happy for you," Aspen said.

"Me being scared makes you happy?" Devyn deadpanned.

"No. But it means that you really care about Lucky. And we've all been there," Gillian reassured her. "You want my advice?"

"Do I have a choice?" Devyn asked with a huge grin on her face to let the other woman know she was teasing.

"No, bitch, so sit back and listen," Gillian quipped. Then she leaned forward and got serious. "Don't question it. Our men are intense and they move fast. But they're doing it because they can't stand the thought of not having you by their side. Almost like, if they don't 'claim' us, they risk someone else coming along and catching our eye. But what they don't realize is that there *is* no one better. That there's no way we're gonna want anyone else. But it's cute to let them do whatever they can to try to prove how much they're into us."

Devyn nodded. "But what if the opposite happens? Some other woman comes along that he can't resist? I mean, Gillian and Kinley, your guys met you on missions. What if Lucky rescues some beautiful woman from the clutches of a terrorist and falls head over heels for her? That would tear me apart. And I can't compete with that either. I'm not brave. When shit gets too overwhelming, I run. That's why I came to Texas in the first place. To be near my brother. I knew Fred would have my back if I truly needed him to, but when I got here, I was too scared to even tell him the real reason I'd left Missouri."

"Breathe, Dev," Riley said.

Devyn realized she'd just word vomited way more than she'd intended. But with every person she revealed even a little bit of the truth to, more weight seemed to lift from her shoulders.

"First, you're the only woman Lucky's had his eye on since the second you two were introduced," Riley told her. "They've been on several missions since you guys met, and he's just as besotted with you now as he was then. Also, I didn't meet Porter on a mission. He was my neighbor. I don't think you can get any more boring than that. And sometimes, running *is* the smart thing to do."

"Yeah, that's basically what I did," Kinley said.

"Going into witness protection isn't the same thing," Devyn said with a snort.

"You know we're here if you want to talk about it," Gillian said gently.

"I know. And I appreciate it," Devyn said. And she did. These woman were some of the most open and friendly people she'd ever met. Some days she had a hard time believing they'd accepted her as readily as they had.

"Oh!" Aspen gasped out of the blue.

Everyone turned to look at her.

"What?"

Aspen's eyes were wide and she'd gone pale. "I...something's wrong." She was holding her belly and bending over slightly.

"The baby?" Gillian asked urgently.

Aspen nodded. "It's too early, I've still got another month or so to go...but either my water just broke or I'm bleeding."

Devyn flinched when Gillian put her fingers up to her mouth and let out a loud, ear-splitting whistle. As if it'd been planned, all of the guys' heads came up, then they were hurrying toward the house. Oz had lifted his niece in his arms, and Logan ran beside them, doing his best to keep up.

"What's wrong?" Trigger asked as he approached the porch.

"Aspen's baby is coming," Kinley said.

"Aspen?" Brain asked, taking the steps two at a time to get to her. "It's too early!"

"I know," she said. It was obvious she was freaked out, but was doing her best to stay calm. "It's early, but not too early for him to survive."

Devyn didn't know if it would be worse to have the medical knowledge that Aspen had from her training as a combat medic and paramedic, or to be in the dark as to what was happening.

"I'll get my Expedition," Oz said, as he turned and ran for the line of vehicles parked in the driveway.

"I don't have any of my stuff here," Aspen said as Brain helped her stand.

"We can bring your things," Gillian reassured her.

"My bag's already packed," Aspen told her, right before she doubled over with a painful contraction. A dark red stain on her pants was growing steadily, even in the seconds she'd been standing.

"Pick her up," Doc ordered.

Brain swooped his wife up into his arms. "You're gonna be fine," he told her. "Both of you."

Aspen nodded and lay her head against her husband's shoulder.

"I'm coming with you," Doc said.

"Me too," Gillian said.

"We'll all meet you at the hospital," Kinley said.

"It's okay, I'm sure it'll be a wh—" Aspen's words were cut off by a long moan.

"We're going," Brain said as he carefully headed for the stairs. Trigger took his elbow in his hand to help guide him, and to make sure he didn't fall with Aspen in his arms.

Gillian and Riley hovered behind them, and everyone watched as they got settled in Oz's car. He backed up so fast, he almost hit a vehicle that was just turning into the driveway.

Oz swerved around the gray Buick LeSabre and took off with a squeal of his tires.

"Oh, shit," Fred said.

Devyn couldn't take her eyes off the new vehicle. She knew exactly who was inside.

"He called before everyone got here and said he was in Texas," Fred told Devyn apologetically. "He doesn't have a place to stay, so I said he could bunk down with me."

Devyn wanted to tell her brother that it was a bad idea. That he should lock up every damn thing that was worth anything so Spencer didn't steal and pawn it. Now wasn't the time to have that conversation. But she was obviously going to have to sit down and have a chat with her brother. Soon.

"We need to go," Lefty said urgently.

"You guys go," Fred told him. "I'll greet my brother and tell him what's going on, then I'll come on over to the hospital."

"Dev?" Lucky asked quietly as he put an arm around her waist.

She shook her head, trying to pull herself out of the trance she'd entered the second she saw Spencer's car. "I'm okay," she told Lucky softly.

"Looks like you guys are planning on heading out," Spencer said with a shit-eating grin as he walked up to the porch. "Did I interrupt something?"

"Drive safe, Grover," Lucky said as he steered Devyn out of Spencer's path and toward his truck.

Devyn heard Fred greet their brother and say, "It's great to see you, bro, although your timing's shit."

"Breathe, Dev," Lucky told her as he started up the engine.

She let out the breath she'd been holding. "I can't believe he's here."

"We'll deal with him after," Lucky said, pulling onto the road.

Devyn nodded. She had a bad feeling he was here about the fifty thousand dollars he needed to pay back the loan shark. But she honestly didn't have that kind of money to give him. She wasn't sure what he was going to do, but harassing her about it wouldn't work. At this point, she honestly wasn't sure she'd give him the money if she had it. And that made her feel like the worst sister on the planet.

"Look at me," Lucky ordered.

Devyn turned her head. He had dirt smeared on the side of his face and his hair was sticking up in every direction. He'd thrown his T-shirt back on as he'd headed for the house, but it too was extremely dirty.

It struck her then, how every single guy on the team had come running at the slightest sense of danger. She was proud of Lucky, just as she was all the others.

"We'll deal with Spencer together. You don't need to think about him right now."

"I know, I just...if he steals from Fred, I'll feel horrible that I didn't warn him!"

Lucky shook his head and split his attention between the road and her. "Personally, I think this is good. Grover's not an idiot. If Spencer pulls anything, he's gonna know. And it'll take the burden off your shoulders about whether or not to tell him about Spencer's gambling habit. But again, nothing your brother does is on *you*, understand?"

"That's easy to say, but not as easy to truly believe," Devyn said.

"I know. But you aren't alone in this anymore," Lucky told her. "If you want me there when you talk to Grover, I'll be there."

"Thanks. Lucky?"

"Yeah, love?"

"I'm in this for the long haul."

He blinked in surprise. "That's good, because I am too."

"I just wanted you to know. I know it took me a while to give you a shot, but I don't think I've ever met a better man than you."

He smiled, and it almost took her breath away.

"I'm not letting you go," he said reverently. "I mean, if you decide you hate me and you really don't want to be with me anymore, I'm not going to be one of those guys who says if I can't have you, no one can...but it'll kill me, and I don't know if I'd be able to date anyone again for a very long time. But as long as you want to be with me, I'm not gonna fuck it up. I'm yours, Dev. For always."

She smiled at him. "When did we get to be so damn sappy?" she asked.

"Must be Angel and Whiskers. I swear I wasn't so mushy before I adopted them," Lucky told her with a grin.

"Yeah, sure, blame the dog and cat who can't defend themselves," she teased. It was hard to believe, but Devyn felt ten times better than she did even a few minutes ago. Somehow Lucky had a way of making her see what was most important. She was still worried about Spencer showing up out of the blue, especially after he'd told her he needed fifty thousand dollars or someone would hurt him, but with Lucky by her side, they'd figure something out.

She was done keeping Spencer's secret. The only way he was going to get better was if his problem was brought out into the light. And the first step was telling Fred. Then their parents. Then their sisters. If everyone knew and put pressure on Spence, he'd get help.

He had to. He couldn't continue on this way.

Lucky pulled into the emergency room parking lot and just like that, Devyn's thoughts turned to Aspen. She hoped her baby was all right. She and Brain had been looking forward to their son's birth for months. She couldn't imagine how scared they were right now.

Lucky parked and she jogged around the back of his truck to meet him. He grabbed hold of her hand and they headed for the waiting room. There was no discussion about whether they would wait to hear something, or how long. They'd be there for their friend and his teammate, no matter what.

* * *

Lucky paced the waiting room. They'd all been led to a separate, smaller room while they waited to hear how Aspen and her baby were doing. He wasn't alone in his anxiety. Gillian, Kinley, Riley, and Devyn sat huddled together in the corner, talking in low voices and doing their best to keep their spirits up. He, Oz, and Doc were all pacing, while Trigger, Lefty, and Grover sat off to the side, hyper alert, their gazes glued to the door.

They'd been there for two hours, and while Lucky was worried about his friends, he was also pissed off that Spencer was in Texas. He hadn't come to the hospital with Grover, but just knowing he was there, and that Devyn was probably stressed out about his sudden appearance, had Lucky on edge. He wanted to take Grover aside and tell him everything. To warn him. To tell him to keep Spencer way the fuck away from Devyn. But he'd made a promise.

He hated keeping secrets from Grover. It went against everything he knew. Everything their team stood for. But for Devyn, he'd break every fucking rule he'd ever known. She was that important to him.

The last week had been one of the best in his life. He seemed to have everything now. His work, which he loved. And when he came home at night, he got to relax and laugh with a woman who just made him feel so damn good. Not to mention the nights, when he got to make love to her and sleep with her in his arms.

And today had started out just as great. Lucky loved hanging out with the guys on the team in a relaxed atmosphere. They worked well together, both on the battlefield and in their downtime. And looking over at the front porch of Grover's house and seeing the women there, laughing and enjoying spending time together, had made something within him...settle. There wasn't a word for how he'd felt seeing Devyn smiling and laughing with some of the best women he knew.

But the second they'd heard Gillian's whistle, they'd all instinctively known something was wrong. They'd all taken off for the house the second they'd heard it. Seeing the blood coating Aspen's pants wasn't something they'd been prepared for. But the former combat medic had kept it together, and the team had done what they always did...worked in tandem to get shit done.

Then Spencer rode up in the midst of the chaos...

He hadn't been expected or welcome.

As if reading his mind, Grover got up and approached Lucky. "When Spence called this morning and said he was on his way down, and would be here in just a few hours, he caught me off guard," he said urgently. "If he'd answered any of my previous calls, I would've told him it wasn't a good idea to visit right now, and done what I could to make him tell me what the hell's going on between him and Devyn. The second I agreed he could stay with me when he got here, he thanked me and hung up."

"You should've given her a head's up," Lucky told his friend.

Grover sighed. "I realize that. I just forgot when everyone arrived. I can't get the look on her face when she saw him out of my mind."

Lucky nodded. He'd seen it too. Shock. Betrayal. And fear. It was the fear that he hated most. He'd heard all the stories about her wild days in her early twenties. All the daredevil things she'd done. His Dev wasn't scared of anything. But the second she'd seen her brother get out of his car, she'd been terrified.

"I'm thinking you need to have a heart-to-heart talk with your brother," Lucky said as diplomatically as possible.

"Yeah, that's on my agenda," Grover said.

"How long is he staying?" Lucky asked.

"I don't know. He didn't say."

"I promised Devyn I wouldn't butt in, that I would keep things between us, but if your brother says or does *anything* to hurt her...things are gonna get ugly," Lucky warned.

Instead of getting upset, Grover replied calmly, "I said it before and I'll say it again, I love that you and my sister are together. I know you better than just about anyone, and I know that you'll do whatever's necessary to protect her...even from her own family, myself included."

Then he clapped Lucky's shoulder and headed over to sit down once again.

Lucky was surprised, but then again...he wasn't. Grover was a good man. And while he loved his family, he wouldn't let that stand in the way of doing what was right. Which was another reason he needed to get Devyn to talk to him. Grover would understand and would make sure Spencer stopped harassing their sister. Dev needed him in her corner, and Lucky needed to convince her to share her burdens.

"It's a boy!" Brain exclaimed as he burst into the room. He was wearing a set of scrubs and he had an ear-to-ear grin on his face.

Everyone surged to their feet and began talking at once.

"Guys, hush!" Gillian exclaimed. "Let him talk!"

"Thanks, Gillian," Brain said, still smiling. "They took Aspen right up to do a C-section, and Chance Kane Temple was born without too many issues. He's underweight, since he decided he was ready to come into the world a month early, but his lungs sound good. He'll be in NICU for a while, but the doctors say they don't expect any long-term issues."

Everyone sighed in relief and extended their congratulations.

"What about Aspen?" Devyn asked. "How's she doing?"

"She's okay," Brain said. "The doctor said the bleeding was

a result of the placenta covering the cervix. I'm not exactly sure of all the details, but the bottom line is that she's gonna be fine."

"When can we see her?" Riley asked.

"I don't know yet. But I know she'll be excited to show Chance off," Brain said.

"*She'll* be excited to show him off?" Doc asked.

Everyone laughed. The mood in the room had lightened immediately after they'd heard both mother and child were all right. Lucky made his way over to where Devyn was standing and put his arm around her waist. She immediately leaned into him, and he loved that she didn't mind touching him and making it clear how much they were into each other in front of their friends.

"You okay?" he asked quietly as he bent down to kiss her lightly.

She nodded, but said, "No," softly.

"You want to stay or head back to my place?" he asked.

She looked up at him. "I'm sure you want to be here for Brain."

"Not what I asked, love."

She stared at him for a long moment before saying, "I love that you'll leave if that's what I want, but I don't want to steal this moment from you. Brain's the first in your group to have a baby. I know you want to share that with him."

"There will be more babies. And I'm sure we'll all be sick of hearing how smart Chance is within a week," Lucky said with a smile to let her know he was teasing. "I'm more concerned about you right now. I know Spencer showing up threw you for a loop, and I want to make sure you're okay."

Devyn sighed. "There's nothing I can do about Spence right now. And I think if we went back to your place, I'd probably stress about him, wondering what he's up to now. I have no doubt this isn't a casual, 'maybe I'll go to Texas to see my brother and sister' trip. He needs money—lots of it—and he's probably got something planned to get it. But for now, I want to celebrate the birth of my friends' baby. Is that okay?"

"Of course it is," Lucky told her. "But anytime you want to go, just say the word."

"I will. Lucky?"

"Yeah?"

"Thank you."

"You don't have to thank me for looking after you, Dev. It's my pleasure," Lucky told her gruffly. He kissed her forehead and gave her a little push toward the other women. "Go do your thing. There will be time later for worrying."

"Love you," she said softly after taking a step away and looking back.

"Love you back," he returned. And he also loved the small smile that crossed her face before she turned to rejoin the other women.

CHAPTER THIRTEEN

"Do you want kids?" Devyn blurted that night.

She and Lucky were lying in bed, both too tired to do anything more than hold each other as they tried to wind down from the day. It had been busy. From Lucky working his ass off to help build the barn they didn't get to finish, to the stress of Spencer's arrival, then worrying about Aspen and the baby. And they'd stayed late at the hospital to take turns going up to see Aspen and chatting with Brain.

It was late when they got back to his townhouse and neither had the energy to do more than grab something quick and easy for dinner, love on the animals a bit, and fall into bed.

But, of course, the second she went horizontal, Devyn's brain kicked in and wouldn't let her sleep.

"Do you?" Lucky countered.

Devyn chuckled. "I did kind of spring that on you, didn't I?" she asked. "Truth?"

"Always," he said.

She tightened her arms around him and felt him hug her in return. She loved this. The sex with Lucky was amazing.

Out of this world. The best she'd ever had. But that didn't mean she wanted to have it every night. She needed this connection with him just as much, maybe more. "I don't know. I mean, I had a big family growing up, and it was sometimes a pain in the ass. Money was always tight and there were times I felt as if I'd missed out on having a really close relationship with my parents because they were always working one of their several jobs. I know they love me and would do anything for me, but Mom and I aren't really friends...if that makes sense."

"It does," Lucky reassured her.

"But then again, I loved always having someone to play with, once I went into remission, of course. I wouldn't trade my relationship with Fred for anything in the world. But there are times when I think I'm barely keeping *myself* together; how in the world can I have a child? I don't know anything about being a mom, and I'm worried about screwing my kid up. Maybe I've watched too many of those true crime shows, where the girl starts dating a boy her parents don't like, so she conspires with him to kill them."

She felt Lucky chuckle under her cheek. Devyn knew she was being ridiculous, but the thought of being a mother was scary. "But then again, when I looked at little Chance today, I thought of how amazing it would be to bring a life into this world. Yeah, it'd be tough, but the rewards would outweigh the disadvantages, I think."

"So, are you asking me so I'll make the decision for us?" Lucky asked.

"Maybe?" Devyn said, wrinkling her nose as she tilted her head back and looked at the man she suspected she already loved more than she thought she could love someone.

He smiled and leaned down to kiss her nose. "I haven't thought about it much, honestly. I'm a guy, we don't sit around wondering if our biological clock is ticking or not.

And I've been so focused on missions and my job, that it just hasn't really been something I've had much of an opinion about, pro or con."

Silence stretched between them.

"And now?" Devyn asked after a while.

"Honestly? I'm like you. I'm on the fence about kids. At this point and time, I'm loving having it just be the two of us. You fill my life so much, I feel selfish and want you all to myself for the foreseeable future."

Devyn nodded and tightened her arm across his belly.

"I liked being an only kid. I'm surprised I didn't turn out to be completely spoiled. But I was lonely at times. If we do have kids, I'm thinking maybe two. Fairly close together. That way they'll have each other to play with, but it won't be overwhelming for them or us."

Devyn chuckled. "You wanna plan their gender too?" she teased.

"A boy first. Then a girl," Lucky said immediately. "Not that girls can't be protective, but I want to teach my son what it means to look out for those younger and not as strong as him."

"What if our daughter ends up being taller and more outgoing?" she countered. "I don't want to teach them to conform to sexist roles right off the bat."

Lucky laughed, and Devyn's head bobbed up and down on his shoulder as he did so.

"What?" she asked, lifting her head once more to look at him.

"We're being ridiculous," he said with a smile. "We're talking about children we may or may not even want or have."

Devyn returned his smile. "We *are* being crazy, aren't we?"

Lucky brought a hand up and brushed it over her hair. "I love you, Devyn. While we aren't exactly young, we aren't old either. We've got time to figure out the rest of our lives. I normally wouldn't push my luck by saying that, because you know, karma. But it's true. I love having you to myself. I love being able to fuck you on the sofa downstairs if I want to without worrying if someone might walk in on us. I love coming home to your energy and smile and not having to play referee with squabbling kids. I love watching you with Angel and Whiskers, and how much they've come out of their shells simply because you've been around them. After we're married for a few years, we can revisit this conversation, okay?"

Devyn's eyebrows rose. "We're getting married?" she asked.

"Yup," Lucky said without tensing up in the least. "Not tomorrow. We've only been dating a short while. But I already know I totally want to spend the rest of my life with you. Wake up with you every morning and go to bed at night, talking about our days."

"Um, wow. Okay."

"Shit. I'm freaking you out, aren't I?" Lucky asked.

"A little. But in a good way. I didn't expect to get a marriage proposal after only a couple weeks of dating."

"Well, in my defense, I've wanted you for a year. And I didn't exactly propose. I just let you know that this relationship isn't casual. Not for me. I'm looking for long term. Very long term. Unless you're freaked because it isn't the same for you."

Now his muscles tensed under her.

"I love you, Lucky. I don't go around casually telling men that I love them if I don't want things to work out long term," she told him quickly, wanting to reassure him.

"Whew," he said, running a hand over his brow as if he were wiping off sweat.

She smiled and felt relieved when his muscles relaxed once more.

"I'm happy for Aspen and Brain. And Riley and Oz too."

"Me too," Lucky agreed. After a moment, he said, "Do you want to talk about your brother?"

Devyn knew he wasn't talking about Fred. She shook her head. "No. I'm comfortable and relaxed right now. Thinking about Spencer and his motives will stress me out. Can we table that conversation?"

"Of course. But one thing before we do."

Devyn sighed and nodded against him.

"You need to talk to Grover. I know you don't want to damage the relationship he has with Spencer, but he already knows something's up. And if the guy's here to try to get money, Grover deserves to know, since Spencer's staying in his house."

"I know," Devyn said. And she did. Fred was going to be upset that she hadn't talked to him before now, even if she was doing it to avoid making waves in the family.

Lucky kissed the top of her head. "What's your schedule like this week?" he asked.

Glad he'd changed the subject, Devyn said, "I'm working ten to three tomorrow, then the morning shift the next day, then I have three days off."

"Damn. We've got that night-training exercise coming up. We'll be at work all day and night during your days off."

"Will you get to come home at all?" she asked. "And can they do that? Make you work twenty-four hour days?"

He chuckled. "The Army can do whatever they want. We've had quite a bit of time off recently, actually. And we'll be a man down with Brain taking paternity leave. We'll need to prepare for the training the day before we go out, then run through the exercises with an infantry company. Then we need to debrief the day after and set up new training based on what happened the night before. *Then* we'll do the training again, this time with another Delta team and an Infantry battalion."

"I can't ever remember the difference between squads, brigades, platoons, battalions, and companies," Devyn complained.

"Some are bigger than others," Lucky said, unconcerned.

"You aren't going to quiz me later on them, are you?" she quipped.

"Hell no. I don't care if you don't know every little thing about the Army. It's kind of refreshing that you have no idea about how everything is structured," Lucky said. "Anyway, so yeah, the Army can keep us working as long as they want. We do the same when we're on a mission, so this isn't much different."

"It sucks that you'll be here, but not," Devyn pouted.

"I know. But my point is, I'm not sure when you're going to find the time to have that talk with your brother."

"Shit. I'll try to see if I can catch him in the next couple days."

"I really want to be there when you talk to him," Lucky said.

"Why?"

"Why?" he echoed. "Are you seriously asking?"

Devyn frowned in confusion and nodded. "Yeah."

"Because I want to have your back. If Grover loses his shit, I want to be there to rein him in. I can't stand the thought of you being upset, and I know this is gonna upset you, so I want to be there to support you. Shit, Dev, I can't believe you asked me that."

"I'm sorry," she said, sitting up and staring down at him. "I just...I've been dealing with Spencer and his addiction by myself for so long, and even though you said you'd come with me to talk to him, it still kind of felt like it was something I should take care of by myself."

"I want to be involved in every damn thing in your life.

Big decisions, small ones, it doesn't matter. Wait...do you *not* want me there? Because it's family stuff?"

"No, it's not that," Devyn told him, hating that he'd think that for even a second. "I want you there. But I just don't want to do anything this soon in our relationship that would make you have second thoughts, or have you see me as weak."

"You aren't weak," Lucky said. "Damn, woman, I have no idea why you'd ever think that about yourself. Come here," he said, pulling her back into his arms. "Okay, we'll do what we can to find time to have the chat with Grover before we head out into the field. If Spencer tries to talk to you before that, put him off. We both know he's gonna ask you for money, and I think once Grover knows what's going on, he'll be a big factor in putting a stop to Spencer taking advantage of you."

"I hope so. I love my brother, but it's killing me that he's destroying his life by gambling. I know it's an addiction, and he can't help it, but the fact that *he* can't see that, and isn't doing anything to fix it, is painful."

"We'll get him help, love. Promise."

Devyn opened her mouth to say more, but a huge yawn interrupted her words. "Sorry," she mumbled.

"You're tired," Lucky said unnecessarily. "Sleep. We'll figure things out in the morning."

"Okay. Love you, Lucky."

"Love you back."

"Lucky?"

He chuckled. "I thought you were going to sleep."

"I am, but one more thing...does it bother you that I call you Lucky and not your given name, Troy?"

"Nope, not in the least."

"I've just heard Fred talking about his teammates so much, you were already Lucky in my mind before I met you. It would be weird for me to call you anything else."

"It would be weird for me too. I don't feel like a Troy.

Only my parents call me that, and it still somehow makes me think I'm in trouble," he said.

"Okay. Good. I just wanted to make sure."

"Anything else you just have to talk about right this second?" he asked.

"Nope. I think I'm good."

"You're more than good," he said. "Now go to sleep."

Devyn inhaled deeply and exhaled, enjoying the feel of Lucky next to her. She had on a tank top and a pair of panties, and all he wore were his boxer briefs. She loved how warm he was, how his skin felt against her own. Her cheek rested on his skull tattoo and the dichotomy between that and how gentle his fingertips were as they played with her hair made her smile.

Lucky was a badass Delta Force soldier, but he was also gentle and loving. She adored every side of the man, and had a feeling she'd love almost everything else she learned about him as time went by. She knew he wasn't perfect, and that each of them would discover things about the other that annoyed them, but she suspected those things ultimately wouldn't matter.

What mattered was how he made her feel...and she felt valued and cherished. There might be times when his job would take him away from her, when it had to come first in their relationship, but Devyn knew Lucky would make up for it in so many other ways.

She was all right with being a military spouse. She was almost thirty, and had been independent most of her life. She could mow the grass and change light bulbs. She'd even learned how to replace a toilet when the one in her last place went kaput and the landlord said it would be a week before he could get the maintenance man in to replace it. She hadn't been willing to wait that long and had done it herself.

No, Lucky's commitment to the Army didn't bother her.

Especially not when she knew she could go to Gillian, Kinley, Aspen, or Riley. They'd stick together, especially with children in the mix. Riley would need help with Logan and Bria, and her baby when it was born, and Aspen would need the same with little Chance. Their world was growing, and Devyn couldn't be happier about it.

"Love you," she mumbled, half asleep.

She felt Lucky's lips against her temple, then his hand crept under her tank top to the small of her back, warm and comforting, holding her against him. "Love you back," he told her.

CHAPTER FOURTEEN

As it turned out, Devyn didn't have the chance to talk to her brother before his Delta Force team had to report to post for their nighttime training exercise. By the time she had to say goodbye to Lucky for a few days, she was cranky and irritated that the conversation had to be put off, anxious to get it over with.

She'd stayed late at work the day after Aspen's baby was born, and when she called Fred afterward, he and Spencer had been drinking, and she didn't want to have the talk when they weren't completely sober.

Then one of the other vet techs got sick, and she'd volunteered to work a full day's shift to cover for him. Later that evening, when she'd called again, Grover said Spencer was out, and he didn't know when he'd be back. She could've gone over and talked to Grover then, but Devyn had already decided she wanted Spencer there. Wanted him to own up to his issues.

Now, Grover, Lucky, and the rest of the team would be out of contact for the next forty-eight hours, at least. It sucked that she had to put off the discussion, but it couldn't be helped.

"You're sure you're okay staying here in my townhouse?" Lucky asked the morning he was heading off to the post to report to duty.

"I'm sure. It's easier on Angel and Whiskers for me to stay here. Less traumatic than leaving them alone all day. Are *you* sure it's okay for me to be here when you aren't?" she asked.

Lucky grinned. "As far as I'm concerned, you can stay here as long as you like."

She gave him the side eye. "Was that your manly way of asking me to move in with you?" she asked.

"No. *This* is. Devyn, you are welcome to move all your shit in anytime you want. I know most of it is still in boxes in your apartment anyway. I love you, and I want you here all the time. But if you're not comfortable with that yet, that's okay too. Me, Whiskers, and Angel will be here when you're ready."

Devyn shook her head. "You're crazy. You know that, right?"

"Crazy about you? Yup."

"Lord, that was so corny," she protested.

Lucky reached out and yanked her into him. Her breath whooshed out with an *oof* as she collided with his chest, then he picked her up and twirled her around in a circle.

Devyn laughed. "Stop, I'm gonna puke!"

He stopped immediately and stepped back in concern. "Seriously?"

"Nope," Devyn told him with a grin. "But it made you stop."

"True. But seriously, I love having you here. I've got good locks and I know you'll be safe here. I don't want to rush you into anything, but you've already got a key. As far as I'm concerned, if I get back in a few days and all your stuff is here, I'd be over-the-moon excited."

"I...I like being here, but I'm not sure I'm ready for officially moving in yet," Devyn told him uncertainly.

"It's okay. I'm pushing, and I know it, but I can't help it. I'm just ready to get on with spending the rest of my life with you."

That was sweet. Devyn went up on her tiptoes and kissed him. Hard.

They'd made almost desperate love that morning. They weren't even going to be apart for that long, but Devyn realized she'd miss him. She'd gotten used to waking up with him in the mornings and being held by him all night.

She knew she was kidding herself by saying she wasn't ready to officially move in yet, but that seemed like such a huge step. Staying over every night, and having her shampoo and conditioner in his shower, and a few things in his closet and their underwear mixed together in the wash didn't *seem* fast...but ending her lease and moving all her knickknacks and stuff over here did. It made no sense, but she appreciated that he wasn't pushing her on it.

Lucky's hand slipped under the hem of her shirt and pressed against her back. He did that all the time, and she loved that he couldn't seem to keep his hands off her. His tongue dueled with hers and they were both breathing hard by the time he pulled back.

"Shit, now I have to go to work with a hard-on," he complained.

"I could help you with that," Devyn volunteered, her hands moving down his chest toward the fastening of his uniform pants.

He grabbed them, halting her downward progress. "If I let you do that, I'm gonna want to reciprocate, then fuck you.

Then we'll both be late," he said regretfully. "I'll be back in two days."

"I know," Devyn said with a pout.

He chuckled. "It's nice to know you're gonna miss me."

"I'm gonna miss you," she agreed without pause.

"Stay safe. Don't spoil the kids too much," he warned, talking about Angel and Whiskers.

"Who, me?" Devyn asked, all wide-eyed innocence.

"Yeah, you. I think they like you more than me," he said without heat.

"Of course they do," Devyn told him.

He laughed. "You going over to see Chance in the hospital after work?"

"Not today. Gillian's going over today, and Kinley's going tomorrow. I'm going to do some housekeeping at Brain and Aspen's place tomorrow, and Riley's gonna come to keep me company."

"I love how you're all helping out," Lucky told her.

"That's what you do for friends," Devyn said with a shrug.

"Yup. Okay, I really need to get going. Have a good few days off."

"I will. My plan today is to take the girls for a long walk if they'll let me, then I'm gonna nap, read, and maybe take a bath."

"Sounds good. Love you," Lucky said.

"Love you back," she returned, secretly thrilled that they already had a tradition when it came to sharing their declarations of love with each other.

Lucky kissed her once more, then gave her a chin lift and headed for the door. He stopped to tell Angel and Whiskers to be good for "Mommy," then he was gone.

The townhouse seemed too quiet and empty without him there, but Devyn pushed that thought to the back of her mind. She didn't mind being by herself. At least, she hadn't before she'd met Lucky. Still, she was glad to have a few days to relax. She liked her job at the vet clinic, but it was hard work. And it had been a while since she'd done full shifts.

She had to decide what to do about that too. Did she want to keep working part time, or go full time? At first she'd been all for going full time. Now she was having second thoughts. The money would be nice, but she'd get to spend less time with Lucky and the others.

It was ridiculous, really. Most people worked full-time jobs, but she'd been doing okay with only part-time hours. And if she moved in with Lucky, a lot of the bills she had now would disappear.

She shook her head. No, she wouldn't move in with Lucky just to save money. That was the wrong reason to move in with someone.

Pushing *that* topic to the back of her mind also, Devyn turned to the box of doughnuts Lucky had picked up the night before. He'd gotten them for her, to tide her over while he was gone. He was in the same state, even the same town, but somehow it still felt as if he was a million miles away. Devyn knew if there was an emergency, and she really needed him, she could get Gillian or one of the others to contact his commander, and he could come out of the field and get home quickly, but she didn't expect to have any kind of emergency. She could handle whatever life threw at her for the next few days.

* * *

That afternoon, after a walk, and while she was in the midst of an extremely hot chapter in the book she was reading, Lucky's doorbell rang.

Devyn had no idea who it might be. She'd already talked to Gillian and Kinley, and texted Aspen and Riley that day. Everything had been fine with them, though they were all a bit grumpy from having to say goodbye to their men. Even though they were all relieved they didn't have to worry about their lives being on the line, as they would be in a real mission, it still sucked to have them gone.

Putting her book aside, Devyn headed for the door. Looking through the peephole, she inhaled sharply.

It was Spencer.

She hadn't expected him to show up at Lucky's house. She had no idea how in the world he'd figured out where she was. Fred would never have given him Lucky's address, so...he had to have followed them at some point.

Sighing, not really wanting to talk to Spencer, but not wanting to leave him standing on the front step either, Devyn opened the door.

"Hey, sis," Spencer said when he saw her.

"Hi," she returned.

"Can we talk?"

Devyn wanted to refuse, but she stepped back from the door, holding it open. Spencer walked in and headed toward the living area on the other side of the kitchen.

He turned, and before she could tell him under no circumstances would she give him any money, he spoke first. "I'm sorry."

Devyn blinked. "What?"

Spencer ran a hand through his short dark hair and repeated, "I'm sorry."

"For what, exactly?" Devyn asked. She was glad to hear him apologizing, but if he was trying to butter her up before he asked for more money, she wasn't going to fall for it.

He sat on the edge of the couch, and Devyn did the same next to him.

"I came to Texas with the intent of asking you for more money," he said.

Devyn tensed. She knew that, but hearing him admit it was still surprising.

"I knew you wouldn't let me stay with you, not after I hurt you the last time I saw you, so I called Fred, half expecting him to tell me to fuck off. You didn't tell him, did you?" Spencer asked.

"About your gambling problem? No," Devyn said.

"Why not? I mean, I'm grateful, but I don't understand. You guys are really close."

Devyn sighed. "The last thing I want is to be the cause of our family being in turmoil...again."

"Again?"

"Yeah, when I was sick, things weren't all that great in the family. Mila and Angela resented all the time Mom and Dad were spending with me in the hospital, you weren't exactly thrilled that you were being ignored, and Mom and Dad almost got a divorce."

"I'm not an expert," Spencer said, "and I've said some pretty shitty things to you in the past, but I'm thinking none of that was your fault. You didn't ask to get leukemia, and I would think a kid being that sick would strain the best of relationships."

"I guess. But regardless...what I wanted was for you to get help, Spencer. Then, if it ever came up, you could tell the others, 'I had a problem, but I'm better now.' *Are* you better now?" Devyn couldn't help but ask.

Spencer looked down at his lap. For the first time, she noticed how tired her brother looked. He had dark circles under his eyes and she wasn't sure his clothes had been washed recently.

"Spence? Are you okay?"

"No," he said softly. "I didn't want to do it...but it was too tempting."

When he didn't elaborate, Devyn asked, "What was?"

"Fred was at work, and I knew my time was running out. He has one of those money jars...you know, where you throw your spare change? You had one too, back in Missouri. Well, there were also bills in there. I went through it, taking the quarters and the paper money...as well as some of his DVDs. I knew I wouldn't get a lot for them, but I pawned them anyway."

He looked up then, and Devyn could see the desperation in her brother's eyes.

"I went to an underground gambling hall. I knew if I just had the chance, I could win the money back and more. And I could at least make enough to give Rocky a down payment on what I owed him."

Devyn's stomach clenched. She'd had a small hope that her brother had finally realized how destructive gambling was, but apparently he hadn't. "Is Rocky the loan shark guy from Missouri?"

Spencer nodded. "Yeah. But, I didn't win. *Again*. I don't know why I keep thinking my luck will change. I'm in big trouble, sis. I know I already told you that on the phone, but I owe Rocky a lot of money, and he's getting impatient. I don't know what to do."

"Well, I'll tell you what *not* to do," Devyn said, a little harsher than she'd intended. "Don't steal any more money from Fred. Gambling is what got you into this mess; you aren't going to get back what you owe by throwing away more cash."

"You don't understand," Spencer mumbled. "I *know* I can do it. But since casino gambling is illegal down here in Texas, I had to make do with a second-rate underground circuit. I'm sure they've got a racket going. Have their games set up to fail."

"Spencer, they're *all* set up to favor the house. Literally everywhere! You *aren't* going to win. And if you do, it's only going to be a few bucks here and there, just enough to make you think you're on a lucky streak, and to make you continue to bet."

Her brother shook his head. "You don't understand—" he started.

"No," Devyn interrupted, angry now. "*You* don't understand. I would think being in debt to this loan shark guy, your life literally in danger, would finally help you get your head out of your ass! You need *help*. Gambling is an addiction, just like drugs. You can't kick this on your own, and even if I forced you into rehab, it wouldn't work until *you're* ready to change your life."

Spencer turned his head and stared at her for a long moment. His shoulders were hunched and he looked like he'd hit rock bottom. Then he said, "I need to pay Fred back. Can you help me? *Anything* will help at this point."

Devyn wanted to cry. "What were you apologizing for when you first sat down?" she asked, needing to know. He never really said earlier when she'd asked.

"For hurting you that last time. I didn't mean to push you so hard."

"And?"

"That's it."

Devyn's throat closed up and she stood, heading into the kitchen so her brother wouldn't see her cry. She'd thought he was apologizing for asking her for so much money. While she appreciated the fact that he was sorry for pushing her, that wasn't what she wanted. She wanted her older brother back. The one who was protective and who cared about *her*, not how much he could get from her.

Not once since he'd walked in had he asked how she was doing. How she liked Texas. Or even about Lucky. He obviously knew she was dating him, since he'd come to Lucky's townhouse to see her, but it was as if he just didn't care.

He was as selfish as ever.

Ever since Spencer had come into the townhouse, Angel had given her brother a wide birth. But she walked into the kitchen now as Devyn did her best to regain her composure.

"What am I gonna do, sis?" Spencer asked as he followed, leaning against the other side of the island.

"About what?" she asked, doing her best to get control over her emotions.

"About Rocky. He wants his money."

"I don't know," Devyn told him, bending down to pet Angel's head. The dog was leaning against her legs, and Devyn needed the comfort as badly as the dog needed hers. It was impressive that she hadn't disappeared up the stairs when Spencer came in. Angel had gotten more and more protective with Devyn over the last couple weeks, and while she was still skittish and standoffish, it was adorable how the dog wanted to stay by her side, even when she was scared.

"He's not a good man," Spencer went on.

"I didn't think he was," Devyn replied, straightening and looking her brother in the eyes. "You're gonna have to talk to him. Explain that you're going to get him his money, but it might take a while. You need a job, Spence. You're going to have to earn that money the old fashioned way."

"But it's *fifty thousand*," Spencer said, his eyes going wide. "I'm not going to be able to find a job that pays that."

"What do you want me to say?" Devyn asked, having had enough of her brother's idiocy. "I don't have fifty grand I can pull out of my back pocket and give to you to bail you out. No one does. Not Fred. Not Mom and Dad. Not Mila or Angela. Not that you'd ask *them*, would you? No, because then you'd have to explain why you need it, and that would embarrass you. But you have no problem coming to *me*, because you obviously don't give a shit about me. You made your bed, Spencer. You're gonna have to lie in it."

"He'll hurt me," her brother said, not seemingly moved at all by her speech.

"I. Don't. Have. The. Money," Devyn enunciated. God, she wished Lucky was here. Not that she needed him to fight this battle for her, but it would've been nice to have him at her back. "I don't want you to get hurt, but I honestly don't have a solution for you. Borrowing more money to try to get what you need isn't the answer either. That obviously hasn't worked in the past, and it won't work now."

Spencer's shoulders slumped. "So when my dead body is found, you won't be surprised when you're called to identify me," he muttered.

"Don't do that," Devyn said fiercely. "Don't you dare give me a guilt trip. I honestly don't know what you want from me."

"Five hundred," Spencer said desperately. "I can turn that into a few thousand and can give that to Rocky. That'll buy me some time!"

God. It always came back to this. No matter how many times she told him she didn't have the extra money, he just didn't stop. "No."

"This time is different—" Spencer began, but Devyn held up her hand, stopping him.

"*No*," she repeated.

Brother and sister stared at each other for a long, tense moment.

"So that's it?" he asked.

"That's it," Devyn confirmed. "*Maybe* if you were willing to admit you have a problem, and that you wanted to get help for it, I might feel differently. I might go with you to talk to

Fred and add my support. Maybe we'd see what we could do to try to raise some of the money you owe this Rocky guy. But why should I bail you out—why should *any* of us—when you're just going to turn around and do the same thing again?

"Until you admit that you have a problem, you're always going to owe someone money. Hell, you owe *me* money, Spence. I guess you've forgotten the couple thousand dollars I gave you before I caught on and moved away from Missouri. I moved because of *you*. Because I couldn't take your begging anymore. Because you resorted to violence the last time I saw you! I get that you didn't mean to shove me so hard, but you *hurt* me. Do you even care?"

For the first time, she saw remorse in her brother's eyes. "I do. I apologized for that. That's why I came over here."

"No, you came over because you wanted money," Devyn said sadly.

Then, for the first time since he'd walked in, Spencer got mad. "This is bullshit! I thought family was supposed to help family!" he yelled.

Devyn's voice rose in response. "Yeah, they are. But I *have* helped you. I didn't even ask what you wanted the money for when you first started borrowing; I gave it to you without question. But that wasn't enough. It's *never* going to be enough. Don't you get it?"

"One of these days I'm gonna hit it big, and I'm not gonna share *anything* with you," Spencer seethed, smacking his hand on the countertop angrily.

Angel yelped and cowered against Devyn's side. And that pissed Devyn off even more. "You've said that before, Spencer. But news flash—you aren't going to hit it big. You're gonna end up homeless and begging for money on the streets to get your next hit. You might as well be throwing money into the trash can, and you can't even see it!"

"Better to throw it away than to be miserly with it,"

Spencer returned. "Besides, you're shacking up with Lucky now. You're trying to ride the military gravy train, admit it."

Devyn wanted to explode. Any tears she'd shed earlier were long since dried up. "Grow up, Spencer," she hissed. "You don't have the first clue as to what my relationship with Lucky is. You roll into town, intent on begging for more money, and you come here and insult me? You're a joke. *Pathetic*."

Spencer stood up straight and took a step sideways, as if he was going to come around the counter toward her, but just then, there was a knock on the door.

Devyn was frustrated...and a little bit scared of her brother. She was glad for the reprieve. She had no idea who was at the door, but opening it would give both her and Spencer a break from their intense conversation.

Shifting sideways, she scooted around the island and headed for the front door of the townhouse. Without bothering to look through the peephole, Devyn opened it.

She had no idea who the two men were, standing there. She'd never seen them before.

"Can I help you?" she asked.

"Is Spencer here?" one of the men asked.

Devyn frowned in confusion. How in the world had they known her brother was here? Had they followed him...? "Can I ask who you are?"

"Nope," the second man said. Then he cocked his fist back—and that was the last thing Devyn remembered before everything went dark as pain blossomed in her face and she went unconscious.

* * *

"Fuck, she's heavy," Bruce said for the millionth time as he and Darrell hiked through the forest, looking for the perfect place to stash the woman they'd kidnapped.

"Shut up," Darrell told him. "I'm sick of hearing you bitch."

"Then maybe *you* should carry her," Bruce retorted.

"I've got the chain, the shovel, and the bag with the other shit," Darrell said.

Bruce mumbled under his breath. He was done with this. He wanted to go home and have a beer. Or fifteen. The day had been very long already. He and his brother, Darrell, had been contacted by an acquaintance who knew a guy who knew a guy who needed a job done. And they were always up for making a quick buck. And in this case, they were making a cool twenty-five hundred for one day's work. Simple job. It was a no-brainer.

They'd left their East Texas house early that morning and had driven over to Killeen, waiting outside the illegal gambling house where their mark had been spotted. Then they'd simply followed him to a townhouse, where they'd made their move.

Knocking out his girlfriend, or whoever she was, hadn't been planned, but whatever. And Bruce had loved beating the shit out of their mark. He'd cried and blubbered and begged them to stop. Dumb pansy. While he was half-conscious on the floor, they'd called their contact about the unexpected woman, who in turn had called whoever had ordered the job in the first place. The brothers hadn't signed up for kidnapping, but since their payment doubled from twenty-five hundred to five grand if they took the broad, they couldn't turn it down.

They'd passed along a message to their mark, picked up the woman, and left.

They'd had to drug her after she almost woke up on their way back to the eastern side of the state, but luckily she'd never fully regained consciousness. The last thing either of them wanted was her waking up and being able to identify them, their car, or any other details about her little trip.

But this walking through the Davy Crockett National Forest was *bullshit*. They had to choose a remote section so no one would accidentally find her. Which meant tromping through brambles and undergrowth, instead of walking along a nice hiking path. Not to mention, Bruce wasn't exactly in shape and didn't enjoy working out. Not in the least.

"Come on, man, we've gone at least three miles from that dirt road where we left the car. This is far enough."

Darrell shook his head and stopped walking.

Sighing in relief, Bruce immediately shrugged and let the woman fall from his shoulder. He didn't let her fall all the way to the ground, but he wasn't gentle with her either. Why should he be? She was a means to an end. That end being five thousand bucks.

"Fine. Start looking for a tree. It needs to be big enough that her hands won't touch when they're wrapped around it."

"She's tall," Bruce commented.

"I see that, asshole," Darrell said as he smacked his brother in the head.

Bruce shoved him. "Don't."

"*Don't*," Darrell mocked, laughing. "You're so easy to rile."

"Fuck you!"

Darrell just laughed. "Come on, help me find a fucking tree and we can be done with this. You sure she's still out?"

"Yes. She's been dead weight over my shoulder for three miles. I think I'd know if she woke up. Trust me. She hasn't."

"Good. God, I love those date-rape drugs. Makes everything so much easier," Darrell mused.

Bruce eyed the woman on the ground. He had no idea what her name was. Didn't care. "She's pretty good-looking. We've got some time..." He let his words trail off.

Darrell snorted. "She ain't got any tits. I like my women to *look* like women. But anyway, we don't have no time to play," he said regretfully. "My ol' lady's expecting me back soon."

"Damn," Bruce said. He would've liked to at least get his rocks off in return for carrying the bitch for miles through the damn forest.

"Come on, let's go check over there. The trees look a little thicker," Darrell ordered.

Bruce nodded and followed his brother. The sooner they got this done, the sooner they'd be able to get home. He would head down to the local watering hole and find him a bitch he could take home and fuck.

Then a thought struck him. "Shit...you got the GPS, right?" he asked Darrell.

His brother froze and looked at him with wide eyes. "I thought *you* had it."

"*Fuck.* No, you said *you'd* grab it! I got the girl, you were supposed to get all the other shit!" Bruce yelled, panic taking over.

His brother stared at him for a long moment—before he burst out laughing. He doubled over and smacked his leg as if Bruce's panic was the funniest thing he'd ever seen in his life. "Damn, you should've seen your face! I wish I had a camera," Darrell said when he could talk.

"Fuck you!" Bruce swore. "You're such an asshole."

"Of course I've got the damn GPS," Darrell said, still chuckling. "We wouldn't be able to mark the coordinates to give to our man to pass on if I didn't. And no way I'd hike three miles back to the car for the GPS, then back here, then back to the car again. Six miles is enough for one day, don't you think?"

"Yeah," Bruce mumbled. He would've been more upset with his brother if he hadn't been so relieved. He knew Darrell would've made *him* walk back to the car to get the

GPS if it had come down to it. And because he knew him so well, he also wouldn't have given him the car keys. Darrell knew Bruce would've been tempted to leave his ass.

"Great. Keep an eye out for—hey...what about that one?" Darrell asked.

Bruce would've agreed with just about anything his brother suggested at that moment, just to get the fuck out of there, but when he saw the tree Darrell was pointing to, he knew it would be perfect.

The brothers worked quickly to wrap the chain they'd brought with them around the tree. Tired of carrying the woman, Bruce just grabbed her arms and dragged her through the undergrowth to the spot they'd prepared. It didn't take them long to prop her up with her back against the wide tree trunk, then wrap a thick chain around her, securing it with a padlock behind the tree. Then they pulled her arms behind her, attached a set of handcuffs to each wrist, and secured *those* to the chain.

Bruce smirked as he stood back and looked down at the helpless woman. With both the chain and the handcuffs, there was no way she'd be able to escape. Her head lolled to one side and she would've fallen over sideways if her arms hadn't been stretched back around the tree.

Darrell fiddled with the GPS for a moment, then nodded in satisfaction. "Got it," he said. "I'll send these coordinates to our guy when we're back on the road." Then he looked down at the unconscious woman on the ground. "She looks kinda pathetic," he noted emotionlessly.

"Should we leave the water we brought?" Bruce asked.

Darrell snorted. "No. I'm not gonna waste it. Besides, with her arms behind her like that, she wouldn't be able to drink it anyway. If her man doesn't come up with that money he owes, she's not gonna last long anyway. I give her four days. Tops. And that's if some hungry creature doesn't find her first. Come on. We've got a long walk back to the car, and after today, I need beer, food, and a good fuck. In that order."

Bruce agreed. He turned his back on the woman they'd kidnapped, transported across the state, hauled into the remote backwoods of the national forest, and chained to a tree. She wasn't his problem anymore. Never was, really. He was being paid for a job and that job was now done. He was as ready as his brother to get his dick wet. But unlike Darrell, he had a whole bar full of women he could choose from. Poor Darrell was stuck with the same chick every night.

Well, that wasn't exactly true. Bruce knew his brother paid for sex all the time, but that wasn't the same thing as free pussy.

His thoughts full of how many times he might get laid later that night, Bruce followed his brother out of the dense forest back toward their car. He felt no remorse for his actions. It was a dog-eat-dog world, and they were entitled to make a buck, just like everyone else.

* * *

Devyn came back to consciousness slowly. But she kept her eyes shut, trying to analyze the situation before she let whoever might be nearby know she was awake. That was something Fred had taught her. She'd laughed at him at the time, saying she would never be in that kind of situation, but he'd merely shaken his head and said you couldn't predict what life had in store, and it was better to be prepared for anything.

The only thing Devyn could hear was the sound of wind and a few birds chirping in the distance. Her arms hurt. And her stomach. *And* did her face. She vaguely remembered opening Lucky's door, but that was it. She wrinkled her nose

—and barely kept herself from crying out in pain. Her face *really* hurt.

When she felt something crawling on her arm, all pretense of still being unconscious was forgotten. Her eyes popped open and she looked down, releasing a little squeak when she saw a spider on her biceps. She tried to jerk her arm to flick the little bugger off, but was stopped short when something made a loud clang in the quiet air around her.

Confused, the spider forgotten, Devyn tried again to move, realizing that she couldn't. Her arms were wrenched behind her, wrapped awkwardly around a large tree.

"What the hell?" she said out loud, more to hear her own voice than anything else. Looking around, she saw that she was sitting on the ground in the middle of some sort of forest. She had no idea how she'd gotten there, or even where "there" was.

"Hello?" she called out, beginning to panic. She didn't know if it was better to stay quiet and not let whoever had brought her there know she was conscious, but she didn't like being alone. Never had. It reminded her too much of waking up in the hospital and being scared and in pain...and not having anyone there to comfort her. Her parents had stayed with her as much as they could, but with four other kids at home, they couldn't always sleep in the hospital.

"Is anyone there?" she cried out.

She heard nothing but silence.

Devyn jerked on her hands, hearing clanging again—chains. Looking down, she saw thick links wrapped around her waist, following them with her eyes as far as she could around the tree. Then, using her fingers, she felt what she thought was a pair of handcuffs on her wrists. She panicked harder then, pulling as hard as she could on her shackles, trying to free herself.

But after several minutes, all she'd managed to do was

hurt herself more. Her wrists throbbed and she was still stuck in the awkward position. The tree at her back wasn't comfortable to lean against at all, and her ass was on an exposed root. Her shoulders were screaming from her arms being wrenched backward.

When she'd tired herself out, Devyn rested her head against the tree bark and looked up. She had no idea what time it was, only that it had to be early evening, based on the setting sun. It was going to be dark soon. Was someone going to come find her before then? The thought of sleeping out in the open, tied up and helpless, was horrifying. It wasn't as if she wanted whoever had kidnapped her to come back, but even that might be better than being utterly alone.

The tears started then. Devyn wanted to be strong, but she was *terrified*. Was this how Gillian had felt when she was on that hijacked plane? How Kinley felt when she'd been attacked and left for dead? She'd never truly understood what they'd gone through...until now. And despite her tears, she knew what she was going through didn't seem as bad as what her friends had experienced. She'd been hit in the face, obviously, but not beaten to a pulp like Kinley. And there weren't people with guns in her face, threatening to shoot her and throw her out of a plane like she was nothing but trash.

But still, being left alone in the woods, tied up and helpless, was enough to make Devyn's throat close up, making it hard to breathe. Whoever had chained her to this tree had to come back at some point...didn't they?

"Help!" she yelled. Then, in a stronger voice, "Is anyone out there? Hello? Help me! I need help!"

She got no response except for a few birds taking off from the tree branches they'd been sitting on.

Devyn yelled for help until her voice was hoarse and her stomach hurt from the effort it took to scream.

When she finally realized no one was out there, no one

was coming to help her, she cried again. Huge sobs that shook her entire body.

She couldn't believe this was happening.

"Please, someone help me," she whispered, her words getting lost in the slight breeze blowing through the trees.

As darkness fell, she began to shake, realizing that for the first time in her life, she was truly and completely on her own. No nurses, no doctors, no siblings or friends. No parents.

No Lucky.

She was terrified...but something deep down inside shifted.

She wasn't ready to die. Not now. Not when she'd finally found a man she wanted to spend the rest of her life with. She wanted to see Lucky again. And Fred. Even Spencer. She was in this situation because of him...but the thought of what the men might've done to her brother after they'd knocked her out haunted her. She was upset with Spence, but she didn't want him dead. She just wanted to get him some help so he could go back to being the brother she knew and loved.

The resolve to live increased, as if someone were blowing up a balloon inside her. She had no idea how she was going to get out of this situation, but she'd do whatever it took. She wasn't quite ready to gnaw off her arm yet, but if it came to that...she might just do it. Devyn didn't want to die in this forest.

Even though the will to live had settled deep, that didn't mean Devyn wasn't scared out of her mind. Tears continued to fall down her cheeks as she looked into the sky. The light was waning quickly; soon it would be pitch dark outside. "Thankfully you're in Texas and not Maine," she said. But of course, then another thought hit her. She had no idea if she *was* still in Texas or not. She could be anywhere. She had no idea how long she'd been unconscious.

"No, I'm still in Texas. Probably the Hill Country. Maybe around Austin somewhere," she mused to herself.

Trying to use her shoulder to wipe her face, Devyn sighed in frustration when she couldn't even do that. Taking a huge breath, she tried to get control. "Lucky's looking for you," she said out loud. "And Fred. And their team. They're gonna find you. Somehow. Just have faith."

CHAPTER FIFTEEN

Lucky was exhausted. The nighttime training had been brutal, but also very good. They ran through several scenarios, and even though the platoons they'd been training with had known they were out there in the darkness, trying to infiltrate the mock city, his team had still been able to get into the building where the "hostage" was being held undetected.

Trainings like this were essential for keeping the Delta Force team's skills up to par, but it also helped the soldiers they trained with as well. Lucky had only been able to catch a few hours of sleep here and there, and was ready to crash.

But he couldn't wait to see Devyn. To see how the last two days had gone for her. How work was going. He wanted to see Angel and Whiskers. He was just happy to be *home*. He'd never really thought of his townhouse as much of a home before; as much as he liked it, the townhouse was still just a place to lay his head. But with Devyn, Angel, and Whiskers now taking up residence, it was much more than that. The empty spaces teemed with life and energy and it made all the difference in the world. Lucky had never thought he was lonely before, but he now realized *that* was the empty feeling he'd had all along, deep down inside.

He unlocked his door, frowning when he realized the dead bolt wasn't engaged. He'd asked Devyn to please make sure she always completely secured the door, because he never wanted anyone to be able to kick the door in while she was inside.

He pushed the door open and called out, "Dev? I'm home!"

Only silence greeted him.

"Devyn?" he called again. Her Mini Cooper was sitting outside in the same place she always parked it. He couldn't remember if she was working today or not, but he guessed one of the other women could've picked her up if they were going to hang out.

He threw his keys on the kitchen counter and headed to the fridge. He opened the door and took out a bottle of water. He'd been hydrating like crazy the last two days, but he always seemed to be thirstier than usual after a mission or intense training.

Turning, Lucky tilted the bottle up to his mouth and took a long swallow as he rested his ass against the counter. He lowered the bottle and happened to glance down—and froze.

There was a pile of dog shit on the floor of the kitchen. And a puddle nearby.

He'd missed it before, intent on greeting Devyn and getting a drink.

"Angel?" he called out, putting the water bottle down and stepping out of the kitchen. He didn't see the dog or cat anywhere. They weren't in their favorite fluffy bed in the corner of the room, and they weren't curled up under Devyn's favorite blanket on the couch.

But Lucky did see another pile of poop near the back door, leading out into the backyard.

"Whiskers? Angel?" he called again, a little more desperately now.

Taking the stairs two at a time, Lucky headed for the master bedroom. He walked in and could immediately smell that something was definitely wrong. The scent of urine and feces was almost overwhelming.

Walking into the bathroom, Lucky's heart nearly broke.

Angel and Whiskers were huddled behind the pipes of the toilet, shaking, and his dog was whimpering. Fuck. They hadn't done that since the first day he'd brought them home. He had no idea what had happened, but whatever it was had freaked his pets way the fuck out. He could see little footprints all over the room where the animals had walked through their own feces. The cheap rug he'd put on the floor was scrunched into a corner, and if the smell emanating from it was any indication, both animals had used it to pee on.

"Oh, my poor babies. What happened?"

There was no answer from them, and Lucky spent the next few minutes trying to get either of them to come out from their hiding spot. Angel was the first to move, inching toward him on her belly.

"That's it, come 'ere. I'm not gonna hurt you. I'd never hurt you," he said in a soft and easy tone. The terrier mix was shaking uncontrollably, and it almost broke Lucky's heart all over again.

When she finally rested her head on his knee, Lucky saw what looked like blood on her front paws.

"What happened here?" he asked softly. His pets were obviously traumatized—and suddenly, Lucky had a horrible thought. "Where's Devyn?" he asked.

Angel looked up at him and whimpered.

"Shit," Lucky said. He needed to give his girls attention and clean up the house, but first he needed to find Devyn. He gave Angel and Whiskers one last pet then stood and headed back down the stairs. He grabbed his phone and immediately dialed Devyn's number.

It rang...and Lucky's blood ran cold. Her phone rang in his ear through his earpiece, but he could also hear the ringtone coming from the living room. Walking into the other room, he saw Devyn's phone sitting on the small side table next to the couch.

"*Fuck*," he swore, ending the connection and immediately pushing the button to call Grover. As the phone rang, Lucky looked around more closely, a dark stain on the floor catching his attention.

"Hey? You missed me so much you had to call twenty minutes after you saw me last?" Grover said in lieu of greeting.

"Is Devyn at your house?"

"No, why? Is she not there?" Grover asked, any hint of teasing gone from his tone.

"No. My animals are freaked and it doesn't look like they've been let out in at least a day. Maybe more. I called her but her phone's still here."

"Don't panic. Maybe she went back to her apartment," Grover said.

"She wouldn't leave Angel and Whiskers," Lucky told his friend. "And her car is here."

"Okay, we need to call the team. Maybe something happened with one of the other women and she got wrapped up in helping them. You call Oz and I'll call Trigger."

"Grover, I'm telling you, something happened here. There's a stain on my rug and—" Lucky walked back toward the door, remembering that the bolt hadn't been turned when he'd gotten home. "Oh, shit."

"What? Lucky...what?" Grover asked impatiently.

"Blood spatter just inside my door," Lucky whispered.

"Don't panic," Grover repeated, sounding like he was

doing just that. "Get out of there so you don't contaminate the place."

"I'm not leaving Angel and Whiskers," Lucky said firmly. He was about to come unglued. Something had obviously happened inside his townhouse while he wasn't home, but he wasn't going to abandon the dog and cat that both he and Devyn loved so much. They'd been through an emotional hell.

"Okay, go get them and bring them to my place. I'm still going to call the others, but if they haven't heard from her, I'm gonna call the cops. Get over here as soon as you can."

"I will," Lucky said.

He felt as if he were in a fog. Where was Devyn? What had happened?

He couldn't understand what was going on. She had no enemies. Had someone targeted his place to rob? And she'd been in the wrong place at the wrong time? If so, where was she now?

He was under no illusions; something awful had happened to Devyn. She wouldn't have left Angel and Whiskers, she wouldn't have left without her phone, and she would've called Commander Robinson if something serious had happened.

Unless she had no choice and was forced out of the townhouse.

Willing himself to calm down, Lucky took a deep breath and spun to grab the crate he'd set up in the corner of the room for the animals to go to when they needed to feel safe. He hated to use it to transport them, but he wasn't leaving them here.

It took longer than he would've liked to coax the animals into the crate. Lucky knew he should probably feed them, as they most likely hadn't eaten since Devyn had left, whenever that had been, but he also wasn't sure they'd eat at all. Not with as tense as they were.

Grover had called back to let him know none of the other women had heard from Devyn. They'd only spoken briefly, and Lucky hadn't been surprised no one had been able to reach her. Yet, it was totally out of character for Devyn to just up and disappear. "Riley said she'd tried to call Devyn yesterday and she hadn't answered," Grover had told him. "She figured she was busy, or had been called into work on her day off. She didn't think too much about it."

The fact that Devyn had been missing for at least twenty-four hours was like a knife straight to Lucky's heart. He was well aware the longer a person was missing, the less likely the chances of recovering them became.

"Please let her be all right," Lucky whispered as he headed for his truck with the crate in his hands. Saying the words out loud wouldn't make them true, however. He hated to be a pessimist, but this wasn't looking good.

He should call the cops himself, have them come to his townhouse to start looking for clues, but he needed to be around his team. Needed their support. And he knew without a doubt they'd do everything in their power to help him find Devyn.

He couldn't live without her. He'd just found her. It wasn't fair.

Lucky drove way too fast toward Grover's house. He apologized to Angel and Whiskers as he took turns too sharply and accelerated too quickly from stoplights. Every second he took was one more second Devyn could be out there hurting, waiting for him to find her.

He raced down Grover's driveway and saw most of the team was already there. Gratitude welled up inside him. Thank God. He even noticed that Brain's vehicle was there. That the man would leave his wife and premature baby to come help him meant the world to Lucky.

When he walked up the stairs onto the porch and opened

the door, Lucky saw that it wasn't just his team who'd arrived. All the women—minus Aspen, who was still recovering from giving birth—were also there.

Gillian immediately reached for the crate. "Let me take them."

Lucky handed over his animals.

"Oh, you poor babies," Gillian cooed through the slats. Then, looking up at Lucky, she asked, "Are they hurt?"

"I don't think so. Just scared to death. Probably hungry too. Angel has some blood on her paws, but I don't think it's hers." Just saying the words made the anxiety rise up within him once more.

"I've got them. Don't worry, you guys just do your thing. Angel and Whiskers will be fine," Gillian said, her voice only wobbling a little.

"Thanks," Lucky said.

Gillian nodded and headed toward the back of the house with Kinley and Riley. He briefly wondered where Logan and Bria were, but assumed Riley and Oz had found someone to look after the kids for a while.

Grover opened his mouth to ask his teammates how they should start trying to figure out where Devyn had gone, but just then, the door behind Lucky opened.

All seven Deltas turned to see who'd arrived.

Spencer.

He looked like absolute hell.

Someone had beaten the shit out of him. Both his eyes were almost swollen shut and his lip was busted. His nose was crooked and he had blood in his hair, all down his shirt, and he was limping.

"What the fuck?" Grover asked as he headed for his brother.

But Spencer held a hand up. "They took Dev—and it's my fault," he rushed out, his voice shaking. "I'm done trying to hide what a shithead I am. I figured he'd come for me...but instead he took *her*. I'm sorry. I'm so sorry!"

Lucky didn't give a shit *how* sorry Spencer was. Everything made sense now.

He took a step toward the man, ready to physically make the asshole tell them everything, but Grover got there first.

"What are you talking about, Spence? What's your fault? Who is *he* and why was Devyn taken?"

Doc grabbed ahold of Lucky's arm and held him back.

"Let go of me," Lucky growled, trying to shake off his teammate's hold.

"You'll kill him, and we need answers," Doc said calmly.

He was probably right. Lucky wanted to take his turn with Spencer. Continue beating on him, but that wouldn't help them find Devyn.

"I'm pretty sure she's alive...at least for now," Spencer said, refusing to look at Grover.

Grover surprised all of them by swiftly cocking his fist back and slamming it into his brother's face.

Spencer went down like a sack of potatoes, crumbling to the floor and not even trying to get up or defend himself.

Grover reached down and hauled him upright. He put his hands on his brother's shoulders and looked him in the eye. "Whatever happened, we'll make it right. But you need to tell us *everything*."

Spencer nodded. "I will. It's time. I'm done. Dev was right the whole time, I need help, and if she dies because of what I've done, I'll never forgive myself."

"We'll worry about forgiveness later," Grover said. "For now, we need information."

Spencer nodded.

"I've called the cops, they'll be here any second. Let's get you an ice pack and a wet towel in the meantime."

Lucky wanted to protest. He wanted to shake Spencer

until he told them what he knew. Who took Devyn. Lucky knew the why, but not the other info.

As glad as he was that it seemed Spencer was finally ready to get help for his addiction, it was too little, too late. Devyn was in trouble. He knew it deep down in his gut.

He needed to find her. She was out there somewhere. Hurting. Possibly dying. It ate Lucky up inside and he felt completely helpless. He needed information. Now.

* * *

Thirty minutes later, Spencer was holding an ice pack to his face and sitting on Grover's couch surrounded by seven very intense Delta Force operatives and two detectives from the Killeen Police Department. Gillian, Kinley, and Riley had bathed his pets and were now standing off to the side, also listening. Trigger had called their commander, Colonel Robinson, and while he wasn't there, he'd told them whatever they needed, he'd do his best to get for them.

Lucky didn't give a shit if the entire town of Killeen was listening, he just needed Spencer to get on with it already.

"What happened today?" the detective asked.

"It wasn't today. It was two days ago," Spencer said softly.

Lucky suspected Devyn had been gone a while, but hearing it verified made his blood boil. His fists clenched at his sides.

"I went over to see her. I knew she was dating Lucky, and I'd already followed her home from work the day before, so I knew where he lived. I went over there the afternoon you guys went out into the field. I wanted to apologize for what happened back in Missouri and—"

"Wait, what happened in Missouri?" Grover asked.

Spencer sighed. "I hurt her. I didn't mean to. You know how we are; when we argue, we get handsy. I pushed her and she fell backward into her table. I guess she got a big bruise or something. But I didn't mean to shove her so hard! I was just so *irritated*. And she pushed me first," Spencer added, as if that made it all right.

"You put your hands on our sister?" Grover growled.

Lucky realized for the first time that while he was pissed at Spencer, it was Grover they probably needed to be worried about right now. He glanced over at Doc and Oz, and they nodded, moving closer to Grover so they could prevent him from doing something in front of the two police officers that might get him thrown in jail.

"I didn't mean to!" Spencer protested again.

"I thought she got that bruise from her boss," Lefty said with a frown.

"She lied," Lucky said, not waiting for Spencer to respond. "She didn't want Grover to think badly of his brother, so she made up that story."

"So why'd she leave Missouri then, if it wasn't because of her boss hitting on her?" Brain asked.

"Spencer?" Lucky asked, looking at the man with one eyebrow raised. He'd be damned if he was going to tell Devyn's secrets; it was up to Spencer to man up and admit what he'd done.

"She left because of me," Spencer confirmed. He looked down at his lap as he spoke, not meeting anyone's gaze. "I'd been on her to borrow money, and it got to the point where she didn't think I was ever going to leave her alone, so she bolted."

"Why'd you need money?" Grover asked in a low, deadly tone.

"I swear I thought I'd be able to pay her back almost immediately, but it didn't turn out that way! I...I've run into some trouble paying back my debts," Spencer said.

"Stop fucking around and say it like it is," Lucky ordered

savagely. "The longer you sit there and hem and haw about your pathetic shit, the longer Dev's in trouble—because of *you*."

Spencer took a deep breath and nodded. Then he looked up into his brother's eyes. "I'm a gambling addict. I thought I'd be able to make back what I lost. But the next thing I knew, I was deeper and deeper in debt. Devyn gave me money at first...but then she got suspicious when the amounts got higher and higher, and she started asking questions. I finally admitted why I needed it. She cut me off. I got upset, she got upset...and she left."

"Are you shitting me?" Grover asked.

"No," Spencer said in defeat. "I didn't want to ask Mom and Dad, and I knew Angela and Mila didn't have anything they could lend me."

"And you didn't ask me because you knew I would've told you to pound sand," Grover bit out.

Spencer nodded. "After Devyn left, I started borrowing from a guy I knew."

"What's his name?" one of the detectives asked.

"Rocky."

"What's his real name?"

"I don't know. He goes by Rocky. That's all I know. I swear. Anyway, I kept losing, and it got to a point where he wouldn't give me any more and wanted me to pay back what I'd already borrowed. I didn't have the cash, and he started threatening me. I figured it would be good to get out of town for a while...give me some time to earn it back."

"So you came here. To ask Devyn for more money?" Grover asked bitterly.

"I didn't want to but I was in a bad spot," Spencer said. "You don't understand! Rocky's got a reputation of always getting what he's owed. And I just needed some more time."

Grover shook his head in disgust.

Lucky had known about Spencer's gambling problem. Devyn had told him about the fifty grand, and he'd suspected the debt would lead to nothing good for her brother. But never in a million years did he think it would touch Dev. Not when the loan shark was in Missouri. Hindsight being what it was, it was a stupid assumption to make, and one that could end up hurting the person he loved most in this world. If he'd known how dangerous the situation had become, he would've told Grover. It could've changed everything.

As if the man could read his mind, Grover turned to glare at Lucky.

"I didn't know about Rocky," Lucky told him. "I knew about Spencer's problem, but it was *his* problem. We certainly didn't think a loan shark would come after Dev. She didn't want to tell you, something about ruining your family dynamics. She's been holding guilt about being sick when she was little for a long time, and I think she saw this as one more way she would somehow be breaking up the family," Lucky explained.

"That's bullshit. This is Spencer's issue, not Devyn's," Grover said with a shake of his head.

"We know that. But she didn't," Lucky said. "She tried to find the time to talk to you about Spencer before our night training, especially because he was staying with you."

"She's going to be all right," Riley said firmly. "She might not be here right this moment, but Oz and I know firsthand that sometimes things turn out all right in the end."

She didn't raise her voice, but Lucky knew she was right. When Logan and Bria had been kidnapped, they'd all thought the worst, but by some miracle, they'd been returned relatively unscathed. Lucky had to believe that would be Devyn's fate as well.

"Can we get back to what happened the other day?" the detective asked. "You borrowed money from a loan shark who wanted it back. You didn't have it, so you came to Texas. What happened then?"

"I hung out with Grover and when he left for his thing on the Army post, I..." Spencer's head lowered again. "I took some money and tried to earn enough back to appease Rocky for now."

"You took some money?" Grover asked. "Shit, this is getting worse and worse. You *stole* from me, Spence?"

"It wasn't a lot! Just some bills from your change jar. And I took some older DVDs that were in the back of your case and pawned them. I'm sure you don't even watch them anymore."

A muscle in Grover's jaw ticked as he stared down at his brother in disbelief.

"I had to get Rocky off my back! I asked around and found out where I could hopefully make some quick cash," Spencer hurried, trying to defend his actions.

"Where?" the detective asked.

"Um..."

"Do *not* hold back now," Doc bit out. He'd been quiet up until that moment. "This is your sister we're talking about. You need to tell the cops where this illegal gambling house is, the names of anyone you met there, and what games you played. This is serious shit, Spencer. Very serious shit."

"You think I don't know that?" Spencer yelled. "I do! Look at me! This is the least of what could happen to me if they don't get their money!"

"Look at *you*?" Trigger sneered. "Look at Devyn. Oh, that's right, we can't. Because we don't know where she is and you still haven't told us! Quit fucking around and tell us what happened at Lucky's place. We get it. You're a gambling addict, in it up to your eyeballs. That ship has sailed. Now fucking *talk* before Grover or Lucky lose their shit!"

Spencer's gaze met Lucky's for a split second before he

looked back down at his lap. When he began to talk again, his words were monotone. "You're right. I fucked up. I *am* a fuck-up and I got Devyn into this. I tried to make some money, but lost it. So I went over to see Devyn. I apologized for what happened in Missouri and tried to make her see how serious the situation was, that Rocky would kill me if I didn't give him the money I owed him. We fought—nothing physical," Spencer said quickly, sensing the animosity in the room.

"Someone knocked on the door and she answered it. One of the guys hit her and knocked her out before she could really do or say anything. Then they came after me. They did this," he said, gesturing to his face, "then left, taking Devyn with them."

"Did they say anything?" Lucky asked desperately. "Where they were going or why they took Dev?"

Spencer nodded. "They said that Rocky sent them, and that when he got his money, he'd tell me where I could find Devyn. I think they thought she was my girlfriend or something."

"Fucking hell!" Grover yelled, spinning around and running a hand through his hair.

"What did they look like?" one of the detectives asked.

"They were both big. At least three hundred pounds, and tall too. One guy picked Devyn up and swung her over his shoulder as if she weighed nothing. He had brown hair, the other had black."

"And you've never seen them before?" the same detective asked. "They weren't at the illegal gambling hall you went to?"

"No," Spencer said dejectedly.

Lucky could only stand stock still, vibrating with anger. His worst nightmare was coming true—and there wasn't a damn thing he could do about it. The thought of Devyn being kidnapped was enough to make him lose his mind.

He couldn't think. Couldn't decide what the hell he was supposed to do now.

Luckily, his teammates and the detectives didn't have that problem.

"Do you know the names of the men who beat you up and took your sister?" a detective asked.

"Darrell and Bruce, I think. At least, that's what they called each other. I hadn't ever seen them before," Spencer repeated almost desperately.

"What kind of car were they driving?"

"I don't know. I never saw a car. I couldn't get off the floor for a while after they beat on me," Spencer explained.

"So where have you been for the last day or so?" Lefty asked. "Why didn't you immediately call Grover to tell him what happened? Or the cops? Devyn's been gone two days and you haven't done shit to help her?"

Lucky wanted to know the answer to that too. He glared at Spencer, even though the other man didn't see it. He kept his eyes on his hands in his lap. "I was wigged out. And hurting. I had to think. Try to figure out what to do. I stayed in my car overnight." Then he looked up at his brother again. "I know I fucked up. That's why I came here. I need help, Fred. Not just to get Devyn back, but to stop this incessant voice in my head that keeps telling me I'm one bet away from making it big. I never wanted to be this guy! The fuck-up in the family...but here I am. I need to make it right. I'll do anything, *anything*, to get Devyn back."

"Then tell us exactly what the guys who beat on you said. How much do you owe and how do we get it to this Rocky guy?" Grover asked.

Lucky wasn't sure he believed Spencer. It was one thing to want to change when you were faced with the condemnation of your family, but it was another once the heat died down. The urge to gamble would always be there for him. He'd have to work damn hard to overcome it...and Lucky wasn't sure the guy had the strength.

"I thought it was fifty G's that I owed Rocky, but Darrell told me with interest, and because they had to track me down, it was now sixty," Spencer said quietly.

"*Sixty thousand bucks?*" Grover shouted, his eyebrows shooting up. "Fuck, Spencer. I don't have that kind of money!"

"Where are you supposed to make the drop?" one of the detectives asked.

"I'm supposed to call Rocky and make the arrangements," Spencer explained.

"We can track it," the detective said to his partner. "And tail him when he makes the drop."

"If you pay the money, this Rocky guy will tell you where he stashed Devyn?" Lucky asked, not giving a shit about the logistics of the drop. All he cared about was Devyn.

"Yeah, I guess," Spencer said.

"Will he honor his side of the bargain?" Lefty asked.

Spencer shrugged.

"Maybe he can call Rocky and say he has the money, and we can trace the call, get him to admit where they've taken Devyn," Oz suggested.

"Or we can beat the shit out of him and *make* him tell us," Doc muttered.

"Um, how about we leave the tracing and coercing to the police," a detective said.

The Deltas ignored him.

"We could see if anyone around your townhouse has security cameras, to find out what kind of car they were driving," Brain said.

"Then we can find these Darrell and Bruce guys and make *them* tell us what they did with Dev," Trigger suggested.

Lucky had been searching on his phone while his team

brainstormed. He appreciated them doing what they did best, trying to figure out a way to manage the op, but he had only one objective in mind. Not finding the loan shark. Not even finding the men who took Devyn, although he'd love to have five minutes alone with them. His one objective was Devyn herself. She was the only thing that mattered.

When he finished on his phone, he looked up and caught Grover's gaze. "I've got seven thousand in my savings."

He saw an immediate look of understanding in his friend's eyes. Grover immediately said, "I think I've got four. I would've had more, but I used it on the house and to buy materials for the barn."

And then the other men began to chime in.

"I've got seven-five," Trigger said.

"I think I have three. I'm sorry it's not more. We just bought all the stuff for the nursery," Brain added.

One by one, Lucky and Grover's teammates offered up their own hard-earned money to try to come up with the sixty thousand they needed to save Devyn's life.

Lucky's eyes watered at the deep devotion of his friends. They all knew they'd probably never see the money again. And yet they still offered it with no strings.

"I've got some too," Gillian added.

"Me too," Kinley and Riley said at the same time.

"I'm not sure paying this Rocky guy is the best option here," one of the detectives said.

"Right, paying a kidnapper means you're giving in. There's no guarantee he knows where your sister is or that she's even still be alive," the other officer said.

Lucky turned to the two men. He was beyond furious, but he did his best to hold his temper...for Devyn.

"This asshole isn't asking for a billion dollars. Or even a million. He wants what he's owed. And that's it. He could've told Spencer he wanted two hundred thousand, or even more.

I don't trust him, not for a second, but we literally have no other choice. The guy's in another state. There's no telling where his goons stashed my girlfriend. They could be hurting her right this second, and I'm not willing to sit around and wait while people are interrogated and the search commences, especially when we have no idea where to even start looking and Devyn's been missing two days. I'd give *any* amount of money to Rocky if there's even a one percent chance he's telling the truth. Right now, it's all we've got."

"But—" the senior detective started, and Grover interrupted him.

"Lucky's right. I don't like this any more than you do, but right now, this Rocky guy holds all the cards. And I want my sister back. If paying off my brother's debt is the only way to make that happen, so be it." Then he turned to Spencer, dismissing the detectives. "When we raise the money, you'll call Rocky and tell him you've got it and demand to know where Dev is," Grover told Spencer.

The other man immediately nodded. "Of course. I'll do anything."

"You'll also go into rehab," Grover said sternly.

The hope in Spencer's eyes dimmed, but he nodded weakly.

"I mean it, Spence."

"I know. Me too. I know I fucked up. But I truly never thought they'd do anything to anyone else. I borrowed the money, so I thought Rocky would come after *me*. I wouldn't have come here if I thought he'd do something to you or Dev," Spencer said quietly. "I can't get the image of Devyn lying unconscious on the floor out of my head."

The shit thing was, Lucky believed him. He wanted to hate the other man, but he looked absolutely devastated about what happened.

This wasn't how he'd wanted Grover to find out about his

brother, but he wasn't upset it was finally out in the open. Now he just needed to get Devyn back. Her family would have to deal with Spencer's addiction, but at least it was no longer Devyn's dirty little secret.

"I'm assuming Rocky isn't going to take a traveler's check," Trigger drawled.

"He deals in cash only," Spencer confirmed.

"Right," Grover said on a sigh. "If we're going to do this, we need to get to our banks before they close. We can meet back here as soon as possible afterward."

"Wait, we need to talk about this some more," one of the detectives protested.

"Here are the keys to my place," Lucky said, tossing his keychain to the officer closest to him. "There's blood on the floor in the living room, where I'm assuming Spencer was beaten. There's also splatter in the foyer, which I'm assuming is my woman's blood. My pets were cooped up in the house, so there's shit and piss everywhere. Try not to track it around, would you? I didn't take the time to clean it up before I came over here."

He was done playing nice. He appreciated the detectives' presence and their wanting to help, but he knew they would take too long. They needed to find Devyn before it was too late.

"I'll fill out whatever form I need to in order to give you access to my townhouse," he said. "But we can't wait. I feel it in my bones. Maybe they've already killed Devyn, maybe they haven't, but I won't take the chance."

"Right, so if we can stop standing around talking about where my sister might be and get to the banks before they close, maybe we can find her before something *does* happen to her," Grover said impatiently.

Lucky tuned out the rest of the conversation between the

detectives and glared at Spencer. The man must've felt his gaze, because he looked up.

"If one hair on her head's been harmed, you're gonna be sorry," Lucky growled.

"I'm *already* sorry," Spencer said. "For what it's worth—and I know it's not much—I love my sister. She's a pain in the ass, as all little sisters are, but I'd do anything for her. I never meant for this to happen."

"But it did," Lucky said.

"I know," Spencer said, slumping over.

Lucky was done with him. Berating Spencer wouldn't bring back Devyn. The only thing that might possibly get her back was money. Lots of it. The sooner they could collect the sixty thousand, the sooner Spencer could call this Rocky guy to get Devyn's location. Hopefully it wouldn't be too late.

CHAPTER SIXTEEN

"How much do we have?" Grover asked Kinley as she finished counting the stacks of cash sitting in front of her.

It had been hours, and the sun was setting again, and all Lucky wanted to do was go find Devyn. She had to be terrified. Hell, *he* was scared out of his mind for her.

"Sixty-two thousand, four hundred," Kinley said.

Lucky sighed in relief. It was enough. Thank fuck.

"Where's Spencer?" Lefty asked.

Lucky looked up in surprise. He'd had no idea Grover's brother wasn't there. A lot of people were coming in and out of the house, so it wasn't surprising he hadn't kept tabs on the other man. Lucky had been gone for a while himself, visiting his bank and making a stop at Devyn's apartment. He had no idea where they'd find her, or in what condition, but from experience, he knew she'd need a change of clothes.

He'd been a POW once. And after he'd been rescued, the first thing he wanted was to get clean. To take off the clothes he'd been wearing for way too long and get into fresh ones. It was a mental thing as well as physical. Personal cleanliness wasn't high on terrorists' lists of things they cared about, and he'd pissed himself more than once while being interrogated. Lucky had no idea where Devyn was or what she was going through, but the one thing he could do for her when they found her was to make sure she had some dignity. A change of clothes wasn't going to take away the memories of whatever she'd been through, but he knew from experience that it went a long way toward making things better right after being rescued.

He'd gone from worrying that they'd find her too late, to pushing those negative thoughts away and only thinking positive. This Rocky guy wanted his money, and they wanted Devyn; he truly believed the man would give them the location where his people had stashed her after he'd gotten the cash Spencer owed him.

"Fuck, who last saw him?" Doc asked.

"He wasn't here when I got back," Brain said. "And I was the last one to return, since I stopped at the hospital to check on my son and to update Aspen on what was happening."

"Is she going home soon?" Oz asked. "When I took Riley home to get off her feet and rest—the baby's really been tiring her out lately—she was asking about Aspen."

"Yeah, she should be there now. Gillian and her friend Wendy, along with Logan and Bria, picked her up and brought her home. They're staying with her."

Lucky was relieved to hear that. As much as he was worried about Devyn, he was glad to know the others were taking care of their own.

"I didn't see Spencer when I got back," Lefty said.

"Me either," Trigger added.

"Fuck. Okay, I saw him sitting at the kitchen table earlier," Grover said, "but I didn't see him when I got back from the bank either."

"His car's not in the driveway," Lucky barked, dread filling him as he peered out one of the front windows.

"Damn it!" Grover swore, kicking a chair as hard as he could. It launched across the floor, breaking as it crashed against the wall opposite where he was standing. "I'm going out to find him," Grover said between clenched teeth. "He's gonna regret this. I swear to God, I don't care that he's my brother. He's the only one who has Rocky's number. Fuck, we should've gotten it from him. I'm such an idiot!"

"Calm down, Grover," Brain said.

"I can't!" Grover said roughly. "It's *his* fault my sister is out there somewhere, probably scared out of her skull and hurting. I can't believe he bolted!"

"I'm here."

Everyone turned to stare at the front door. Spencer had just walked in and was standing there facing them all. "I'm sorry, I didn't think I'd be gone so long."

He still looked terrible. He'd changed clothes and was no longer wearing the blood-soaked T-shirt he had on earlier, but his face was still swollen and bruised all to hell. He limped as he shuffled toward Kinley, who was still sitting at the table holding the money they'd all withdrawn from their bank accounts. Lefty shifted so he was standing slightly in front of his wife, as if to protect her if Spencer made a move to grab the cash.

But instead of looking at the cash with greedy eyes, Spencer reached forward and put a stack of bills down next to the others. "I know it's not enough. It's not nearly enough... but it's all I could get. I sold my car. They'd only give me five hundred for it, but I had to do *something*."

Lucky couldn't help but be shocked. Spencer Groves would never be his favorite person. He wouldn't be invited to Thanksgiving anytime soon, not after his direct actions had gotten Devyn kidnapped, but he still appreciated the gesture.

"How'd you get back to the house?" Grover asked.

Spencer backed away from the table and shrugged. "I hitchhiked."

No one told Grover's brother that they didn't need his money. That they'd already gathered the sixty thousand dollars Rocky wanted. It was obvious Spencer had wanted to help, even if it was too little, too late.

"We've got the money," Grover told his brother. "It's time to call Rocky."

"Should we call the detectives and let them know?" Doc asked.

"No," Lucky and Grover said at the same time.

Lucky nodded at his teammate. They were on the same page. They might get in trouble for keeping the cops out of the loop, but if something illegal had to be done in order get Devyn back, they were both willing to risk it. Not to mention, the money drop was going to be tricky. If the cops were there and watching, it was possible whoever Rocky sent to get the money would get spooked. And the longer it took for the money to change hands, the longer it would be until they could retrieve Devyn from wherever she'd been stashed.

Spencer slowly lowered himself into a chair at the other end of the table from Kinley. He put his cellphone on the table in front of him and clicked on a few buttons. Within seconds, the sound of ringing filled the room from the speaker.

Lucky saw Spencer wipe his hands on his jeans several times. It was obvious the man was nervous. As he should be. There was a lot riding on this call. Devyn's life.

"Rocky," a deep voice said from the other end of the phone.

"It's Spencer."

"Ah, Spence. It's good to hear from you...especially since it seems you cut out of town. You weren't trying to avoid me, were you?" Rocky asked.

"No, of course not," Spencer said nervously.

Lucky couldn't help himself; he leaned over and broke into the conversation. "We've got your money. We want Devyn back."

"And who do I have the pleasure of talking to?" Rocky asked.

"Name's Lucky, and Devyn's my girlfriend," he spat out.

"I'm terribly sorry things got to the point they did," Rocky said congenially. "I always hate when my clients don't take me seriously and refuse to pay what they owe."

"Where's Devyn?" Lucky asked between clenched teeth.

"Here's the thing—I don't know you, and I don't trust you. No offense. Spencer's been a pain in my ass for a while now. I loaned him money in good faith. He knew the consequences of not paying me back, and here we are. I don't like resorting to violence, but I also can't let my clients get away with ripping me off. If word gets out that I've gone soft, *no one* would bother to pay me back and that'd be bad for business. You understand that this was strictly a business transaction, right?"

"What I understand is that your goons beat my girlfriend unconscious then kidnapped her. We've got your money, and I want to know where she is. Now."

"Tsk, tsk, tsk, that's not how this is gonna work, and you know it," Rocky said, his voice a bit harder now. "I get my money first, then I'll send word as to where you can pick up the woman. Spencer, you still there?"

"Yeah, I'm here."

"Good. You're gonna make the drop. You and *just* you. If there's anyone else with you, the deal's off. If I get word that there are cops watching, the deal's off. If you do *anything* to make my guys nervous when they go get that money, the deal's off. It's been a couple days. How long do you think your sister can last without food or water? Time's a tickin'."

Without food or water...

Lucky wanted to reach through the phone and fucking kill this Rocky asshole.

"I understand," Spencer said quietly.

"Tomorrow morning, at ten o'clock sharp, you're to be in Austin. The North Lamar area. There's an apartment complex called Longspur Apartments. There'll be what looks like a homeless man, panhandling for money. He'll be wearing a Dallas Cowboys jersey and a black baseball cap. You'll walk up to him, put the cash into his collection bucket, then walk away. When you get back to Killeen, you call me, and by then I'll know if all my money was paid back and I'll give you the GPS coordinates for where you can find the chick."

"Tonight. We'll make the drop tonight," Lucky said, not wanting to wait another fucking second to get to Devyn.

"You aren't calling the shots, are you?" Rocky retorted. "I'm going out on a limb here. I don't trust you as far as I can throw you. You could be a cop for all I know. If you want to see the woman again, I've told you what you need to do."

"How will we know for sure he's your man?" Grover asked. "Dallas Cowboy jerseys aren't exactly rare around here."

"I'm not surprised there's a roomful of you there," Rocky said with a slight laugh. "And you're right. When you walk up to the man, he'll say, 'Interesting morning this morning, isn't it?' That's how you'll know."

"One of us will have to drive him to Austin," Lucky told Rocky. "He sold his car."

Rocky laughed outright. "I'm actually surprised it took him so long to sell that piece of shit. I figured he'd have gotten rid of it a while ago to get cash to gamble with. Fine, one of you can drive him. *One.* If anyone tries to grab my guy to get info from him, you'll never find your missing girl.

Besides, he doesn't have the information. The only people who do are me and the two men who stashed her for me—and you'll *never* find them."

The shit thing was, Lucky believed him. "Fine. We agree. But you need to swear that after this, you forget all about Spencer and anyone he knows and loves."

Rocky laughed again, like all this was a game to him. "I'm good at forgetting stuff," he said. "But I'm guessing little Spencer will be knocking on my door sooner or later, wanting to do business again. An addict's an addict, and I depend on people just like him for a living. He'll be back. Mark my words."

"I'm done," Spencer said firmly.

Rocky just laughed yet again. "I'll see you soon, Spence. And hopefully I'll be talking to the lot of you again tomorrow morning." The other man clicked off the connection without another word.

Kinley made a small choking sound, and Lucky saw that she was crying. They probably should've sent her home, but when she'd returned to the house with Lefty, no one had thought to make her leave.

As Lefty comforted his woman, Lucky's thoughts returned to Devyn.

She was going to have to spend another night in whatever hell she was going through. He *hated* it. Wanted to go to Austin right this second and get this shit done. But they had no choice but to wait until tomorrow.

"I'm driving," Grover said.

"No fucking way. I am," Lucky told him.

"Wrong. No way in hell are *either* of you driving down to Austin tomorrow," Doc said. "I'll go." He held up a hand when everyone began to protest. "Brain, you have to be with Aspen. Chance will be coming home soon, and she just got home. She'll need rest. Oz, you need to be with Riley. The last thing you want is her baby coming prematurely because of all this stress. And there's your niece and nephew to consider. As for you two," he said, eyeing Grover and Lucky, "I'm seriously worried about either of you being alone with Spencer right now."

Lucky reluctantly nodded. Doc had some very good points. Especially that last one. There was no telling what he'd say or do to Spencer if he had to spend forced time in a car alone with him. He might be Devyn's brother, and she might love him, but it would be a long time before Lucky forgave him for putting Devyn into the position he had.

Grover's hands were fisted, but he nodded.

"I'll keep you guys informed the entire time," Doc said. "I'll keep my phone on speaker so you'll know what's going on."

Lucky happened to glance at Spencer—and saw that his stare was glued to the stacks of cash on the other end of the table. "Don't even think about it," he said in a low, lethal tone.

Spencer's gaze whipped up to meet his.

"I mean it," Lucky warned.

Spencer nodded, swallowing hard. "I just...I never thought I had a problem. I blew off Devyn's worries. I wasn't addicted to gambling. I just wanted to make a few bucks. But sitting here, seeing all that money...my hands are shaking and I literally want to grab it up and go find a casino."

The man sounded lost. Beaten.

"Sometimes you have to hit rock bottom before you can claw yourself upward," Lefty told him.

Grover walked over to the money and began gathering it up. He looked at Doc. "Don't let him anywhere near it until it's time for him to get out of the car. The last thing we want is him absconding with it."

"I wouldn't do that," Spencer said, but it was easy to hear even *he* wasn't that sure of what he was saying.

"I'll take it home with me tonight," Doc said.

"It looks like it's about sixty miles to the North Lamar neighborhood," Trigger said, looking up from his phone. "I'm thinking if you leave around eight, that will give you time in case there's traffic, and you can find a place to stake out the apartment complex. Since Rocky didn't say exactly where this guy would be, you might have to search for him."

"I'll be here at quarter to eight tomorrow," Doc said with a nod.

"I'll update commander tonight. Let him know what's going on. He's not going to be happy we didn't call him right away, but I have no doubt he'll do what he can to help us once we get Devyn's location."

Lucky nodded. Colonel Robinson would definitely help them. He remembered how frantic the man had been to get to his *own* woman, Macie, when she'd been in trouble.

"And tomorrow, after Doc and Spencer leave, I'll get in touch with the detectives," Lefty said.

Lucky felt like he should volunteer to do something. But the only place he wanted to be was here at Grover's house. Waiting for Spencer to return so they could call Rocky and finally go get Devyn.

Everyone began to say their goodbyes, but Lucky couldn't do anything more than stand woodenly against the wall. Finally, it was just him, Spencer, and Grover left in the house.

Spencer, not being completely dense, mumbled, "I really am sorry about everything," before slinking down a hall to the room he'd been sleeping in.

Grover sighed and went to the kitchen. He reached into the fridge for a bottle of water. "Want one?" he asked Lucky.

"No. There're a lot of things I want right now, but a drink isn't one of them."

"I get why she didn't want to tell me about Spencer," Grover said softly as he propped his ass against the counter. "I don't like it, but I get it. She's always been the peacekeeper. Not liking when anyone was fighting. That doesn't mean she couldn't hold her own when she was in the midst of a fight, but she always preferred for all of us to get along."

"I truly didn't think this loan shit would blow back on Dev," Lucky told Grover. "I never, *ever* would've kept that from you if I'd thought for one second she'd be in trouble."

"I know. We're good, man."

Lucky let out the breath he hadn't realized he'd been holding.

"She's tough," Grover said. "She doesn't think she is, but my sister went through hell with those cancer treatments when she was little. Even when she was throwing up and had no hair, she was reassuring everyone else that she was fine. That when she grew up, she was gonna find a cure for cancer so no other little kids would have to go through what she did."

Lucky chuckled. "That sounds like her. Except the whole being a doctor thing."

"She's much happier working with animals," Grover said.

The talk of animals suddenly made Lucky wonder where *his* were.

"They're in the guest room on the other end of the house," Grover said, reading his friend's mind. "After Gillian and the other women cleaned them up, they put their crate in there and made a comfortable nest for them. They were taking Angel outside to do her business, and Kinley set up a litter box for Whiskers when she and Lefty got back from the bank. I also saw them taking a bowl of tuna back there earlier, and some leftover baked chicken I had in the fridge."

Lucky appreciated their thoughtfulness, feeling guilty that

he hadn't thought about Angel or Whiskers in several hours. "I can stay?" he asked.

"I'd be pissed if you didn't," Grover responded. "But...I'm gonna ask you not to kill my brother in the middle of the night."

Lucky wasn't sure if his friend was kidding or not. "I won't. I'm pissed as hell at him, and I can't believe he put us all in this situation, but I won't kill him."

"Appreciate it. I'm gonna make sure he gets his ass into rehab," Grover said. "And he's gonna pay every cent of that money back to everyone, even if it takes the rest of his life."

"I don't give a shit about the money," Lucky said. "I just want Devyn back."

"Me too, brother. Me too."

They were both silent for a moment before Grover said, "We're gonna find her."

Lucky nodded in agreement. Because the alternative was unthinkable.

He gave his friend a chin lift good night then headed down the hall toward the guest room. He slipped inside and took some solace in the fact that Angel lifted her head, then actually got up to come to him.

Kneeling down, Lucky scratched the dog under the chin. "It's been a shitty day, hasn't it, girl?"

Her tail wagged tentatively.

"You guys wanna sleep on the bed with me tonight?" He and Devyn didn't allow the animals on their bed at home, but he needed their comfort...just as he thought they might need his. He had no idea where they'd been while Spencer was getting beaten up, or what they'd done in the days they'd been locked inside the house, but it had obviously traumatized them.

He lifted Angel onto the mattress then reached for Whiskers. He grabbed two of the towels they'd been nested in and climbed into bed next to them. He settled onto his side, and Angel actually crawled closer, snuggling against Lucky's belly. Whiskers joined her companion, and the three of them lay there quietly, trying to relax after everything that had happened.

Lucky knew he wouldn't sleep. He was beyond tired, but all he could think of was Devyn. Was she sleeping? Was she hungry? Scared? Cold? Was she being hurt? Tortured? Sexually assaulted...?

He had no idea. Rocky didn't seem all that concerned, but that meant nothing. The man was ice cold and had no compassion whatsoever.

"I love you, Dev," Lucky whispered.

His heart hurt when he didn't get the usual "love you back" in response.

* * *

Devyn's mouth was dry and it was a struggle to swallow. A light rain had fallen earlier that day and she'd sat against the tree with her mouth open, trying to swallow as much water as she could. Every muscle in her body hurt and she felt as weak as a kitten.

But she refused to give up.

It was dark again. Night three. Every now and then, she'd scream her head off, hoping against hope someone would be hiking in whatever forest she was in and hear her and come to her rescue. But no one ever came.

She'd talked to herself for hours, just so she wouldn't feel quite so alone. She'd counted from one to five thousand, and back down to one. Anything to pass the time and to keep her mind occupied. She refused to give up. She couldn't.

The first night she'd fallen asleep and had a nightmare that she'd given up and died. But even though she was dead, she still saw Lucky appear out of nowhere and find her. Even in her dream, she'd felt his horror and devastation. She didn't want Lucky to have that kind of memory when it came to her.

She'd woken up determined to do whatever was necessary to survive. Grover and Lucky would find her. They had to.

Moaning when she moved and her shoulders screamed in agony, Devyn sighed. She hadn't thought this was going to be easy when she'd first woken up, but she'd underestimated how *not* easy the experience actually was.

She was in pain, and hungry, and thirsty.

And embarrassed and revolted beyond belief...

When she realized she had to go to the bathroom, she'd done her best to hold it, but it was no use. There was no way she could hold back her body's natural functions forever. She'd cried after she'd done it. Knowing she had to sit in her own filth. She couldn't get her pants down, couldn't do anything but sit trussed up against the tree as if she were a piece of trash.

There were moments when she hated her brother. She swore she'd never forgive him for getting her into this situation. Then she'd cry and promise out loud she was sorry, that she didn't mean it. Her emotions were all over the place, and Devyn knew if she wasn't found soon, she probably wouldn't last...

"Just hang on, Dev," she whispered. "The big rescues never happen in the middle of the night. They're probably doing what they do best...planning and getting ready to come get you. Just hang on one more night. You got this."

She wasn't sure she did, but she was doing her best to pretend.

Then, closing her eyes, and trying to convince herself she wasn't sitting in the middle of some forest somewhere, Devyn thought about Lucky. How much she loved lying against him

215

in bed. They'd listen to Angel and Whiskers circle and scrunch their blankets before settling down. Both animals snored, and several nights she'd fallen asleep with the feel of Lucky's bare chest against her cheek and the amusing sound of snoring from the animals in the room.

Just before she fell into an uneasy slumber, she heard Lucky say in a deep, husky, sleepy voice in her head, *I love you.*

"Love you back," she said softly.

CHAPTER SEVENTEEN

"We found him," Doc said the next morning at ten-fifteen.

The entire team was gathered around Grover's table listening as Doc gave a play-by-play of the money drop.

The pair had arrived at the Longspur complex around nine-thirty. They'd scoped the place out and then parked, waiting. Doc told them he knew why Rocky had chosen this place for the drop. There were homeless men and women everywhere. There was a sort of tent city in a field nearby, and it wouldn't seem out of place for a homeless man to be panhandling along the road.

Lucky began to sweat at ten after the hour, when Doc had said they hadn't seen anyone who was wearing a Cowboys jersey and black hat.

But then suddenly, he was there. Spencer got out, clutching the money, and Lucky prayed he didn't try to do something stupid, like run off with the cash.

"Spencer is talking to the guy...and he just put the envelope in the guy's bucket. They nodded at each other...now he's coming back to the car."

"What's the other guy doing?" Grover asked.

They'd talked about it that morning, worried that the guy they gave the money to would double-cross Rocky. Take the money for himself. But they literally had no control over that and had to pray Rocky's reputation was scary enough that no one dared go against him.

"He's still standing there."

"Seriously?" Grover growled.

God, the guy was either an idiot, standing on the corner in this neighborhood with sixty thousand dollars, or he was a genius. Lucky had to admit that he was probably doing a damn good job of not making himself stand out.

"Yup. He's hitting up other people who are walking by," Doc said.

They all heard the car door shut through the speaker of the cellphone.

"It's done," Spencer said.

"We're headed back now. We'll be there in about an hour," Doc said. "Out." Then he clicked off the connection.

Lucky wasn't sure he could wait an hour. He wanted to go get Devyn now. He prayed she was all right, and that Rocky's henchmen hadn't abused her in any way in the few days they'd had her. He'd slept like shit the night before, waking up frequently, wondering where she was and what she was thinking. He prayed she knew they were doing all they could to find her.

"She's gonna be all right," Trigger said quietly from next to him.

"She's tough," Lefty added.

"And stubborn," Brain said.

"She loves you and will do everything in her power to hang on until we get there," Oz threw in.

Lucky waited for Grover to add something positive about his sister as well, but when he looked over at him, his friend had his head bowed and was leaning on the table with both hands, as if it was the only thing holding him up.

"Grover?" Lucky said in concern. He felt sick inside, and he knew his friend was feeling the same way.

"I haven't told the rest of my family what's going on," Grover said after a beat. He looked up. "Maybe I should? I'd be pissed as hell if something happened to Mila, or Angela, or anyone else, and I wasn't told."

"I'm thinking it would be better to wait until you had something to tell them," Trigger said. "If you tell your parents that Devyn has been kidnapped, and you have no idea where she is or how she is, that's just gonna stress them out. I'd wait until you have something concrete to tell them."

Grover nodded. Then said, "Spencer's going into rehab if I have to drag him there kicking and screaming."

"I don't think you'll have to do that," Brain said. "He seems pretty devastated by all this."

"Did you see the way he looked at the money?" Grover asked no one in particular.

"Addiction's a bitch," Lefty murmured.

Lucky agreed with everything his teammates were saying, but he couldn't participate in the conversation. All he could think about was Devyn. Where she might be and what might be happening to her.

"Hang in there, man," Oz said quietly, putting his hand on Lucky's shoulder. "Thinking about the what-ifs is the worst part."

His friend would know too. When his nephew and niece had been taken, he had to have been thinking the same way Lucky was now. "We've been taught to think through every outcome," Lucky said softly. "The good, bad, and ugly. And as much as I want to stay positive, I can't stop running every scenario through my head."

"I know," Oz agreed. "I was the same way when Logan and Bria were missing."

"And then I feel guilty for hating how slow things seem to be moving, because while at least I know we're doing something, *Devyn* doesn't know that."

"Wrong," Lefty said. "She knows you and Grover and the rest of us are doing everything possible to get to her."

Lucky took a deep breath and nodded. He glanced down at his watch. Fuck. Only three minutes had passed since he'd last looked at it. He needed time to speed up. For Spencer and Doc to get back here so they could call Rocky and get the coordinates to wherever Devyn was stashed.

He hated sitting around waiting. He needed to be moving. To be *doing* something. They couldn't even make a plan, because they had no idea where they might be going to find her. Around the block? To Missouri? Mexico? She could literally be anywhere.

"Fifty-four minutes until they're back," Grover said under his breath.

It was actually comforting to know he wasn't alone in his impatience. The other guys on the team were worried about Devyn too, but it was different for him and Grover.

Not able to stand still, Lucky began to pace.

* * *

Another day and she was still chained to this damn tree. Devyn was sure she'd gone through all the stages of grief. Denial that she'd actually been kidnapped—although that phase hadn't lasted long, since she was sitting in the middle of nowhere with her arms behind her back. She'd cried, she'd bargained with God, she'd gotten depressed thinking she was going to die, and now she was just plain mad.

How *dare* someone think it was all right to punch her in the face.

How dare they think it was okay to kidnap her and chain her to this tree.

How dare this tree be so big, she couldn't get her arms all the way around it.

How dare no one want to hike this section of the forest and find her.

How dare her wrists not be small enough to slip out of the cuffs.

She took out her anger on anything and everything.

She wanted to get out of there. Didn't want to be stuck in the forest another day, and *definitely* not another night.

Nights were the hardest. When the bugs came out and crawled over her legs and up her arms. When she couldn't see a damn thing. When she worried about a bear deciding she would make a great snack. Devyn had no idea if there were any bears out here, since she had no idea where she was in the first place, but still, the thought wouldn't leave her mind. She'd been sleeping like shit. She'd done her best to shift positions to make sure she didn't lose blood flow in her arms, but they hurt from being wrenched backward for so long.

And the birds...the damn birds! They never stopped singing and chirping. Didn't they know how upset she was? They needed to shut the hell up, but they wouldn't. They flew around her, chirping as if everything was perfectly all right. But it wasn't. *It wasn't.*

And just like that, her anger drained away and she was depressed again. She had no idea if Spencer was okay. She had no doubt that what had happened to her was because of the money he owed. He'd said that his life was in danger, and she never even considered that being around him could endanger her as well. If she had, she would've said something to Lucky or Fred. They would've done everything in their power to protect her.

But now maybe Spencer was dead. Maybe the people who took her had killed him. Would he still owe money if he wasn't breathing anymore? She had no idea how loan sharks worked. Maybe the debt was passed down to the family when the borrower died. She honestly didn't have the kind of money Spencer owed, but she'd find it somehow.

Throughout her captivity, Devyn rarely allowed her thoughts to turn to Lucky. She knew he would be trying to find her, but the thought of how devastated he probably was tore at her insides. He'd be blaming himself, which she hated.

Devyn hadn't even had time to defend herself after she'd opened his door. She'd been too irritated with Spencer—and yes...scared—for caution, which was just dumb. She knew better. After everything that had happened to the other women, and after everything Fred had taught her, she'd just opened the damn door and invited whoever was there to kidnap her.

What day was this? Three? Four? Time seemed to crawl out here in the forest, and Devyn was having a hard time concentrating. She needed water...more than she'd been able to swallow in the two light rains that had fallen. She was dizzy and her mouth was completely dry. Her lips were dry and cracked, and she could feel her heart beating just a little too fast. If she wasn't found by someone, anyone, soon, she'd probably fall asleep and never wake up.

That thought jolted her. "No!" Devyn said out loud, the nightmare she'd had of Lucky finding her corpse chained to this tree still fresh in her mind. She didn't want that for him. Or Fred.

"Hey!" she called out. "I'm here! Is there anyone out there? Help me! Fire! Fire! Fire!" Didn't people respond better to a fire than for a generic call for help? A fire could affect them, but getting involved in an assault was more dangerous. At least that's what Fred had taught her.

But no one answered her cries for help. The birds seemed to mock her, chirping merrily as if nothing was wrong.

Closing her eyes, Devyn rested her head against the tree trunk behind her. "I'm here," she said softly. "Right here."

But once again, no one answered.

* * *

"I appreciate your business," Rocky told Spencer over the phone. They'd called the loan shark the second he and Doc had arrived back at Grover's house. Thankfully, the man had answered right away. He'd verified the amount of money Spencer had given his contact.

"Where's Devyn?" Lucky growled.

"Got a pen?" Rocky joked. "I've got the coordinates." Then, without waiting to make sure the men were ready, he rattled them off.

Both Brain and Lefty were quickly writing the numbers down as Rocky read them off.

"If I were you, Spencer," Rocky said congenially, "I'd find another line of work...because frankly, you aren't a very good gambler." Then he hung up without another word.

Spencer stood against the wall, his lips pulled into a frown, looking much older than his thirty-one years.

At the moment, Lucky didn't care one whit about what Spencer was feeling. He was completely focused on his teammates. "Did you get it?" he asked impatiently.

"Yeah, hang on," Brain said as he pulled his laptop in front of him and typed in the coordinates Rocky had given them. He sat back and frowned at the screen. "That can't be right. What'd you get, Lefty?"

"The same thing," Lefty said, looking down at his phone.

"What?" Grover barked.

Brain turned his laptop around and they all stared at it.

"Where the fuck is that?" Lucky bit out. All he could see on the screen was a huge patch of green.

Brain fiddled with the settings and the map changed. Going from a close-up to a more expansive view. Lucky moved to stand behind him. Slowly, what he was looking at registered.

"Holy shit—she's in East Texas?"

"If the coordinates he gave us are correct, yeah," Brain said. "The Davy Crockett National Forest. The southern section, which isn't very popular with tourists because it's overgrown and there aren't many hiking trails. The campgrounds are all north of that location. It's hillier there too."

"Fuck," Grover said, running a hand through his hair.

"Colonel Robinson? This is Trigger."

Lucky turned to see his teammate talking into his phone.

"We need a chopper...I know it's short notice...we found Grover's sister...she's in East Texas...yes, I understand...great, we appreciate it...No sooner? Right...How many? Okay...we'll be ready. Thank you, sir."

"What?" Grover asked impatiently when Trigger had hung up.

"That was the commander," Trigger said unnecessarily. "He's going to get with the aviation unit and set up a training exercise. We'll have a chopper in two hours...max."

Lucky's heart both soared and sank at the same time. He was glad to have a helicopter at their disposal so they could get to Devyn sooner, but hated to wait even five minutes for it. Two hours would be torture.

"He has to get the paperwork turned in," Trigger said, as if he could read Lucky's mind. "Get approval from the base general. He knows time is of the essence and he's going to do everything in his power to get us off the ground even faster.

The chopper will only hold four of us," Trigger said. "Grover, you and Lucky are in, obviously. I think Doc should go so he can give first aid if necessary."

"And you," Lucky said immediately. He trusted all his teammates, but Trigger was their leader, he could get shit done if Devyn was in worse shape than they'd hoped.

Everyone else nodded in agreement.

"I'll stay here with Spencer," Oz said. "Look after Whiskers and Angel."

"Me too," Lefty agreed. "Brain can go home to be with Aspen, and if we need him, he'll have his laptop."

Lucky nodded, satisfied with the arrangement. It appeared as if Spencer meant it when he'd said he wanted to help, but he still didn't want the man running off the second he found out his sister was all right—*please let Devyn be all right* —and having Oz and Lefty stay at the house would assure that didn't happen.

And Brain needed to be home with his wife. Lucky hated that this drama was happening in the middle of what should be a happy time for his friends after the birth of their first child. Though he also knew Brain would never just sit at home and ignore what was happening. He'd do whatever he could to help.

"We're gonna head over to the post then," Trigger said. "We want to be ready to head out the second the paperwork is approved."

Lucky was never so thankful for their team leader as he was right that moment. Trigger knew exactly what to do and how to get it done.

Meanwhile, Lucky felt like a mess. All he could think about was that blue dot on the computer. In the middle of fucking nowhere. The satellite image showed nothing but trees and more trees. He hoped like hell the image was old, and there was a cabin...or *something*. Because the alternative was unthinkable.

Bodies were dumped in forests. In the middle of *nowhere*, so they'd never be found.

Lucky prayed they weren't headed out to find Devyn's gravesite.

His teeth ground together so hard, he knew he'd have a headache later, but he refused to voice his concerns out loud. Not that he really had to. Each and every person in the room, maybe except for Spencer, knew the odds were low of finding Devyn alive.

Damn Rocky and his henchmen...Lucky would spend the rest of his life hunting the men involved, making sure they paid for their crimes. Permanently.

Looking over at Grover, Lucky could see his friend was thinking much the same thing. Their eyes met, and Grover nodded. Yeah, they were definitely on the same page.

Thinking about what Devyn might've gone through—was *still* going through—both terrified and enraged Lucky, so he pushed it to the back of his mind. He and the others headed for the door and he picked up his pack along the way. He had supplies for Devyn in there; he had to stay positive and believe that she'd need them. Anything else literally made him feel sick.

* * *

Devyn was tired. She kept going in and out of consciousness. She wanted to stay alert, just in case, but the entire time she'd been chained to this damn tree, she hadn't heard or seen anything that might help her escape.

She started counting down from five thousand again, hoping it would keep her awake.

She got to three thousand two hundred and eighteen

when she thought she heard something. Looking up past the leaves on the tree, she couldn't see a thing—but the sound of an engine got louder. Then she heard a *whomp whomp whomp*.

The unmistakable sound of a helicopter.

It wasn't very close, but her heart still leaped in excitement.

"I'm here!" she screamed. She couldn't stand up and wave her arms. She couldn't light a signal fire. And Devyn knew there wasn't a chance in hell anyone in a helicopter or low-flying aircraft would be able to see her through the trees, but she still yelled and carried on as if they could.

Her head was on a swivel, trying to spot the chopper, but she had no luck. Within moments, the sound got softer, until she couldn't hear it anymore.

"*No!*" she wailed. "I'm here!" she cried. "Right here. Please don't leave me!"

But it was no use. The forest was silent once more, the damn birds resuming their chirping and flying around above her head, mocking her with their freedom of movement.

Devyn didn't have any extra liquid in her body to cry, so she closed her eyes and forgot about trying to stay awake. What was the use? She was going to die out here. Alone and afraid.

She had so many regrets. The biggest was, she'd never get to have a life with Lucky. She knew, deep down, that he would've made the best partner. Supportive and generous. It wasn't fair that she'd found him, only to lose him before they had a chance to really start their lives together.

* * *

"We can't land near the drop zone," the pilot said through the headphones.

Lucky's eyes were glued to the terrain. He couldn't see

past the leaves to the ground below. He was holding a GPS and knew they were about a mile from the DZ, the coordinates they'd been given for where Devyn was located. The pilot had flown in a large circle around their destination and was lining up the chopper to land as close as he could get to Devyn.

"This is gonna be tricky," the copilot chimed in.

Tricky was an understatement. There were trees and hills everywhere. The pilot was literally putting them down on top of an outcropping of rocks. All around them were tall trees, any one of which could snag the rotor blades and send the helicopter hurtling to the ground. They'd considered rappelling down and using a rescue basket to get Devyn back into the chopper after they found her, but the forest was just too damn dense. The pilot swore that while landing would be tricky, he could do it.

But Lucky wasn't thinking about that. The Nightstalker pilots were some of the best in the Army. If anyone could get them on the ground safely, it was these guys.

Lucky strapped his pack on and prepared to climb out of the chopper so he could get to Devyn. Every second that passed was one more second she could be in pain and suffering.

Looking over, he saw Doc had his medical pack on his back as well, and Trigger and Grover were just as ready to head out. The chopper rolled a bit and the blades kicked up dust and wind as it neared the ground. The second the landing skids bumped on the rocks, Lucky had the door open and was moving.

His teammates were on his six, then they were jogging through the forest. No one said a word, each focused on their mission. The underbrush was thick and it was a challenge to get through in places, but the four men never slowed. Lucky heard the pilots talking through the radio in his ear, but he tuned them out. Trigger would update them as to their progress, as soon as they reached Devyn.

It took longer than Lucky would've liked for them to traverse the mile or so to where they hoped to find her, the terrain slowing them down. But the team moved like the well-oiled machine they were. Completely silent, each one hoping against hope they'd find Devyn alive and well.

When they got within two hundred feet of the coordinates, Lucky held up his fist to halt the others behind him. His heart thumping in his chest, he listened.

All he heard was the sound of birds merrily chirping overhead. He smelled no fire, had no other indication that anyone was nearby.

Bile rose in his throat, but very slowly, Lucky pressed forward.

He had to know. Had to get to the woman he loved...even if he was too late to help her.

Looking down at the GPS, he saw he had forty feet to go. He put the device in his pocket and crept forward.

Ten feet later, he swerved around a large tree and blinked at the sight before him.

Devyn was sitting awkwardly against a tree, her head lolled to the side and her arms stretched behind her. Her eyes were closed, and he couldn't tell if she was breathing from where he stood. His own breath caught in his throat. Her face was swollen, but he didn't see any blood and she looked relatively unscathed.

But it had been days. And if she'd been out here in the middle of nowhere, chained to the damn tree she was leaning against, she could still very well be dead.

He felt more than heard the movement next to him, and Lucky automatically put out his hand to keep Grover from rushing toward her. He knew he had no right to keep Grover from his sister, but she was *his* woman. His responsibility. His to protect and to take care of. Even if that meant making sure she had the dignity she deserved in death.

He also wanted to protect Grover from being the one to find out, God forbid, she hadn't made it.

He took a step forward. Then another.

And then he broke, rushing toward her, causing enough noise to make the birds stop chirping and fly off in fright.

One second he was sure he was too late, that Devyn had passed away, and the next, her beautiful blue eyes popped open...and she was staring up at him in disbelief, and a little bit of fright, as he approached.

* * *

Devyn was lost in a semi-conscious state. Part of her was aware of exactly where she was and that she needed to stay awake, and the other part was more than happy to float in a blissful happy place where it was just her and Lucky, sleeping together in his large bed.

She wasn't sure when she realized something had changed, but it was the sudden explosion of birds taking off from the branches they'd been mocking her from for days that had her opening her eyes.

At first, she thought the men who'd kidnapped her had returned. All she saw was a large shape moving toward her at a fast clip. Then she looked into the wide eyes of the man before her—and realized it was Lucky.

Devyn had no idea how in the world he'd appeared out of nowhere, but she'd never been so happy to see anyone in her entire life.

"*Lucky*," she croaked. Then he was there.

His hands were on her face and he was staring into her eyes as if she were a ghost. *Was* she a ghost? Why wasn't he saying anything? Was this her dream coming true? She'd really died and he'd found her dead body?

"Dev..." he said after a long moment.

She wanted to reach up and touch him more than she wanted anything else in the world, but her hands were still bound behind her. She couldn't do anything but stare up at him with love, gratitude, and the most extreme relief she'd ever known.

"You found me."

"I did," he whispered.

Jerking in surprise, Devyn looked up at the other three men who suddenly appeared above her.

"Hey, sis," Fred said in a choked voice. "If you wanted more excitement in your life, I probably could've arranged for you to go skydiving again or something."

She snorted lightly. "I'll remember that for next time," she whispered.

"You feel like gettin' out of here, beautiful?" Trigger asked as he disappeared out of her line of sight behind her.

"Yes," she said emphatically.

"It might hurt when your arms are released," Doc warned.

"I've got her," Lucky said.

Devyn relaxed. He did. Lucky had her. She wasn't looking forward to the pain she knew Doc was downplaying, but she wanted to be free more than she cared about a little discomfort. She couldn't see what Trigger was doing behind her—but she knew the second he'd cut and loosened the chain that held her prisoner.

Her arms fell to the ground. She tried to lift them, and couldn't stop the gasp of pain that left her lips.

Lucky dug his thumbs into her shoulders, and she tried to arch away from him, but there was nowhere to go.

"I know it hurts. Hang on for just a bit longer, love,"

231

Lucky murmured, as he attempted to get the blood flowing through her arms by massaging the joints.

Closing her eyes, Devyn did her best to breathe through the pain. And then she realized Lucky was right. It hurt to have him manipulating her shoulders, but before long, she felt tingles in her hands and knew that was actually a good sign.

"She's gonna need an IV," Doc said.

Lucky nodded. "I know. Give me a sec."

Trigger appeared in her line of sight once more, holding the chain that had bound her to the tree. He kneeled down and unlocked the handcuffs that were still around her wrists and then stuffed her shackles into his pack. Then he whistled. "You really fought to get free, didn't you?" he asked.

Devyn nodded and turned her head to look at her right wrist. It was pretty gruesome. She had bruises almost up to her elbow and deep red gouges in her skin.

"I'll put some painkillers in the IV," Doc muttered.

Devyn tried to move her arms and was pleased when the muscles worked as she wanted. She lifted her hands and gripped Lucky's biceps as hard as she could, which she was aware was pretty pathetic. "I love you," she told him softly.

"Love you back," he returned.

Closing her eyes, Devyn sighed in contentment. She'd dreamed of this moment so many times, had begun to think it would never happen. But it had. Lucky had actually found her. She didn't know how, but she was so damn grateful.

She moved on the ground, wanting to stand, to stretch her back—and then she smelled herself. Embarrassment swept over her like a shroud. It was stupid. She was so happy to have been found, to see Lucky and her brother. But she suddenly wanted nothing more than to hide her face in shame.

"What's wrong?" Lucky asked, always so damn observant.

Devyn glanced over at the other men, then back at the pulse beating in Lucky's throat. She couldn't say it out loud. Not in front of the others.

But again, Lucky seemed able to read her mind. "Can you give us a second, guys?"

Trigger nodded and moved away.

Before Doc joined him, he warned, "She needs medical care as soon as possible, Lucky. We need to get moving."

Fred stayed where he was.

Lucky stood up, pressing his ankle against her thigh, as if he didn't want to lose contact with her for even a moment. "We need a second," he told her brother.

"She's my sister," Fred said. "She can tell me anything."

The two men stared at each other, neither backing down.

Devyn hated to be the reason her brother and the man she loved were butting heads, but she couldn't talk about what was bothering her with Fred. She just couldn't.

"I'm okay, Fred."

He looked down at her, his eyes watering. "I love you, Devyn."

"I know," she told him, begging with her eyes for him to give her some privacy for just a second.

He sighed. "I get it. I'm just your brother." He leaned down and kissed the top of her head. "I'm so glad you're all right, munchkin. You scared me."

Devyn nodded, her throat too tight to speak.

"Two minutes," Fred told Lucky, who'd crouched down in front of her again.

He began to back away, and suddenly Devyn found her voice. "Fred? Is Spencer okay?" she called.

He stared at her for a long moment before sighing. "Yeah, sis. He is. You know he's the reason you're here, right?"

She nodded. "Yeah. But he's still my brother, and I love him. I'm assuming you know everything?"

Fred inclined his head.

"He needs help," she said softly.

"And he's gonna get it," Fred told her. "Now hurry up and let your man know what's bothering you so we can fly home."

"You guys were in the helicopter I heard? I thought it was just a random chopper," Devyn said.

"That was us. And we have a two-hour or so flight to get back to Killeen, so let's not take all day, okay?"

"Two hours?" Devyn said in confusion. "Where are we?"

"East Texas," Lucky said softly, and Devyn turned her attention back to him.

"Seriously?"

"Yeah."

"Wow. I had no idea I was unconscious for as long as that," she said.

"I'm guessing they drugged you when they got you into their car. Being knocked unconscious by a punch to the face wouldn't have kept you under as long as it would've taken them to drive you out here. Did they touch you when you got here? Sexually assault you?" Lucky asked.

Devyn saw Fred back away to join his other teammates, leaving her and Lucky to talk privately. She shook her head.

"You can tell me, Dev. It won't make me think any less of you."

"I know, and I'm telling the truth. When I woke up, I was alone and chained to this tree. I never saw the guys again. I didn't even get a good look at them before they knocked me out. I don't hurt...down there, if you know what I mean. So I don't think they did anything to me. My stomach was a bit sore the first day or so though."

"One of them probably carried you over their shoulder, which might account for the pain. Now...what's wrong? You looked horribly uncomfortable a minute ago."

"I just...I smelled myself," she whispered.

Lucky's face lost some of its tension. "You haven't had a shower in days, it's normal."

"You don't understand...I..." God, Devyn *hated* this. Didn't want to admit it. But the second she stood up—if she could even stand after all this time—it was going to become really obvious and uncomfortable.

"You can tell me anything, love," Lucky said softly. "Trust me."

"It's embarrassing. I've been chained to this tree. I couldn't move. And when I had to use the restroom...I couldn't get my pants undone." Devyn knew she was probably beet red, but she couldn't help it.

Lucky shrugged the pack he'd been carrying off his shoulders as he spoke. "I was held hostage once. I can't tell you where or what we were doing there, but needless to say, it wasn't fun. They tied my hands to a beam over my head and left me standing there for days. They took great pleasure in beating the shit out of me and laughing when I couldn't do a damn thing to defend myself. By the time I was rescued, I'd been there long enough to have pissed my pants several times...and I had also shit myself." He pulled out a pair of her sweatpants, a T-shirt that was too big to be anything other than one of his own, a pair of socks, her sneakers, and a package of wet wipes.

Lucky put one hand around the nape of her neck and leaned down so his forehead rested against her own. "You did what your body was made to do. Do *not* be embarrassed about that. I'd be more worried if you *didn't* go while you were out here. I had no idea what condition we'd find you in, and I'm more thankful than I can say that you're conscious and you mostly seem to be all right. But I brought some clothes for you, just in case. I know how it feels to be dirty, and I wanted to do everything I could to make this easier for you, even if that was just bringing a change of clothes."

Gah. This man. Devyn wanted to cry, but again, her body wasn't capable of it right this moment. "Thank you," she whispered.

"Don't thank me yet; you're gonna have to let me help you," Lucky warned.

Devyn crinkled her nose.

"It's either me or Grover...or Doc or Trigger," he told her.

"You," Devyn said immediately.

"Right. Let's get you changed so we can get the fuck out of here. Sound good?"

It definitely did.

"First step, let's see if you can stand," Lucky said without seeming too concerned.

Devyn wasn't too sure how that would go, but she nodded anyway. Lucky did most of the work, basically lifting her off the ground, then holding her around the waist until she stood, using the damn tree as a prop to keep her upright.

"Okay, we're going to have to do this quickly," Lucky said. "First, because I don't think your brother is gonna wait much longer."

Devyn looked over and saw that Trigger, Doc, and Fred all had their backs turned to them, giving her some much-needed privacy.

"Second," Lucky went on, "you aren't going to be able to stand on your own for long. I'll hold you steady while you get your pants and underwear off, okay?"

It wasn't, but Devyn nodded anyway. She was going to have to strip and clean herself with the wet wipes while Lucky held her upright, but that was much better than the alternative...staying in her soiled clothes for a second longer.

Surprisingly, the entire process of changing and cleaning up went much faster than she could've imagined. Lucky was all business, and he did his best to keep his eyes on her face, which made it much easier. By the time she had on clean underwear, sweatpants, and had donned his T-shirt, Devyn was completely drained. Her entire body shook, and she felt extremely dizzy.

"Doc?" Lucky shouted as he put one arm under her knees and the other behind her back, picking her up and holding her against his chest.

The other man was there in seconds. "What's up?"

"We need that IV. Stat."

Lucky knelt on the ground, still holding Devyn, as Doc got to work attempting to find a good vein to insert the IV.

"Once he gets this in, you'll feel much better," Lucky told her, distracting her from what Doc was doing. "We'll get some fluids in you, get you to the hospital, and you'll be right as rain in no time."

"No hospital," Devyn said insistently.

"Not an option," Lucky told her with a frown.

"Please! I'm okay. I swear I am. Yes, I'm dehydrated and hungry as hell, but they didn't hurt me. All I want is to go home and sleep for days. I won't be able to sleep in a hospital. I hate them." She looked up into Fred's eyes. He and Trigger had approached the same time Doc did. "Please, Fred! Tell him how much I hate hospitals."

"She does," Fred said quietly.

"I need to make sure she's okay," Lucky insisted. "She could have internal injuries. Her organs could be shutting down from lack of water."

"I managed to drink some of the rain," Devyn said. "I don't have internal injuries. I swear."

Lucky closed his eyes and looked up at the sky.

Devyn loved this man so much. She hated to stress him out, but she honestly didn't think she needed a hospital. She wrapped her hand around his neck and stroked the sensitive skin there. "I know I probably look like hell, but you got here in time. You found me," she said softly.

"I'm in," Doc said as he taped the needle to her inner arm. "For what it's worth, it wasn't as difficult as I thought it might be to find a vein. I can monitor her on the way back to Killeen and if I think there are any complications, I'll let you know."

"Please," Devyn begged. She knew she wasn't being fair, that she should go and get checked out for Lucky's peace of mind, but she only wanted to go home and be held. That was all the medicine she needed at the moment.

"Fine," Lucky said. "But if Doc says you need to go, you're going."

"Okay," Devyn agreed. She wasn't an idiot. She didn't want to die after finally being rescued, but although she was weak and shaky, she truly felt as if she was okay. She'd learned a lot about her body when she'd been sick, and right now, it wasn't telling her that anything major was wrong, other than needing nutrients and water.

"It's gonna be even slower going back to the chopper," Trigger said. "With that IV in, and you carrying her, it'll be tricky."

"We've got her," Doc said. "All you need to do is lie there," he told Devyn with a wink.

"Thank you all for coming to get me," she told the men as they all started walking. She held on to Lucky even tighter, though she knew he wouldn't drop her.

"No thanks necessary," Trigger said. "You're one of us now, and we'll always have your six."

"My what?" Devyn asked in confusion.

The four men chuckled.

"It means we've got your back," Lucky told her. "It origi-nated in World War One. Fighter pilots referenced the rear of the airplane as the six o'clock position. If you think about a clock face, and you're standing in the middle, twelve o'clock is in front of you, three is to your right, nine to your left, and six is behind you. On a battlefield, your 'six' is the most vulnerable position because you don't have eyes in the back of your head. So when someone says they have your six, they mean they're watching your back."

"That actually makes sense," Devyn said as she put her head on Lucky's shoulder.

"Of course it does. Everything we say makes sense," Fred told her.

Devyn rolled her eyes. "Whatever."

"And there she is," Fred said with a huge smile. "Gotta say, I never thought I'd see the day when I liked my little sister being annoying."

"Oh, I'm sure it won't last," Devyn said, her voice slurring. She was amazingly comfortable sitting in Lucky's arms. She hadn't even bothered to take a last look at where she'd been held captive for so long. It was done. Over. She was moving on.

"Feel free to take a nap," Lucky told her.

"I won't be able to sleep until we're home," Devyn told him, but with the gentle rocking of Lucky's steps, the knowledge that she wasn't alone anymore, and because she hadn't truly gotten any real rest in days, she quickly fell into a deep slumber.

"You think she's truly all right?" Grover asked Doc softly as they walked back to the helicopter. Trigger had informed the pilots they'd found Devyn and were headed back with her. All four men had heard the pilots cheering through their earbuds.

Lucky had forgotten about the radio when he'd been helping Devyn change, and he knew his team—and the pilots

—had heard every word of her humiliation. But he also knew no one would ever mention it.

He was so damn grateful he'd thought to bring a change of clothes for her, just in case. It was obvious she'd been embarrassed about what had happened.

"I do," Doc said, answering Grover's question. Then to Lucky, "There's no doubt she's dehydrated, but the rain she said she drank must've helped. Other than the bruises on her face and arms, did you see any on her legs that might indicate she's too embarrassed to tell us about a sexual assault?"

"No. Thank God. I think Rocky's goons did just what he claimed they did. Brought her out her and left her. You heard her; she said she never even saw them."

"Makes it harder for the cops to ID them," Trigger mused.

"You know as well as I do that there's no way the cops will find them," Grover said in disgust. "Rocky may be an asshole, but he's clearly smart."

Lucky nodded and shifted Devyn in his arms. She might be tall, but she wasn't a heavy burden for him, not in the least.

"I wasn't sure we would find her," Grover admitted softly. "I thought for sure we'd walk up on a freshly dug grave."

Lucky swallowed hard and nodded. He'd had the same thought even though he'd refused to verbalize it. "I know he's your brother, but it'll be a long time before I want to see Spencer again," Lucky admitted.

Grover nodded. "I know, and I don't blame you. But... Devyn's one of the most loyal people I know. It's why she didn't want to share his secret. She's also a peacekeeper. She wants everyone to get along. She's always been that way. If you want to keep her in your life, you're gonna have to find a way to forgive him, Lucky."

"I know," Lucky said. And he did. "I will. It just won't be this week. Or this month. It might even be years. Going to rehab and kicking his gambling habit will go a long way toward making that happen."

"He's going to rehab," Grover said firmly.

Spencer should feel damn fortunate to have a family who loved him as much as they did.

It took double the time to get back to the chopper as it did to get to Devyn's location, but no one seemed to be overly concerned. Trigger and Grover helped Lucky get into the helicopter without having to let go of Devyn. She stirred when he got settled.

"Are we home?"

"No, go back to sleep," Lucky told her with a small grin. "I'll let you know when we get there."

"Okay. I want to see Angel and Whiskers and give them kisses," she said sleepily.

Lucky chuckled. "Okay, love. I'm sure they'll like that."

He mentally made arrangements to get his animals back home. He wasn't sure how they'd feel about going back into the townhouse after the violence they'd obviously witnessed there, but he hoped Devyn's magic would work once again and they'd be all right.

"Gillian called a cleaning company after the cops were done taking pictures and prints," Trigger told him. "I figured dealing with all that was the last thing you'd want to do once we found Devyn."

That was very true. Lucky appreciated his friends so much. "Thank her for me."

"No thanks necessary," Trigger said. "But I'll tell her all the same."

Doc put a pair of headphones over Devyn's ears and did the same for Lucky, who hadn't let go of his woman for even a second.

When everyone had ear protection on, the chopper

slowly and carefully lifted out of the precarious landing zone and headed west, toward home.

"You know everyone's gonna want to come see her," Trigger warned.

"I know," Lucky said. "I need at least a day to make sure she's all right. If she has complications, I'm gonna take her to the hospital no matter how much she begs differently."

"Good," Trigger said. "Just say the word, and we'll keep everyone away until she, and you, are ready."

Lucky sighed in relief. It wasn't that he didn't want Kinley, Riley, and the others over, he just needed some one-on-one time with Devyn. To reassure himself that she was truly all right. He could've lost her. Almost *had* lost her. If Spencer hadn't gotten his head out of his ass and come forward with the truth about what happened, it was possible they would've found her too late. As much as it was Spencer's fault she was taken in the first place, it'd been because of him that they'd been able to get to her before any long-term damage had been done.

The men fell silent in the chopper and Lucky looked down at the sleeping woman in his arms. Her blonde hair was a complete mess. He knew Devyn would have a hard time getting it clean and brushed, but he'd help her. The black and blue bruise on her face was vivid against her pale skin and her arms would be bruised for quite a while. He knew she still felt dirty; wet wipes couldn't take away the feel of contamination, although they helped a hell of a lot. She needed a shower and some very definite pampering.

But the thought that she felt safe enough to fall asleep in his arms went a long way toward reassuring him that she would be all right. Her chest rose and fell rhythmically, her breathing didn't seem labored, and she'd stopped shaking as the IV in her arm did its best to replace the lost fluids in her body.

Lucky leaned down and gently kissed her forehead, leaving his lips against her skin for a long moment. He loved her so damn much, and he was thankful as hell that they'd gotten a second chance. Life was so damn short; he'd learned that the hard way. He and Devyn were going to live life to its fullest from here on out. He'd make sure of it.

CHAPTER EIGHTEEN

Devyn opened her eyes and blinked.

She saw the light from the bathroom that Lucky had left on. For her. Because she was freaking scared of the damn dark now.

And every night she slept for around three hours, then woke up suddenly. As wide awake as if she'd just had four cups of espresso.

It was annoying.

She'd really hoped that once she was home and safe, she'd be able to get past what had happened. She hated that Spencer had been beaten up, that Lucky had been terrified while she was missing, and even that Whiskers and Angel had to be traumatized by the men who'd come into the house and brought extreme violence with them.

Even though Devyn had been knocked unconscious after one blow and didn't remember anything about her abduction, it still scared her to think about what had happened. She tried to rationalize her experience by telling herself it wasn't *that* bad. She'd woken up tied to a tree and that was that. Hadn't worried about being sexually assaulted. The worst thing that had happened to her was that she'd gotten bitten by bugs and had gone to the bathroom in her pants.

But she was kidding herself. The entire thing had been terrifying. And even though she was safe and back home with Lucky and everything seemed to have worked out in the end, she wasn't all right.

Every night since she'd been found and brought back to Killeen, she'd woken up in the wee hours with her heart racing and having a panic attack. Intellectually, she knew she had nothing to be scared of. Lucky was with her. She could hear the animals snoring on their bed in the corner of the room. The bathroom light was on, so she knew she wasn't in the middle of that forest.

It was the damn birds chirping.

Devyn supposed she heard them unconsciously and her body forced her to wake up, maybe just to make sure she wasn't back in that forest, tied up and helpless. Whatever the reason, she hated it.

The first few nights, she'd tried sneaking out of bed, but Lucky had woken up and been so upset that she wasn't sleeping, Devyn felt guilty. He'd started going back to work on the post and needed his rest. So now when she woke up, she lay in bed for hours, staring at the ceiling and berating herself for being so stupid and weak.

Tonight, Devyn's thoughts turned to her family. Spencer was already in rehab back in Missouri. Her parents had flown down when they'd heard about what happened to two of their children. They'd been disappointed in Spencer, but supportive. Devyn had downplayed what happened to her to make sure the focus was on her brother and getting him the help he needed. For the first time in his life, he was the center of attention, and it seemed he really needed that. Devyn wasn't bitter; she was relieved that she hadn't been seriously hurt, allowing Mila, Angela, and their parents to turn all their attention to Spencer.

He was in a thirty-day in-house treatment program in St. Louis, and after that, the psychologists would assess where he was and see if he needed to stay longer. He wasn't allowed to have any visitors for the first month, so he could completely concentrate on himself and not have any outside factors interfering with his recovery.

Devyn was genuinely happy for her brother. Well, happy might not be the word...relieved, maybe. She'd moved away from Missouri because she'd been scared of what he might do if she continued to refuse him money, and it seemed that wasn't really the best move. Spencer had become so desperate to get his hands on money any way he could, he'd gotten involved with a ruthless loan shark. But on the other hand, everything that had occurred had ultimately led to Spencer seeking help.

And it had led her to Lucky.

Life was slowly returning to normal for the others, during the two weeks since she'd been found. Aspen and Brain had brought Chance home and were getting used to being a family of three. Riley and Oz were preparing for the birth of their child. They had about two more months to go.

Gillian had organized a party for a large local company, which had gone off without a hitch. She'd been getting more and more local business and was as busy as ever. Kinley was working a lot too; she'd gotten a job as an executive assistant and, from what Devyn heard, had changed up everything, making her boss's schedule run much more efficiently.

Everyone seemed to be happy and well-adjusted, even after what they'd all been through, and here was Devyn... scared of a fucking bird.

"Dev?" Lucky mumbled as he rolled over and lifted his head.

"Go back to sleep. It's early," she said softly.

"Not sleeping?" he asked.

"I'm fine," she said automatically.

Lucky rolled toward her and put an arm around her chest. He leaned forward and kissed her shoulder before resting his head back on his pillow. "What can I do to help?"

"Nothing. I'm gonna get up and go downstairs and read," Devyn told him, slipping out from under his arm and throwing her legs over the side of the mattress.

"Dev—"

She ruthlessly interrupted him before he could say anything else. "I'm *fine*, Lucky. Seriously. You have to get up in two and a half hours and go to work. Sleep." She didn't give him time to answer, standing up and heading for the closet. She grabbed a pair of comfortable sweat pants and one of his Army sweatshirts before leaving the room.

Even though she'd been a bitch, she couldn't help but feel a little disappointed when he didn't follow her.

God, she was a mess. If he had come after her, she would've been irritated, yet here she was, upset when he didn't. She really needed to get her shit together.

* * *

Later that morning, after Lucky had gone to work, Devyn sat on the couch with Whiskers purring in her lap and Angel sitting next to her, snoring. She hated how things were going with Lucky, and knew it was all her fault. He was doing all he could to help her, to figure out what was wrong, but Devyn was keeping him at arm's length. She wasn't sure *why*, just that she was struggling with getting back into the routine of her life.

She loved Lucky, that wasn't in question. She needed to

get back to work, decide if she was going to go full time, and get on with her life. But she couldn't. She was stuck.

A bird warbled outside, and Devyn winced.

Shit. Would she never be able to hear a damn bird again without flinching?

Her cell phone rang, scaring the shit out of Devyn, and she laughed nervously as she reached for it. Seeing it was Aspen, she eagerly answered. "Hey! How's mama and baby?"

"We're good, and we're having a girls' day in. Get your ass over here."

Devyn blinked. "What?"

"Gillian's already here, Riley's on the way, and Kinley's coming to your place right now to get you. So if you aren't up and dressed, you better get that way, pronto."

Devyn had to chuckle. "You're awfully bossy today."

"I have to be. Chance is sleeping and I don't know how long he'll be down. I need to talk to someone besides this kid, and I finally convinced Brain to go to work today. You're coming over, so get ready."

Devyn wasn't sure she wanted to be social, but she nodded and said, "Okay, okay. Do I have time for a shower?"

That was another thing. Devyn had been taking two or three showers a day. She couldn't seem to feel clean enough.

"If it's fast, yes. Can't wait to spend some time with you, Dev," Aspen said more gently. "See you soon."

"Bye."

Devyn hung up and couldn't decide if she liked that her friends were pushy or not. Sighing, she gave Whiskers one last pet and gently extricated herself from under the cat. She wanted to be ready before Kinley got there. Angel and Whiskers hated the sound of the doorbell or when someone knocked on the door. They'd been traumatized by the violence that had happened inside what they'd finally seen as their safe space, and it would take a while before they forgot what happened.

Thirty minutes later, Devyn was dressed and waiting when Kinley pulled up. She slipped out of the townhouse, locked the door behind her, and headed for the Toyota Corolla.

Kinley smiled as she climbed in. "You look good," she said.

"Thanks, you too," Devyn replied.

They made small talk as they drove toward Aspen and Brain's house. They'd been talking about buying a bigger one, but neither seemed to be in a huge hurry to make the move. After they'd pulled into the driveway and gotten out, they waved to Winnie—Aspen's elderly neighbor, who was sitting on her porch—and headed for the door.

"It's about time!" Aspen said as she met them at the door and gave them both a big hug.

Devyn eyed Aspen and nodded in satisfaction. Her friend looked great. A little tired but, that wasn't too surprising since she was a new mom.

"Hey," Gillian said, hugging both Devyn and Kinley. "Come on, I've already poured you a glass of wine, and I picked all the yucky cashews out of the mixed nuts for you, Dev."

Devyn smiled. She loved that her friends knew her so well.

An hour later, they were all settled in Aspen's living room and Devyn was feeling much more mellow, now that she'd had two glasses of wine. Chance had woken up twenty minutes ago and Aspen had fed him. They'd talked about how hard it had been for her to breastfeed at first and how she'd had to supplement Chance's feedings with formula. They'd discussed the ickier aspects of childbirth as well. Devyn had been afraid the frank talk would freak Riley out, since she was next up to have a baby, but she seemed grateful for the information, even when it was gruesome at times.

Chance was now sleeping again, and Aspen had put him in a bassinet on the other side of the room.

"So..." Gillian said once the baby was settled. "Devyn, let's talk about you."

Devyn winced. "How about we don't," she tried to joke.

"You aren't doing well," Gillian said bluntly.

Devyn blinked in surprise.

"I'm sure you think you're hiding it, but you aren't. You've yawned about five hundred times today, and you can't blame that on the alcohol. Two glasses of wine isn't enough to make you *that* tired. You aren't sleeping well?"

Four pairs of eyes fixed themselves on Devyn, and she shifted uncomfortably. She didn't want to talk about this. She was *fine*. "I'm good," she told her friends.

All three looked skeptical.

"Right, okay, so how about I start?" Gillian said.

And just like that, Devyn realized that she'd been set up. This wasn't a casual get-together at all. It'd been planned. She wanted to be upset, but she couldn't. Her friends cared about her, even though Devyn wasn't sure they could help.

"After I got home from Venezuela and the plane hijacking, I thought I was good. Ann, Wendy, and Clarissa told me how well they thought I was doing, and I just went with it. I was pretty focused on Walker, and wishing he'd call, to think too much about what I'd been through. Then Walker and I started dating, and that kind of took my mind off everything even more. But after I got taken by Salazar and realized Andrea wanted to kill me, I kind of fell apart. I had horrible nightmares. I felt stupid, because I was safe, loved, and had no reason to be such a baby."

"I have flashbacks," Kinley added. "Of being at the bottom of that ravine and being in so much pain, it hurts to even breathe. There are times in the middle of the day I have to stop, close my eyes, and force myself to remember that I made it out. That I'm okay."

"I've got PTSD. It's not as bad as what a lot of soldiers deal with," Aspen said, "but there are times I can't get the images of what I've done in the past out of my head. The people I've killed. I feel kind of stupid, because what I've done and experienced isn't *nearly* as bad as what a lot of soldiers have gone through, but comparing myself to others isn't healthy. I'm allowed to feel the way I feel about what I did, and I'm still trying to come to terms with it all."

Devyn's eyes filled with tears, and she stared down at the dregs of wine in her glass.

"I still wake up in the middle of the night and have to get up and go check on Logan and Bria," Riley said softly. "I know they're safe inside our house. Porter installed that kick-ass security system and a mouse can't fart without the damn thing going off, but I still wake with a feeling that they're gone."

"Our point," Gillian said, leaning forward and putting a hand on Devyn's knee, "is that no matter how put-together we look on the outside, we're all still dealing with what happened to us. What's that saying, Kinley? The one you like to say?"

"You never know how strong you are, until being strong is the only choice you have," Kinley said firmly.

"Yeah, that one," Gillian agreed. "What happened to you was *horrible*. I can't imagine being left alone out in the wilderness like you were. But then again, I bet you couldn't imagine being in a hijacked plane. Or thrown off a bridge. Or being in battle. It's all a matter of perspective, and if you're comparing your experience to what happened to us, and deciding that you have no right to be traumatized, you're wrong."

Devyn swallowed hard three times before she could

speak. "I wasn't beaten. I wasn't yelled at or threatened. I wasn't raped. I don't even remember being taken. I was punched, then all I did was sit on my ass and wait to be rescued. I shouldn't be affected by what happened at all."

Riley stood from her chair and waddled over to where Devyn was sitting on the couch. She sat next to her, forcing Devyn to scoot over, since Riley wasn't exactly small at the moment with her big baby belly.

"Wrong," she said firmly. "What happened to you was traumatic. I don't give a shit if you don't remember part of it. You still experienced a violent crime against you, as a result of your brother's actions. That's traumatizing."

"Right," Aspen agreed, coming over and kneeling at Devyn's feet. All five of them were now practically huddled together, but it felt comforting to Devyn. Not constricting in the least. "Being alone is its own special kind of hell. I was alone all night in those flood waters with Kane. Every little sound freaked me out. I was both hopeful it was someone coming who could help me, and scared to death that it'd be a looter or someone who would cause us harm. It was the longest night of my life, and I only had *one*. You were out there alone for much longer than that."

"It's the birds," Devyn whispered. "They were constantly chirping. You'd think that would've been a good thing, that I wasn't in complete silence all the time, but I wake up in the middle of the night and hear them and I'm transported right back to that damn forest. I've only been sleeping a few hours a night, and then I lie awake and stare at the ceiling, being afraid. But I don't know what exactly it is I'm afraid of. It's so stupid!"

"It's not stupid," Gillian said. "What about Lucky?"

"What about him?" Devyn asked.

"What does he do when you wake up?"

"Well, at first I tried to slip out of bed so I didn't wake

him up, but you know our guys have the hearing of a bat. I guess because of their training. He wanted to comfort me, to stay up with me, but that makes me feel even more guilty that I'm disturbing his rest. It's...we're...Things are strained right now," Devyn admitted softly. "And I hate that. I love him. So much. And I know I'm pushing him away."

"Well, he won't go," Gillian told her matter-of-factly. "When our men commit, they're in for the long haul. Can I give you some advice?"

Devyn couldn't help but laugh. "You mean you aren't already?"

All of the other women chuckled.

"Right, okay, can I give you *more* advice?" Gillian asked.

"Please do. I'm at my wits' end. I hate that I feel so weak. You guys are all so damn strong! I can't help but compare my situation to yours, and I come up short every time."

"First, stop that shit," Gillian said. "You aren't us, we aren't you. I personally never would've been able to go through what you did with my sanity intact. Not having others there to share in my fear and the experience? No. Just no. But second, from someone who had a hard time sleeping herself, you need to distract yourself when you wake up."

"I've been trying. When Lucky lets me, I go downstairs and read or something," Devyn protested.

"No, you need to let *Lucky* distract you," Gillian said bluntly. "Are you guys still having sex?"

Devyn blushed and shook her head. "He's been really gentle with me lately."

"Right. So the next time you wake up and can't sleep, jump him," Gillian told her.

"Um...I don't feel all that sexy when I wake up and hear those damn birds," Devyn said wryly.

"I know. I never felt like sex either. But you know what? It helps. It makes you stop thinking about what's bothering you.

And it has the added bonus of tiring you out. I'm not saying you need to have an hour-long fuck marathon; a quickie will work just as well. It gets your endorphins going or something. I have no idea how it works, but I swear after one of my nightmares, when Walker takes me, I can't think about anything but how much I love him and how grateful I am to have him in my life. It brings me back to the present, makes me count my blessings."

"When I come back to bed after checking on Logan and Bria, Porter makes me forget my worries. We don't always have sex; sometimes he goes down on me, sometimes he holds me and fingers me to an orgasm...but it works every time," Riley said.

"Before we all sound like a bunch of sex-starved horny bitches, it doesn't always have to be about sex, either," Aspen said, and everyone laughed. "There have been times when I get lost in my head, and Kane simply holds me and tells me how much he loves me and how blessed he is to have both me and Chance. He makes me realize that I've got everything I ever wanted right here, right now. It helps."

"It's so obvious how much Lucky loves you," Kinley said softly. "When I was in witness protection, I longed to be able to simply sit next to Gage and hold his hand. That sounds stupid, but I always loved it when he did that. I missed it a lot. I try not to take anything for granted anymore. Easier said than done, I know, but I force myself to be present in the moment. Life is short, and we could spend it worrying about every decision we've made in the past and our actions, but that's not going to do a damn thing to change them. We have to keep moving forward."

Devyn nodded. "Thanks, guys. I needed this."

"We know," Aspen said with a smirk. "That's why we made you come over."

"You might not think what you went through was all that bad, but it was, Dev," Gillian said. "Cut yourself some slack."

"Talk to Lucky," Riley ordered. "He can help you."

"He *wants* to help you," Aspen corrected. "You'll grow closer if you let him."

"You might think you're doing the right thing by letting him sleep after you wake up, but I guarantee he's not sleeping. He's worrying about you," Kinley added.

"Okay, okay, I hear you," Devyn said with a smile. "I'll talk to him."

"Good," Gillian said with a nod.

Kinley smiled.

Aspen squeezed her knee affectionally.

And Riley said, "Thank God. I need to pee. *Again.* I swear this kid is standing on my bladder. Can someone help me up?"

Everyone laughed, and the serious part of the day was over just like that. The rest of the afternoon was spent talking about their jobs, babies, and the guys' upcoming mission to the Olympics. That was one of the few missions that wasn't super top secret, and the girls were just as excited as the men. It was a nice change of pace for them. Even though they'd have to be on their toes to watch for danger, it wasn't as if they were being sent into a foreign country under the cover of darkness to do surveillance or to try to rescue someone.

By the time Kinley drove her home, Devyn was feeling much better. She made a mental vow to be a better girlfriend. Yeah, she was struggling with what had happened, but Lucky was also struggling as a result, and she needed to open up to him.

CHAPTER NINETEEN

Lucky eyed Devyn critically that night. She looked tired, but somehow...lighter. He really hoped her day with the other women had helped.

"How was your day?" he asked after he'd greeted both Angel and Whiskers. The animals were slowly but surely coming out of their shells. They still didn't like strangers all that much, and when the doorbell rang, they bolted up the stairs, but with time, he hoped that skittishness would fade.

Devyn had been in the kitchen making a salad, and she walked up to him and right into his embrace. Lucky sighed in relief. She hadn't initiated physical contact since they'd come home from East Texas.

"It was great. Lucky?"

"Yeah, Dev?"

"I love you."

"Love you back," he said immediately.

She lifted her head. "I'm sorry I've been such a headcase."

Lucky shook his head. "No, you're good. You've been through a lot."

"But that's the thing...I don't *feel* as if I have. I wasn't hurt, nothing happened to me."

"You don't have to be hurt and beat up to be traumatized," Lucky reasoned.

"I'm finally realizing that. And I wanted to say...thank you for bringing the clothes for me. I heard what you said, and I didn't really acknowledge it then, but I'm sorry you were a POW at one point."

"Thanks. It wasn't the best time in my life, but I'm willing to talk about it if it'll help you." He hated talking about what he'd gone through, but he would if it would help her. He'd do anything for her.

Devyn shook her head. "No, I didn't bring it up to make you discuss it. I just wanted to make sure you knew how much it meant to me. I'm still embarrassed about going to the bathroom in my pants, but I'm trying to get past that. And...I wanted to ask you a favor."

"Anything."

"You know I've been having trouble sleeping. I go to sleep just fine, but then I wake up. It's...It'sthebirds," she said quickly, her words running together.

Lucky frowned. "What about them?"

"I hear them singing, and it brings me right back to the forest. I can't get my mind to turn off and it feels as if they're taunting me. I *hate* it. I mean, I like birds, and I used to like hearing them chirping. But now the sound scares me. I want to do something drastic. But I need your help."

Lucky frowned. "What are you thinking?"

"Will you go camping with me?"

"Camping?" he asked.

"Yeah. Just in the backyard," she clarified. "In a tent. Do you have a tent? I just...call it immersion therapy or something. Maybe if I'm in the dark, at night, with you...I can get over this stupid insomnia thing."

"Maybe you should talk to a psychologist about this," Lucky began.

But Devyn shook her head. "No. I *need* to do this. But I know I can't be alone. Will you help me?"

"You know I will. I'd do anything for you."

* * *

Lucky had no idea how he'd let himself be talked into this. He'd borrowed a tent from the supply room at work and set it up in their backyard. Angel and Whiskers were beyond confused, and had refused to come outside after he'd set the thing up. They were upstairs in their nice comfy bed, and he was outside, worrying about Devyn.

They were sitting in camp chairs and looking up at the stars. He didn't think this was a great idea, as Devyn hadn't said much since the sun had set. She looked nervous and tense, and Lucky wanted nothing more than to take her upstairs and hold her tight in their bed. She'd seemed excited about the campout earlier, laughing and joking, but now her shoulders were hunched and she wasn't talking. At all.

Suddenly a line from one of the *Jurassic Park* movies flashed into Lucky's head. It was the one with the chick who wore high heels the entire movie and was running around the jungle as if those spiky heels weren't sinking into the wet soil with every step. It was ridiculous. But, anyway, toward the end of the movie, one of the kids turned to her and said, "We need more teeth."

Picking up his phone, Lucky quickly sent a few texts. It would take some time for his plan to come to fruition, and in the meantime, he needed to have a discussion with Devyn.

He stood and picked her up without a word.

"What are you doing?"

He ignored her question, sitting back down in his own

camp chair. The thing creaked, and Lucky knew it would be a miracle if they both didn't end up on their asses in the grass, but he needed to hold her.

"Lucky? Can this chair even hold us both?"

"I have no idea. And I don't care. If it breaks, it breaks. I won't let you get hurt. Things have been crazy the last two weeks. We haven't had a lot of time to sit and just talk. You haven't gone back to work...can we talk about that?"

Devyn sighed, but she didn't pull away from him, which made Lucky relax.

"I just...I love my job, but I don't know that I want to work full time."

"Then don't," Lucky said easily.

"But I need to."

"Why?"

"Well...because. That's what people do. They work to get money so they can eat and have a roof over their heads."

"I've got money to keep us fed, and for this townhouse."

"Speaking of which...I still can't believe you guys ponied up all that money."

"Stay on point," Lucky scolded. "The money's not a big deal. Spencer will pay us all back eventually. Grover will make sure of that. Besides, I would've paid whatever it cost if it meant getting you back. I would've gotten Tex involved. He knows people, and he could've helped raise three million dollars if that's what Rocky had demanded. Back to your job."

Devyn's eyes were huge. "Wait, seriously?"

"Yeah, love, seriously. You're worth all the money in the world, and I was gonna pay anything to get you back."

Her eyes filled with tears.

"No crying," Lucky chided. "And we were talking about your job. If you don't want to work, don't."

"I need to do something. I can't just sit around all day," she protested after a minute.

"You like your job as a vet tech, right?" he asked.

She nodded.

"And you like your job here in Killeen, yeah?"

"You know I do."

"Then why can't you continue to work part time?" he asked.

Devyn was quiet for a long moment as she thought about his question. Then she said, "I just feel as if I should be working full time."

Lucky shook his head. "Don't. And if working four hours a day is what works for you, then do that. Maybe you can volunteer at the shelter or something if you get bored. Or we can foster some animals to try to help them acclimate. I don't give a shit *what* you do, I just want you to be happy. And it's obvious being around animals makes you happy. We won't starve if you don't work full time, and we won't be thrown out on our asses either."

"You *do* know that I don't live with you, right? I still have my apartment."

Lucky laughed. "Seriously? Dev, you've been sleeping in my bed for two weeks. You haven't even been back to your apartment once. You *do* live with me. And I'm not letting you go back to your apartment now. I've gotten too used to having you in my bed and my life."

"I don't know why. I'm a pain in the ass. Waking you up all the time. Shit, you aren't even getting the perks of having a live-in girlfriend. We haven't had sex since...well, you know."

"I don't need sex to love you, Devyn," Lucky told her. "Simply having you by my side makes me happy and content."

"You haven't asked why," she said quietly.

"Why what?"

"Why I haven't wanted to have sex."

Lucky's heart broke for her. No, he hadn't asked. But it was more than obvious she hadn't been in an amorous mood lately. "I figured when you were ready to talk about it, you would," he said.

"I feel dirty. All the time. I can't get clean. The thought of you wanting to get close to me...down there...gives me the heebie-jeebies."

Lucky hated that. It was weird the way the mind worked. She'd dealt with the fact that she'd been kidnapped and chained to a tree pretty well, the birds and insomnia notwithstanding, but she was having a harder time getting over going to the bathroom in her pants.

"I took two showers a day after I was rescued," he admitted. "I felt the same way. But that feeling fades. I swear it does."

She nodded. "I love you. I don't know too many men who could've helped me out there without batting an eyelash like you did. It wasn't pretty."

"Devyn, we're gonna get old. We're gonna need to hire people to wipe our asses when we can't do it ourselves. It's likely we'll eventually puke all over ourselves when we're sick. I might get an ingrown toenail that you need to help lance for me. Being human is gross. But I love you for *you*, not because you smell fresh as a daisy all the time. And I hope you feel the same...because Lord knows there are plenty of times in my job when I'm a disgusting mess and you're probably gonna get a front-row seat for that when I get home from missions."

"You make it seem so...normal."

"That's because it is. Dev, I've seen the most disgusting things in my line of work, some things you can imagine and most you can't. Bodily fluids don't even register on my gross meter anymore," Lucky told her matter-of-factly.

She sighed against him.

A bird chose that moment to chirp loudly over their heads. Maybe it wasn't happy they were encroaching on its nightly hunting grounds, or maybe it was just saying hello, but whatever the reason, Devyn tensed.

"I'm here," Lucky said, tightening his arms.

"I know," she said.

"Hello?" a voice called out from the other side of the fenced-in yard.

"Come on in!" Lucky returned.

"What did you do?" Devyn asked as Oz, Logan, and Bria walked into the yard.

"You weren't relaxed. I figured maybe if we had more people, a camp-out party, you might forget about the birds and have some fun," Lucky said tentatively.

The smile on her face made his tension disappear. He'd done the right thing, thank God.

"I love you," Devyn told him.

"Love you back. Come on, let's help them get their tents set up." Lucky eyed the yard. "I'm not sure we'll have room."

"Who else did you invite?" Devyn asked with a tilt of her head.

"Um...everyone?" Lucky said, scrunching up his nose. "I wasn't sure who would be able to make it on such short notice."

Devyn laughed. "It's a good thing we went shopping and stocked up on food today, then."

"Yup," Lucky agreed.

* * *

Five hours later, and way past midnight, Devyn smiled as Lucky crawled into their tent. Bria and Logan were the best distractions. They'd made s'mores and ran around with sparklers, laughing and smearing gooey melted marshmallows everywhere. Gillian and Trigger had come, as had Kinley and Lefty, Doc, and Fred. Brain and Aspen were at home with

Chance, and Oz had left Riley at home as well, but she'd insisted he come with the kids. The backyard had been filled with good friends and giggling.

Devyn had gone inside and made frozen margaritas for those who wanted them, and Trigger had brought beers. Everyone had gotten tipsy and, before she knew it, Devyn had forgotten all about the dark, and the birds, and had lost herself in spending time with good friends.

"Happy?" Lucky asked as he took her in his arms. The night was warm, and Devyn could smell the sweat on both her and Lucky's bodies. The scent of wood smoke had also permeated everything, their clothes, her hair, even the tent itself, but instead of focusing on the fact that she was dirty and needed to shower, she was too tired to do more than snuggle into the man at her side.

"Very," she said on a sigh.

"The birds? The dark?"

"What birds?" she asked.

"I wasn't sure it was the best thing to do, but I hoped," Lucky said.

"What? Inviting everyone over? It was perfect," Devyn told him.

"Good." Lucky kissed her forehead and held her closer.

It really was too hot to be snuggling, but Devyn couldn't imagine a place she'd rather be right now.

A bird warbled overhead, and she didn't even flinch. She had no illusions that she was magically cured of her uneasiness, but for the moment, she was completely relaxed.

"I love you, Dev. So damn much. I know talking about stuff is hard, but you have nothing to fear from me. I'll never judge you or think badly because of how you're feeling. You can always talk to me. About anything. I'll protect your heart as well as your body."

Devyn nodded against him. She'd been on her own for so

long, had kept her feelings buried so deep, it was hard to share. But after everything that had happened, she knew she needed to get better at that. If she'd shared with Fred about their brother, maybe he wouldn't have gotten into such trouble with the loan shark. Maybe he would've been convinced to get help before things went so wrong. And opening up to the other women had gone really well. She'd learned she wasn't alone in struggling to come to terms with what happened to her. The others weren't as put together as they seemed from the outside. And opening up to Lucky made her realize that he truly did have her back.

"I love you back," she told him. "And I'll do better at talking."

"Good. Think you can sleep?" he asked.

Devyn nodded against him. Suddenly her eyes were so heavy, she couldn't keep them open a second longer.

"Okay. I'll be right here by your side. You aren't alone, those damn birds won't get you, and the bathroom is just inside the house. You're good."

She was. Lucky had summed up all her fears in one plain-spoken sentence, and then countered each one. She had nothing to be afraid of. Not with Lucky by her side.

She slept then. Deeply. Without waking up once.

EPILOGUE

Devyn opened her eyes, saw nothing but black, and internally groaned. It had been so long, at least three weeks since she'd woken up in the middle of the night and couldn't go back to sleep. Three weeks of bliss. Somehow, camping in the backyard with most of their friends had done what she hadn't been able to do alone...calmed her mind.

She could hear birds without freaking out and being thrown back to the middle of that deserted forest. Even Angel and Whiskers were doing great. Fred had come over the other day, and the animals hadn't darted up the stairs to hide. They hadn't exactly run up to Fred for pets, but they weren't traumatized by a stranger either.

Lucky still kept the bathroom light on for her, and she had thought that soon, she wouldn't even need that anymore.

But now it was dark and she was awake. Was she backsliding? Devyn frowned and turned her head slightly to look at the clock. When she read the numbers on it, she blinked. Five-o-two. She smiled. It wasn't the middle of the night. She'd gotten a full six hours of sleep.

Lucky's alarm was going to go off in twenty minutes or so.

An idea formed in her head then. They'd been going slow in the sex department, mostly because Lucky hadn't wanted to rush her and was taking great care with her mental health. But Devyn felt good. Ready to get her life back.

She'd told her boss she wanted to stay part time, and she was deeply satisfied with her decision. She was still a little worried about money; she didn't want to mooch off Lucky, especially after he'd already shelled out a hefty sum to Spencer's loan shark to get her back, but she had to admit that she was happier only working twenty hours a week. She'd started to volunteer at a local rescue group, playing with the animals and assisting with easy medical issues. It felt good. *She* felt good.

And she wanted Lucky. Now.

Knowing the second she stirred, he'd wake, she moved quickly, sitting up and straddling Lucky's thighs. She pulled off her T-shirt, thankful she hadn't been wearing underwear to bed, then pulled Lucky's boxer briefs down and lowered her head.

"Holy shit," Lucky moaned, one of his hands immediately tangling in her hair.

Smiling, she licked his cock, pleased when it immediately began to harden. Without a word, she got to work, licking and sucking, doing her best to please her man.

"Fuck, Devyn, that feels so damn good."

She'd never done this before. Oh, she'd given a blow job or two, but not to Lucky, because he'd always been too bossy and impatient to let her play with him like this. But she'd never felt the bone-deep need to please a man in this way before. She wanted to thank Lucky for being as amazing as he was. Show him without words how much she loved him. How fortunate she felt to be with him.

They both wrestled his briefs down his legs and off, and Devyn didn't remove her mouth from his cock the entire time.

She leaned down to lick his balls, and he broke.

Lucky sat up and grabbed her around the waist and practically threw her onto her back next to him.

Devyn frowned at him. "I wasn't done," she complained, licking her lips, loving the taste of his slight musk.

"I was about to be," he told her. "Are you sure?"

Devyn nodded. "I woke up and thought it was the middle of the night. But I'd slept another whole night. I feel so fortunate, and I need you, Lucky. In my life, in my bed, and in my body. Please?"

Without a word, he lowered his head and took one of her nipples into his mouth and sucked. Hard. With his other hand, he reached between them and tested her readiness. Devyn loved how considerate he was, but she was more than ready for him. Surprisingly, sucking his cock had excited her to the point that her body was dripping wet.

But Lucky took his time, licking, sucking, and nipping at her small nipples as he played with her clit. When he felt she was wet enough, he sat up, bringing his fingers to his mouth and licking her wetness off them.

Devyn knew she was blushing, but she didn't care. She spread her legs wide and begged him with her eyes to stop fucking around.

He chuckled, obviously reading her look. He inched forward on his knees, forcing her legs even farther apart. "I love you, Dev."

"Love you back," she whispered, gripping his thighs with her hands.

Then Lucky was there. Where she needed him. Slowly pressing inside her as if she was the most precious thing in the world to him. She could see the pleasure on his face as he slipped through her folds.

"This'll never get old," he breathed. "Seriously, you have no idea how fucking good this feels. Being inside you bare."

"I think I have *some* idea," Devyn panted.

Then neither had the breath to speak as he slowly and methodically made love to her. In and out, steadily ramping up both their arousal. Then, without her having to beg, he began to move faster, as if knowing she needed more. His cock felt so big and deep inside her, and all she could do was moan.

Then, as if he wasn't turning her on enough, he began to roughly thumb her clit. Devyn jerked and dug her nails into his skin. She was holding on to his arms now, as if they were the only things holding her together.

"Can I come inside you?" Lucky asked without stopping his thrusts or flicking her clit. "If it'll make you uncomfortable, I can pull out and come on the sheets."

Devyn hadn't thought she could love this man any more, but at that moment, she overflowed with gratitude. She didn't know what she'd done to deserve him, but she was going to do everything in her power to keep him. To be worthy of him.

They hadn't talked much more about her aversion to being dirty, but of course he still knew.

"Inside me," she breathed.

"Are you sure?" he asked.

Devyn managed a nod. *Nothing* about Lucky felt dirty to her.

"So fucking strong," Lucky said under his breath, then thrust into her and held himself there as he manipulated her clit.

Devyn tried to thrust up, but couldn't; Lucky's hips held

her still. She writhed in his grasp and every muscle in her body tensed as her orgasm approached.

"That's it. Let go. I've got you. You're safe with me. Let me feel it. I wanna feel your pussy grab hold of my cock as if it never wants to let go."

Fifteen seconds later, Devyn did just that. She flew over the edge and let out a small screech as she orgasmed. It was so intense, it almost hurt, and Lucky never stopped stroking her clit, forcing the pleasure to keep going until she begged him for mercy.

Instead of fucking her hard and fast like she expected him to, Lucky lifted her ass and somehow got even deeper inside her. She swore she could feel the head of his dick against her cervix. It was almost painful, but in a good way. Then, without even moving, Lucky's stomach muscles contracted and he came.

Long and hard, if the look of pleasured agony on his face was any indication.

His fingers bit into the flesh of her ass and his nipples were hard as rocks on his massively defined chest. Devyn swore even the skull tattoo on his shoulder looked as if it was highly pleased.

She loved when he lost control and fucked her hard and deep, but somehow she loved this even more. He'd come without moving, and that felt pretty damn amazing.

"Damn," Lucky said when he'd stopped coming. "I...*Fuck*."

She giggled and felt his cock slide out of her a little. He was adorable when he was speechless.

"You think that's funny?" he asked, pretending to be affronted.

"No, not at all," she lied.

They smiled at each other, then Lucky rolled over so she was astride him. He was still lodged inside her body, but she could feel he was no longer hard. Wetness slipped out of her body, was probably coating his balls, but he didn't seem to notice or care. His hands came up and he framed her face and pulled her down for a long, deep kiss.

When they were both breathing hard, Lucky said, "I never want you to suffer in the night alone again. I know you've been sleeping fairly well these past few weeks, but promise me, in the future, if you wake up and can't go back to sleep, you'll wake me up too. I can't stand the thought of you lying next to me, miserable and unhappy."

"I'm okay," she said.

He shook his head. "No. I mean, I know you are, but seriously, I love you so much, and even if all we do is talk, I don't want you to suffer alone. Never again."

God, she loved this man. "Okay." What else could she say?

"Thank you," Lucky said, breathing out a sigh of relief. Devyn could see that her response meant everything to him.

"I wasn't going to shower before PT this morning, but I'm thinking now I need to make sure my woman's clean. Inside and out," he said with a smirk.

"It's awfully early," Devyn mock complained.

"You can go back to sleep after I leave," Lucky told her.

Once again, he was making sure she was comfortable and didn't wake up feeling dirty. He was amazing. "Okay. What are your plans for today?"

"More meetings about the Olympics. We're headed out next week, which you know."

"Do...are you guys expecting trouble?" Devyn asked tentatively.

"No," Lucky said without hesitation, which went a long way toward comforting her. "But we never know what will happen, so we plan for every contingency. And the fact that several different teams are switching out over the month or so that the games take place makes things more difficult, as well. Which is why we have so many planning meetings. Honestly, we look forward to this kind of assignment. It's a nice change of pace and it's fun to meet all the athletes."

"You gonna get autographs?" Devyn teased.

"I personally don't care that much about that sort of thing. I mean, I admire their dedication to their sport, and how hard it is to become an elite athlete and to qualify for the Olympics in the first place, but I don't need their signature on a piece of paper to remember them by. But...we're all gonna do everything we can to get Shin-Soo Choo's autograph for Logan."

"Oh my gosh! He would die!" Devyn gushed, knowing all about the little boy's obsession with the baseball outfielder.

"Yup," Lucky agreed.

"Well, with a name like Lucky, I'm sure you'll be the one to track him down and get it," Devyn said with a smile.

"You know," Lucky said seriously, "there have been times when I seriously hated my name. I haven't always felt very lucky."

Devyn reached up and held on to his wrists, locking her gaze to his. "You might've been a POW, but you weren't killed and were rescued. You found me...and I was like a needle in a haystack." She winked. "Somehow out of all the people in this world, we managed to find each other. I'd say you're pretty damn lucky, and I think your name fits you to a T."

"You're right," he said softly.

"I know," she said smugly.

Just then, his cock slipped all the way out of her body, and they both groaned.

"Right, now it's really time to get up," he told her, sitting up with Devyn still on his lap. He scooted over to the edge of the bed and stood, holding her ass with both hands.

"I still can't believe you can haul me around as if I'm as petite as Riley."

"You're perfect for me. I love your long legs, and your tits, and your ass, and your—"

"Right, I get it. My beautiful personality," she said with a laugh.

"That too," Lucky agreed.

He put her on her feet in the bathroom and reached for the tap to turn on the water. Devyn could feel his come dripping down her inner thigh, but for the first time since that awful day in the woods, she didn't feel dirty. Not in the least. She felt loved. Completely and utterly. And that trumped just about everything else.

She leaned into Lucky as they waited for the water to warm. "I love you, Lucky. So much. I may not have been sure about getting into a relationship with you when I got here, for so many reasons, but not one of those was about *you*. I was scared. Scared of finding exactly what I've been looking for all my life and then losing it."

"You're stuck with me," Lucky told her, hugging her to his chest. "Forever."

"Good."

They smiled at each other, then Lucky took hold of her hand and helped her step over the rim of the tub into the shower. She wasn't perfect, neither was he, but somehow, they were perfect together.

* * *

Sierra Clarkson lie panting on the dirt floor of her cell. Once she knew for certain she was alone...she smiled. She couldn't believe her manipulation of her captors had worked. Yes, she was still locked up in the dark. Yes, she was still hungry. But she'd gotten them to do exactly what she'd wanted.

Namely, to cut off her hair.

Most people would think she was insane for *wanting* them to shave off her auburn locks. Maybe she was. But being held captive by Taliban terrorists for months on end tended to do that to a person.

At one time she'd been so proud of her red hair. She knew it was one of her best features. People commented on it as much as they talked about her height, or lack thereof. But after months of being a hostage, and not showering, her hair had become the bane of her existence. When she slept, cockroaches would crawl into the filthy strands and she'd have to shake them loose every morning. Her guards loved to grab hold of her hair and haul her around that way. And she absolutely couldn't stand how disgusting it felt.

She wasn't sure when she'd decided that her hair had to go, but once she did, she focused all her energy and attention on making that happen. When she was first captured, she remembered begging for clean water to wash with. Her captors had laughed and purposely withheld it. Same with food. The more she begged to eat, the longer they made her wait before finally throwing some scraps her way.

She'd learned quickly that showing interest in anything would make the assholes holding her captive take it away simply to make her suffer. So...she'd simply started paying extra attention to her hair whenever they were around. Asking for a comb. A bar of soap. Complaining about the condition of the strands. Begged them not to pull her hair, said she'd do anything as long as they didn't shave it off. It took a month or so—at least, that's how long she *thought* it took; she had no way to gauge the passage of time—but just that morning, they'd shown up with a pair of shears and wicked grins on their faces.

Sierra had done her best to fight them off, not wanting her captors to think she was eager for what they had planned.

In the end, they'd tied her down and done exactly what she wanted them to do.

Shaved her bald.

Running a hand over her head, Sierra grimaced at the unevenness of the hack job, but she couldn't help feeling thrilled with how much lighter and cleaner she felt. The assholes thought they were continuing to torture her, but they'd played right into her hands.

Now, if she could use her psychology degree to somehow convince the Taliban that she *wanted* to be with them, that she never wanted to be released, she would. But she knew that wouldn't happen. She was their prize, even if she was treated worse than a piece of livestock and mostly forgotten in the back of this mountain cave.

As she closed her eyes, Sierra couldn't help but be relieved she wouldn't have to fight the cockroaches out of her hair when she woke up. Today was a good day. A very good day.

She just had to keep holding on in the hopes that soon she'd have a *great* day, and be able to escape from the assholes who'd captured her. Their day of reckoning would come, she hoped. Until then, she'd savor the small victory she'd gained.

* * *

Doc wasn't all that fired up for the next assignment. He knew his teammates were happy to have a more laid-back mission, where they knew the chances of them being shot at or taken hostage were low. He didn't blame them; if he had a woman or child waiting for him, he'd feel the same way. But he didn't. And it kind of sucked.

He wanted what his friends had. Wanted to feel that bone-deep connection with someone. He had that with his team, but it obviously was very different with a woman.

Doc was a quiet man. He'd never been very flamboyant. Outside missions, he rarely shared his opinion unless it was expressly asked for. He hoped to find someone like him. An introvert who was somewhat shy; someone he could sit quietly with and read a book and not feel as if he was holding her back. He'd seen firsthand when soldiers hooked up with women who were complete opposites of themselves. It never worked.

Doc didn't know where he was going to find a slightly nerdy woman who was pretty—but not *too* pretty—who liked fading into the background like he did, and who would think the highlight of her week was going over to one of his teammates' houses to hang out.

Sighing, he shook his head. He was looking for someone who didn't exist. A unicorn of a woman. At thirty-four, he was the oldest on the team, and most days he felt it. His knees hurt almost all the time, and he was dreading the day they'd give out completely and he'd have to leave the team. The thought of not being a Delta, of not working side by side with the men he felt as if were his blood brothers, was extremely painful.

Doc forced his attention back to the meeting he was currently attending. They were reviewing one last time before they headed overseas to the Olympics Games. They were going to be a man down on this mission because Riley's baby was due in the next four weeks or so, and Oz didn't want to take a chance that he'd miss it. He was allowed to take leave time and to skip this deployment since it wasn't a high priority or high risk.

"I just found out which building we'll be assigned to," Trigger said, handing each of them a map of the Olympic Village, where they'd be bunking. "We'll be on the same floor with the US pentathlon athletes and water polo teams."

"Damn, not the beach volleyball players?" Grover quipped.

"Any chance the baseball players are nearby?" Lucky asked. "Since Oz isn't going, it's up to us to find Logan's idol and get his autograph."

"Nearby is relative. But I'm sure we can manage to finagle our way into the building the team is living in. The problem is that a lot of those professional baseball and basketball players aren't staying in the Olympic Village. They're renting high-end, five-star hotel rooms and taking limos to the venue every day."

"Shit," Brain mumbled.

"I have faith in us," Lefty said. "We'll get it."

"Speaking of which, remember that our job is to guard the athletes and venues, not to be starstruck by the famous players," Trigger said.

Doc rolled his eyes. "We know, jeez. You think this is our first rodeo?"

"No, but it has to be said. Some of the men and women who'll be there are quite well known. Especially in the world of social media."

Doc wanted to roll his eyes again, but resisted. He didn't care at all about social media. He saw his friends every day, and if he wanted to know what was going on with them, he picked up the phone and called. Besides, Delta Force operatives were encouraged to not have profiles because of Operations Security. He was out of touch as to which celebrities were popular these days, but he didn't give a shit.

"It's an honor to serve our country in this different way, and I, for one, am looking forward to being able to shower every day and eat hot food," Trigger said.

Everyone laughed and agreed.

Doc joined in, but secretly had the thought that he would much prefer to be slogging through the sand of the Middle

East, hunting down a terrorist. That world, he understood; the one with celebrities and pampered athletes who thought their shit didn't stink wasn't exactly his cup of tea. He knew they weren't all like that, probably even *most* weren't like that, but he'd seen enough who were to make him jaded about the entire assignment.

But like with every mission, he'd perform to the best of his ability. It was what he'd signed up for when he joined the Army.

Pushing thoughts of dating out of his head, Doc looked down at the papers in front of him. He needed to be ready for anything, and while his teammates would never say it, he knew he was the most expendable man on the team. And he was all right with that. He'd give his life so that his friends could live, any day of the week, especially now that they had families of their own.

Ember Maxwell sat in her bedroom in her parents' house in Beverly Hills, California. She was supposed to be meditating, visualizing herself winning the Modern Pentathlon event in the Olympics, which started next week. But instead, she was sitting on the comfortable cushion in the window seat, staring out the window.

She was twenty-five years old and had never lived on her own. Hadn't gone to college. Hadn't done anything but what her parents told her to do since she'd been a young child. They'd single-handedly made her into both a social media sensation—her Instagram account had over ten million followers—and an elite athlete.

She'd started with swimming when she was seven; when she'd proven good, but not great, they'd enrolled her in track.

Then horseback riding. She hadn't excelled in any of them, had only been half decent.

Then they'd watched the summer Olympics one year...and had gotten an idea.

The Modern Pentathlon wasn't a hugely popular sport, which meant there were fewer competitors. If they could train her to swim, run, ride, shoot, and fence even halfway decent, then she'd have a shot at being an Olympian.

It had been *their* goal all along, not Ember's. They'd both been good athletes in high school, but not good enough to earn scholarships to college or be anywhere close to a professional. But apparently they saw potential in their child, which evolved into an obsession with making her a star.

Like a good little girl, she'd done what she'd been told. She'd worked out from morning till night, learned how to fence, how to shoot, swam endless laps in the pool. They'd bought her a horse, making her run to and from riding lessons.

But that hadn't been enough for the Maxwells. No, they wanted their daughter to be *famous*. And being a pentathlete wouldn't do that. So they'd spent hundreds of thousands of dollars buying her followers. Paying influencers to feature her. They'd even managed to get a producer friend of theirs to do a reality show of her life one spring. That had only lasted one season, but it had been enough to cause her Instagram numbers to skyrocket, making Ember famous.

But the thing was...she didn't want any of it.

She hated the way she was photographed everywhere she went. She couldn't even go to the grocery store without someone recognizing her and wanting an autograph or a picture. And God forbid she was seen buying or eating any kind of food. She still remembered the one time she was photographed eating a candy bar. Her mom had lectured her for hours.

So yeah, Ember might be on her way to the Olympics, and she might be famous, but neither had been *her* goal. And now that she'd made the Olympics, her parents—mostly her mom—were already planning for the next one in four years.

It was depressing as hell...and Ember wanted out. Wanted nothing to do with California and fame and the Olympics and Instagram, and even though she was in the best shape of her life, had muscles on top of muscles, she just wanted to live a normal existence.

Sighing, she pulled over the box of the latest letters she'd received. Her parents employed people to read her fan mail and to send out pictures with her autograph, but sometimes Ember liked to read her own letters. Wanted to connect with someone, *anyone*, even if it was through the mail.

Most of the letters she received were nice, but there were always those people who thought she was a bitch, and had no problem telling her so. It surprised Ember how many people still wrote actual letters. She knew she got hundreds of messages and emails a day on her social media accounts, but those were all managed by someone else. Reading the letters made her feel more human, somehow.

The first one was obviously written by a child. The handwriting was big and messy, but the sentiment behind it was touching.

Your my favorite. Your pretty. I want to be like you when I grow up.

Ember read through a few more. Then she pulled out another envelope...and actually recognized the handwriting. The guy had been writing her for years.

· · ·

Hi, Ember. Good job in the Trials. You blew everyone away. I know you're gonna kick everyone's butt at the Olympics. I can't wait to see you on top of the medal stand. You'll bring home that gold medal for sure! I admire you so much. It's not easy to excel in five different sports at one time. Most of the other Olympians are only good at one. I think that makes you amazing. Good luck! ~Your #1 fan, Pat

Ember knew better than to write a personal note back to anyone who sent her fan mail. She was aware of what had happened to Rebecca Schaeffer in the eighties. The very popular young actress had made the mistake of writing back to her future killer, telling him his note had been the nicest one she'd received. That had made him obsess over her, think they had a personal relationship. He'd found her address and had gone to her apartment. When she'd opened the door, he'd shot her dead.

But she couldn't help but smile at Pat's letter. He was always so sweet and kind. She appreciated his notes and encouragement.

Still thinking about Pat's letter, Ember opened the next one and started reading. She was jarred out of her musings by the words typed on the page.

You're a bitch. Think you're so pretty and too good for everyone. I hate you. I hate everything about your lifestyle. Do you even think about all those suffering around you? That the money you throw around as if it's candy could actually feed a needy family for a week? I bet your damn manicure costs more than a month's rent for some people. I hope you come in last in the Olympics. You don't deserve to be there, Mommy and Daddy probably bought your way in. Maybe someone will shoot you in the head so the US doesn't have to be embarrassed to have you represent them. Crash and burn, bitch!

. . .

Ember shivered and shoved the letter back into the envelope. She pushed the box away and sat back, staring out the window again. Tears came to her eyes. She couldn't understand that kind of hate for someone you didn't know. And no matter what people saw on the internet or their TVs, they *didn't* know her.

She wanted to be normal. Wanted a family and kids. She didn't ask to be Ember Maxwell, internet star and elite athlete.

She knew she should be grateful. She'd had a privileged upbringing and had everything money could buy. But the one thing money *couldn't* buy her was happiness. That old saying was true. And what she was doing now wasn't making her happy.

Somehow, she had to find the courage to stand up to her parents. But first, she had to get through the Olympics. Her parents were expecting her to bring home a gold medal, but if that happened, it would be even harder to escape her gilded cage.

She wouldn't purposely perform badly. She was too competitive for that. She'd just have to see what the next few weeks had in store for her, and act accordingly.

Forgetting about the letters, Ember got up and headed for bed. She had to be up early tomorrow for more training. At least in her dreams, she could be who she wanted to be. Normal. Ordinary. Happy.

* * *

Doc and Ember have very different backgrounds. Can a Special Forces soldier and a world famous Olympian make things work between them? Pick up *Shielding Ember* to find out! :)

. . .

And of course Sierra is still waiting to be found. But her time is coming...as is her book, Shielding Sierra!

Want to talk to other Susan Stoker fans? Join my reader group, Susan Stoker's Stalkers, on Facebook!

Also by Susan Stoker

Delta Team Two Series
Shielding Gillian
Shielding Kinley
Shielding Aspen
Shielding Jayme (novella)
Shielding Riley
Shielding Devyn
Shielding Ember (Sep 2021)
Shielding Sierra (Jan 2022)

SEAL Team Hawaii Series
Finding Elodie
Finding Lexie (Aug 2021)
Finding Kenna (Oct 2021)
Finding Monica (TBA)
Finding Carly (TBA)
Finding Ashlyn (TBA)
Finding Jodelle (TBA)

Silverstone Series
Trusting Skylar
Trusting Taylor
Trusting Molly (July 2021)
Trusting Cassidy (Dec 2021)

Eagle's Point Search & Rescue
Searching for Lilly (Mar 2022)
Searching for Bristol (TBA)
Searching for Elsie (TBA)
Searching for Caryn (TBA)
Searching for Finley (TBA)

Searching for Heather (TBA)
Searching for Khloe (TBA)

SEAL of Protection Series
Protecting Caroline
Protecting Alabama
Protecting Fiona
Marrying Caroline (novella)
Protecting Summer
Protecting Cheyenne
Protecting Jessyka
Protecting Julie (novella)
Protecting Melody
Protecting the Future
Protecting Kiera (novella)
Protecting Alabama's Kids (novella)
Protecting Dakota

SEAL of Protection: Legacy Series
Securing Caite
Securing Brenae (novella)
Securing Sidney
Securing Piper
Securing Zoey
Securing Avery
Securing Kalee
Securing Jane

Delta Force Heroes Series
Rescuing Rayne
Rescuing Aimee (novella)
Rescuing Emily
Rescuing Harley
Marrying Emily (novella)

Rescuing Kassie
Rescuing Bryn
Rescuing Casey
Rescuing Sadie (novella)
Rescuing Wendy
Rescuing Mary
Rescuing Macie (novella)

Badge of Honor: Texas Heroes Series

Justice for Mackenzie
Justice for Mickie
Justice for Corrie
Justice for Laine (novella)
Shelter for Elizabeth
Justice for Boone
Shelter for Adeline
Shelter for Sophie
Justice for Erin
Justice for Milena
Shelter for Blythe
Justice for Hope
Shelter for Quinn
Shelter for Koren
Shelter for Penelope

Ace Security Series

Claiming Grace
Claiming Alexis
Claiming Bailey
Claiming Felicity
Claiming Sarah

Mountain Mercenaries Series

Defending Allye

Defending Chloe
Defending Morgan
Defending Harlow
Defending Everly
Defending Zara
Defending Raven

Stand Alone
The Guardian Mist
Nature's Rift
A Princess for Cale
A Moment in Time- A Collection of Short Stories
Another Moment in Time- A Collection of Short Stories
Lambert's Lady

Special Operations Fan Fiction
http://www.AcesPress.com

Beyond Reality Series
Outback Hearts
Flaming Hearts
Frozen Hearts

Writing as Annie George:
Stepbrother Virgin (erotic novella)